SHIVER
HITCH

SHIVER
HITCH

Linda Greenlaw

Minotaur Books

New York

SHIVER HITCH. Copyright © 2017 by Linda Greenlaw. All rights reserved. Printed in
the United States of America. For information, address St. Martin's Press, 175 Fifth
Avenue, New York, N.Y. 10010.

www.minotaurbooks.com

The Library of Congress Cataloging-in-Publication Data is available upon request.

ISBN 978-1-250-10756-5 (hardcover)
ISBN 978-1-250-10757-2 (e-book)

Our books may be purchased in bulk for promotional, educational, or business use.
Please contact your local bookseller or the Macmillan Corporate and Premium Sales
Department at 1-800-221-7945, extension 5442, or by e-mail at MacmillanSpecial
Markets@macmillan.com.

First Edition: June 2017

10   9   8   7   6   5   4   3   2   1

About the Knot
Shiver Hitch

The shiver hitch is an antiquated knot that is no longer used. In its day, the shiver hitch was used to pull masts or spars around a shipyard. The hitch is made with a length of line ("rope," if you are a cowboy) and the sheave (shiv) from a block. To tie a shiver hitch, first thread the bitter end of the line through the center of the block. Tie a stopper knot (typically, a Matthew Walker Knot was used) in the bitter end to keep the end from pulling back through the center of the block when pressure is applied from the standing part. Next, take a hitch around whatever is to be moved, and the shiv will jam when the line is made taut.

I chose *Shiver Hitch* for this title from tens of thousands of knot names because this is the first book I have set in a good old-fashioned Maine winter.

SHIVER
HITCH

ONE

Except for the time I was digging my own grave at gunpoint on the edge of Biscayne National Park, I hadn't much experience with a shovel. Now, my first winter in Maine was providing a cram course in the form of snow. Back in Miami, a sore back was the least of my concerns. And when I was able to crack the gun-toting drug lord's head with the back of the shovel and run for the mangroves, the real terror began. That night spent hiding, half submerged, I was unable to decide which was worse: leeches or mosquitoes. Neither of those was a threat here in deep, dark February in sleepy, frozen Green Haven, Maine.

I had been warned, and was fully expecting and prepared for a "wicked" winter, or so I thought. The locals whose holy books are *The Farmers' Almanac* and *Uncle Henry's*, who had advised me that there would be a record amount of snowfall—as forecast in "FA"—and that I could get whatever I needed to cope with it in "UH," must now be enjoying the fact that I had been skeptical. Of course it didn't help that my parking space seemed to be at the vortex of a snow funnel. Every time the wind blew out of the northeast, which accompanied most large storms, my 1987 Plymouth Duster had been buried. To be honest, my car is actually a Plymouth Tourismo. Plymouth did not make a Duster in 1987. I just think a Duster is more my style—less extravagant, more practical. Today, just the tip of the antenna marked the car entombed in flakes so big I could almost see their individual differences. I laughed to myself. My present situation was a far cry from chief detective of Miami-Dade County. If anyone from my past could see me now—Jane Bunker, bundled up like a goddamned Eskimo—living in an apartment over a trinket-selling tourist trap in this remote outpost—making ends meet financially (just barely) with a combination of insurance consulting/investigation and a job as the assistant deputy sheriff of Knox County—shoveling snow!

My landlords, Alice and Henry Vickerson—Mr. and Mrs. V to me—had been gracious in offering me the use of their snow blower. But that offer had come with the stipulation that it not be fired up until eight a.m., the time at which "anyone with an ounce of civility" should wake. I suspected the ounce of civility was in direct correlation to the ounces of Scotch whiskey consumed the night before, but might also have been age related. The eight a.m. mandate, in conjunction with the price of gasoline to power the blower, had me, at six sharp, digging a path with a red plastic shovel from the door of The Lobster Trappe (the V's gift shop over which I reside) to the antenna under which lived my wheels. Not that I am opposed to Scotch. I have been known to imbibe. But I am frugal; some would say "cheap."

When a crease of golden light warmed the eastern horizon, I figured I had been shoveling for nearly an hour. Not that I was counting, but I was aware that we were gaining over a full minute of daylight every twenty-four hours. I yearned for the four a.m. sunrise that would come again with the spring solstice. I thrive in daylight. And, I've come to find out, I am not crazy about the cold. Mr. V had secured a big red lobster thermometer ("Lobster Thermadore," as advertised in the shop) on the largest spruce tree on the lot. The black line whose height signified the temperature barely showed on the tail, displaying a frigid eight degrees this morning. Exercise within multiple layers of clothing resulted in full warmth by the time I had exposed the hood of the Duster, allowing me distractive thoughts while I found the car's doors.

Maine had become home, again, sort of. Although I still struggled when asked about my past, I had at least confided in the Vickersons and my new friends enough to stop their incessant questions that were born out of curiosity and rumor. People make more of what is unsaid than what is said. Not one to wear my heart on my sleeve, I am weirded out by strangers who bear their souls over a cup of coffee in public, or share intimate and minute details of their daily existence over social media. The surge in popularity of reality TV has everyone thinking their lives are ready for prime time. Just eight months ago, I was the new kid in town. What preceded my arrival was the knowledge that I had been born on Acadia Island, was basically kidnapped by my own mother (along with my baby brother, Wally), and was transplanted to Miami, where I grew up in a predominantly Latino section of the city and worked as a police detective until

3

this past June. Rumors of a highly decorated career in drug enforcement cut short by some undefined, yet insurmountable scandal may have been exaggerated. But I have never been one to kiss and tell.

Although I hadn't yet visited Acadia Island since my move back to Maine, I could see it, as I stood to rest my back in the distance across the bay, looming mysteriously over smaller islands and ledges that dotted the way between it and Green Haven. Someday, I thought, I would initiate a family reunion. Someday, when I could stomach the possibility of having a door slammed in my face. Or worse yet, learning that the Bunkers were not the catalyst that sent my mother sneaking off in the middle of the night, settling at the farthest reach of the Eastern Seaboard, into the looney bin, and finally to suicide. The way my mother told it it qualified her for sainthood. To my five-year-old mind, she had been heroic. At forty-three, I wasn't as convinced. What I "knew" was this: My mother had disappointed my father's family when she gave birth to a girl, as boys were needed to perpetuate both the Bunker name and the heritage of lobster fishing. The Bunkers had fought long and hard to acquire and protect their private sliver of the ocean floor that provided their livelihood and identity, and needed to seed the future with young Bunker men willing and able to carry on the territorial war. I always wondered how my life would have been different if the Bunkers had considered women capable of fishing and fighting. No matter, because when dear Wally was born and it was clear that he was a Down syndrome baby, that was the final blow to our "family." My mother, according to her, was treated like a pariah until she found the courage to escape.

Nearly forty years later, here I was, a short boat ride to the truth, but unable to climb aboard; my fear of disillusionment crippling. Or perhaps it was confirmation I feared.

My move to Maine from Florida was indeed a knee-jerk reaction, and one that brought with it an inherent dichotomy that I straddled awkwardly. What remained constant in my life was my affinity for the law. This passion for fighting crime and solving cases ranging from petty theft to first-degree murder was what bolstered me through all lows. In the short time I had been in Maine, I had seen the crime rate change dramatically. Although the downeast coastal villages were quaint, sleepy havens where tourists enjoyed tranquillity and lobster rolls, there had been an explosion of drug use and overdoses among the young population of year-round residents. Meth labs were being discovered weekly, and synthetic opioids had become the new heroin. I had cut my law enforcement teeth in the era of the War on Drugs in Miami, the highest drug trafficking area in the Continental US. The older folks who live here are shocked by the seemingly rabid increase in drug-related topics in their local newscasts and print. But when you see young people harvesting a very abundant and lucrative resource like the Maine lobster, it was just a matter of time before the drug lords would tap into that cache. Timing may indeed be everything. Or is it location, location, location? Time and place. I was in the right place at the right time to make a difference, I thought.

When I was able to pry the driver's-side door of the Duster open wide enough to squeeze in, I did. Three pumps on the gas pedal with a foot clad in the requisite, insulated L.L.Bean boot, a twist of the key in the ignition, and "Vroom," off she went—purring contentedly. I hated wasting gas, but thought it might be okay to let the engine idle while I dug out the back tires and dished out a couple of wheel wells behind them and out to the main road. The price of gasoline in Down East Maine was all the motivation I needed to throw snow with a real hustle. Just as I was finishing the job, the phone inside the house rang, piercing the stillness of the icy air. I leaned the shovel against the rear bumper and started toward the house. One ring later, the phone stopped. Two rings and a hang-up was the code I had worked out with my boss at Marine Safety Consultants, Mr. Dubois, and was my signal to call him back pronto.

Cell phones are all but useless in this particular nook of coast, so my personal calls all come through a "party line" that I share with the Vickersons. The code was worked out in an attempt to gain a bit of privacy. At first, Mr. and Mrs. V had been discreet about listening in on my calls. But once the cat was out of the bag, rather than stop doing it, they became more blatantly nosy—even jumping into conversations to offer opinions. Most of my first-time callers end up saying "Who the hell is that?" before the end of the conversation. I then have to be polite and introduce whichever one of my octogenarian landlords happened to be near the phone when it rang. At the start it was disconcerting, then it really began to piss me off. Now, I laugh. And of course outsmart them.

Torn between allowing the Duster to remain running and thus climbing into a toasty warm car and shutting it off to feed my frugality, I opted for frugality. Besides saving gas, I needed to toughen up, I thought as I made my way back to the house. Carefully closing the door behind me so as not to wake my landlords, I brushed snow from the bottom of my pant legs, which were frozen stiff, and pulled my feet from my insulated "Beanies" with the lobster claw boot jack. Yup, The Lobster Trappe sold anything and everything lobster related. There were lobster trap birdhouses, lobster beanbags, lobster coloring books, lobster corkscrews . . . Well, you get the picture. The shop was now in its off-season, so the Vickersons were busy researching new items to add to their inventory, which led to many interesting conversations at their dinner table, where I had an open invitation to be any night at 7:30—five o'clock if I wanted cocktails. I tiptoed my wool socks across the shop and started up the stairs to my apartment. Halfway up, the door below that connected to the main house opened and I heard a very cheery, "Good morning, Janey!"

"Hi Mrs. V. I hope I didn't wake you."

"No dear, the phone did. Two rings and a hang-up. Must be your boss. Better call him back right away." Oh no, I thought, they were on to me. I wondered how many conversations they had tapped into since I had schemed the code. The Vickersons were so good to me in every way that I had never been able to bring myself to scold them for eavesdropping. What the heck, I thought, at eighty-two and eighty-six, if they find pleasure injecting themselves into my fairly unexciting life, so be it. It's not as if the happenings in Down East Maine and outer islands (my territory in both my insurance and deputy gigs) required security clearance. The last two assignments I had been given by Mr. Dubois were surveying minor damage to lobster boats in a late January blizzard. One boat's mooring parted and it was blown into another boat before landing luckily on the only patch of sand beach in the county. And the only task I had been assigned as deputy sheriff since September was following up on leads that often led to busting meth labs, arresting addicts, and hopefully beginning to snuff out what had reached epidemic proportions. Often, the entire community knows about a case or incident before I do, I realized. The Vickersons just like to be in the loop. I assured Alice that I had come in to call my boss, and hoped I could discreetly give Mr. Dubois a heads-up that they were listening before they jumped in.

"Hello?"

"Hi, Mr. Dubois. Jane Bunker here, *we* are returning your call."

"Alice?" Mr. Dubois asked.

"Present," Mrs. V said promptly.

"Henry?"

"Standing by," answered Mr. V dutifully. Oh God, I thought, now there wasn't even any pretending. The only thing keeping me from being terminated from either of my jobs was the total lack of anyone else to do them. That, and the fact that I *am* good at what I do.

"Okay team, here's the deal," the boss started. "Jane, I need you to go out to Acadia Island to survey damage suffered in a house fire. It's a summer home owned by a good customer for whom we insure several properties, three vehicles, a boat, and a business. The fire was just last night, and I want to move quickly to accommodate these people."

"Since when do we survey house fires? I thought you handled only marine-related insurance?" I asked to stall, and hoped to conceal an oncoming loss of composure about a trip to Acadia.

"It's called bundling, dear," interjected Mr. V. "Everyone is having to gain bandwidth in *any* business to stay afloat. Insurance is very competitive. Alice and I have all of our insurances under one roof as well—it's the only way we can afford it all."

"Besides," Mrs. V weighed in, "you really should go to Acadia and get that demon off your back."

"I think you mean monkey, dear," Mr. V corrected. "And maybe Jane needs to let sleeping dogs lie."

"Either way," Mr. Dubois interrupted what I had come to know as ping-pong proverbs before Alice could send one back over the net, "I assume the place is a total loss. Not much in the way of firefighting on these islands—all volunteer, and no real training or equipment. All I need from you is to go out and take lots of pictures to document what I already know," said Mr. Dubois.

"Yes sir, I'll get out there ASAP." Yet again, I am reduced to a photographer, I thought.

"Great. When you get off at the dock, take a right on the main road, in about half a mile you'll see a yellow Cape on the right. The Proctors are expecting someone from the Agency. They are caretakers for the Kohls, whose house you'll be surveying. They will get you where you need to be and back to the dock," the boss instructed. I breathed an audible sigh of relief when I registered "Proctor"—not any of the family names associated with my kin.

We all said our goodbyes and hung up, leaving me to

contemplate the trip "home." Within seconds the phone rang again. I grabbed it and was not at all surprised to be speaking with the Vickersons. They advised me of the ferry schedule to and from Acadia, adding that I had already missed the first boat out to the island. The winter ferry schedule to Acadia did not give a passenger many options—the "early boat" departed from South Haven (a ten-minute ride from home) at seven a.m., and the "late boat" was a three p.m. departure from South Haven. Following the forty-minute cruise out, the Vickersons informed me, the boat would remain at the dock on Acadia just long enough to unload people and freight, before returning to the mainland. I thanked my landlords for the info, and told them I would find an alternate ride out, snap a load of pictures, and return on the last and only remaining ferry this evening. "Better get a wiggle on," advised Mrs. V. "Time is of the essence."

"What's the rush? Remember, haste makes waste," instructed Mr. V.

"He who hesitates is lost," admonished Mrs. V.

"Fools rush in where angels fear to tread!"

"The early bird gets the worm!"

"Good things come to those who wait."

"Tide and time wait for no man. And damn few women! There, top that, Henry," Alice challenged.

"I need to deice the Duster. I'll let you know my plans, thanks!" I wasn't quite sure what I was thanking them for, but slammed the phone down, bolted down the stairs, yanked on my boots, and hustled to my chilly and waiting Duster. For all I knew, the old folks were still volleying proverbs. Their game used to irritate me. Now I enjoyed it, I thought as I quietly quipped, "A stitch in time, saves nine."

My warm gloves melted the thin layer of frost on the car's steering wheel, leaving distinct handprints at ten and two. Nothing upsets me more than waste, I reminded myself as I waited for the Duster's defroster to clear a porthole in the windshield. I don't mean global, all-encompassing misuse and extravagance. That does not concern me. I only pay heed to the wastefulness of which I am responsible—me, myself, and I. Perhaps a gut reaction to my very unusual childhood; my personal frugality is just that—personal. I don't preach. I don't boast. I don't admire extreme economy in others. I find nothing more annoying than conversation regarding the "great deal" someone got on something following a compliment on that something, or the fuel economy of any particular hybrid automobile. Nor do I care about membership on the Fortune 500 list, or who the top-paid athlete is at any given time. My mother's routine of frittering away the monthly welfare check from the State of Florida in a single day, leaving us to "get creative" for the remaining thirty days to the next installment, left its mark. Not that I didn't enjoy and look forward to the first of every month and whatever my mother had planned for us, but I knew at a very early age that my mother suffered from chronic immaturity with money. We ate and enjoyed government cheese, and the neighborhood ladies were forever dropping leftovers off for us, which sustained our family of three until I was old enough to work. I heard but didn't agree with the same ladies' whispered, negative opinions of how Wally and I were being raised.

The ladies whose husbands worked long, hard hours, barely making ends meet, knew the value of a dollar. And I remember the look of envy in their children's eyes each and every month when we arrived home by taxi—not the bus, a taxi—armed with gifts, souvenirs, and stories of adventure. They said we couldn't afford such extravagance as a day at the circus. My mother said we couldn't afford not to. I'll never know which is true. But this morning, had I left the car running for fifteen minutes while I was on the phone, I would have been sick to my stomach.

Publicly, I am not big on sentimental journeys. My wanderlust is limited to the future. Privately, I spend a lot of time wondering about my roots, especially since moving to Green Haven. The only family I have left is Wally, I thought. Five years my junior, and an adult with Down syndrome, living in an assisted, yet independent situation, my baby brother has always been more well balanced and adjusted than I have been. He makes friends easier than I do. All of the reasons that I had for *not* uprooting him to come along to Maine when I bailed, were the exact same reasons why I should have done so. He's happy there, I justified as I backed out of the driveway. But Wally is always happy. The last shrink I saw before the big move north told me that I was overprotective of my brother. Maybe so. I just couldn't risk dragging him off into the unknown where, if my mother had been truthful, he would be mistreated by mean people blinded by ignorance—and those were blood relatives! Now I faced the probability of actually meeting what remains of the Bunkers, and hoped some of the hatefulness my mother spoke of had withered in the past thirty-eight years.

I reminded myself that this trip to Acadia was not a quest for the truth or an opportunity for a family reunion. It was work, period.

Normally I would walk the mile to the Harbor Café, but there had been so much snow lately, it was banked high on either side of the street, leaving a gap so narrow that an oncoming vehicle presented a challenge. No sidewalks and not much time to find my buddy Cal were reasons enough to forgo the exercise today. As I nosed the Duster into a too-small parking space, I hoped this latest snow had not disrupted Cal's morning ritual of coffee and a newspaper at the café. Cal had quickly become my go-to guy for just about everything, including a boat ride, which was foremost on my request list this morning. Cowbells swinging on the inside of the café's door announced my entrance along with a good gust of cold, fresh air that formed a wispy vapor where it mixed with air permeated with donut grease. The place was crowded, and I stood in the doorway looking for Cal while I wiped snow from my boots onto a not-so-welcoming doormat that read "Many Have Eaten Here. Few Have Died."

"Close the door!" Yelled a chorus of apparently chilly breakfast guests. Pushing the door closed behind me, I spied at the counter the back of Cal's head with its thinning white hair. Luckily, the only empty seat was next to him. Unluckily, the seat was unoccupied because of the presence of Clyde Leeman, the unofficial town crier, on the other side of it. I tried to be discreet about putting my back to Clydie when I took the stool between him and Cal, like the people on the airplane who stick their face in a book to avoid having to speak to their seatmate.

13

I liked Clydie well enough, just wasn't up to his nonstop complaining and nonsensical jabbering. It was clear to me how and why Clydie had developed a very thick skin. It was virtually impossible to insult the man. And believe me, everyone tried.

"Hi Cal," I said pleasantly, as he lowered the newspaper onto the counter, exposing his quick smile, and removed his glasses to reveal twinkling blue eyes that defied his age. Cal had a natural ability to make everyone feel as though he were genuinely happy to see them, even when he wasn't. Before Cal could speak, Clydie broke in with his usual, too loud voice.

"Well, hellooooo, Ms. Bunker! You must be freezing. You ain't in Kansas anymore, are ya? Hey, I hope you don't have to pee. The pipes are froze in the bathroom." With that, the couple seated on the other side of him got up to leave.

"Clyde Leeman!" shouted Audrey, my favorite (and only) waitress in the café. "Will you stop with the announcements? Every time you open your pie hole, a customer leaves." The sassy, heavily tattooed and pierced Audrey was headed my way with a cup of coffee. Clearing a used paper place mat printed with local advertisements with her right hand, she plunked the full cup onto a clean one with her left, and slid it in front of me.

"Well, I just think it's good to let people know that your toilets are not working. What if someone has an emergency? This coffee is like mud! If anyone makes the mistake of a second cup, you're gonna have an awful mess," Clyde yelled.

"I thought the out-of-order sign on the door was sufficient," Audrey said. "But I guess that would require the ability to read." Audrey rolled her eyes, and sighed in exasperation. "Want the usual, Janey?" she asked, seemingly hopeful to exclude Clyde from any more conversation. I hesitated, not knowing what my usual was. I didn't recall being that predictable.

"I can read!" Clydie defended himself. "And you'd better avoid the prunes this morning, if you know what I mean, Ms. Bunker. Those pipes is froze solid. They won't get a flush down until April at this rate."

"Why don't you take some of that hot air into the bathroom and thaw the pipes?" Audrey asked sarcastically.

All the talk revolving around the status of the toilet was making me nauseous. I quickly agreed that I wanted my usual, whatever that was.

"English or day old?" asked Audrey. When I met this with a puzzled look, she elaborated. "Your usual is the least expensive item on the menu. Today that's a tie between a toasted English muffin and yesterday's special muffin."

"What was yesterday's special muffin?"

"Raspberry, a buck fifty."

"What's today's special muffin?"

"Apricot bran, two bucks."

"I'll have the toasted English, please," I said.

"Ha!" Clyde chimed in. "Good idea to avoid bran with the nonfunctioning facilities." Just as I thought Audrey would pour coffee into Clyde's lap, the cowbells announced another customer, causing Clyde's head to swivel toward the door. The incoming customer looked around in vain for a place to sit other than next to Clyde, and, shrugging hopelessly, shuffled over and took the least coveted seat in the café. As Clyde began chewing an ear off the guy, I turned my attention to Cal.

"Cal, I need a favor," I said.

"You name it. I'm your guy," Cal replied immediately, never breaking eye contact. To my mind, only the best of friends will agree to a favor before knowing what it is. This was testament to the mutual trust we shared; trust that had been won quickly and tested frequently. Not that I had been involved with many investigations since my arrival in Green Haven, but when I had, Cal had been at my service in any way needed.

"It's an easy one today. I need a ride to Acadia Island this morning. Seems that I missed the boat, so to speak." I went on to explain my mission to document damage caused by a house fire, and my plan to grab the late ferry back ashore later. Cal confirmed that I was in luck. He was happy to accommodate my request, especially at the expense of the insurance company who would reimburse all expenditures. I had learned that Cal was delighted to collect money from an insurance company with whom the vast majority of cash flow had always gone in the opposite direction. And since his retirement from a number of careers including commercial fishing, Cal had the time and appreciated a little extra money.

"Besides," Cal added, "the *Sea Pigeon* needs to stretch her legs a bit. And it's a great day for a boat ride. I haven't been to Acadia in years. No reason to go."

Me either, I thought to myself as Audrey delivered a toasted English muffin.

"Not my business, but . . ." Audrey started and hesitated long enough to give me an opportunity to cut her off, which I did not. I really liked Audrey. She is young and quirky, but has great insight—well beyond her nearly two decades of life. And I had confided in her to a small extent about my connection to Acadia, so figured that I had made it her business by doing so. "Are you hoping to catch a glimpse of the mysterious Bunker clan?"

"No," I chuckled. "I wouldn't know a Bunker if I was sitting next to one." I extended my arms to both sides, indicating that Cal and Clydie were more family to me than anyone on Acadia.

A long pause accompanied by Audrey shaking her head was finally filled with, "OMG. The only thing keeping me from genealogy research is the slight possibility that I could be related to Clydie." Cal's shoulders bounced up and down with a silent laugh. "Well, I want a full report tomorrow, girlfriend," Audrey said as she smacked the counter with my tab. Cal ordered a couple of muffins to take to his wife before Audrey was out of hearing range, and we laid out a plan.

I was to go home and ask the Vickersons to deliver the Duster to South Haven so that I would have it upon my return to the mainland this evening. Cal would pick me up at the Lobster Trappe and we would ride together to the dock where his boat was secured. He would get me to the island by ten, giving me plenty of time to take pictures and catch the last boat off. I liked simplicity. And I liked the fact that I would be home in time to join Mr. and Mrs. V for drinks and dinner.

Cal and I paid our respective tabs and stood to leave just as the cowbells rang out. Marilyn and Marlena, or "the old maids" as they were affectionately referred to, stepped in single file; Marlena cradling one of the couple's numerous blue-ribbon Scottish Fold cats. A chorus of "close the door" was met with quick action, and the ladies, whom everyone assumed were gay, came over to take the stools Cal and I had vacated. The sixty-ish gals were regulars at the café, allowing them lenience with pets. Any resident of Green Haven who had engaged in conversation with either of the women knew a lot about Scottish Folds. Even I, in my brief time here, had learned that these cats cried with a silent meow and stood on their hind feet like otters.

Marlena and Marilyn owned Green Haven's only hardware store and gas pump, and were legendary for gouging the locals who had no other shopping options. (My introduction to them several months ago had left me with a comparison to the Baldwin Sisters from *The Waltons*, which I had never been able to shake.) Marilyn had a distinct look: gray hair pulled into a neat braid; Marlena looked like a man. Both of the women had a penchant for tweed. And both pulled off an arrogance that privileged education and upbringing afford by being quite philanthropic.

Before we could exchange pleasantries, Clydie took the floor at full volume. "Hey, Aud," he yelled across the counter to a clearly disgusted Audrey. "That's it! The solution to the problem is kitty litter. If it's good enough for the highfalutin Sir Walter Bunny of Wheat Island, it's plenty good enough for the clientele here."

I choked back a giggle with the reminder of the name of this particular cat. I thought I recalled being told that the ladies' numerous Scottish Folds had been trained to use the toilet, too, but may have imagined that part. Audrey looked stunned, and claimed that it was shock at the inclusion of "clientele" in the dimwit's vocabulary. This was not enough to throw Clyde off his game, though. He added, "Put a litter box back there, and I'll bring in my clam rake for you to use as a pooper scooper."

Audrey scowled and snapped a pointed index finger at the door while Marlena and Marilyn looked on in confusion. Clydie, who was banished from the café nearly weekly, donned his coat and hat, and wished everyone a nice day. Clydie's exit scene was complete when he drew Audrey's attention to two customers who were sitting crossed-legged, suggesting that they might need the restroom.

The door closing behind us clipped fragmented conversations of the village idiot and other daily customers, small talk that I had become accustomed to since my arrival in Green Haven and my frequenting the only breakfast joint in town. Cal was right behind me in his pickup truck as I weaved the way back to my place through high banks of snow made fresh white with this morning's windfall. Although it had been a full nine months since my move here from Miami, I still marveled at the differences. It wasn't the obvious, opposite ends of the spectrum differences of the physical surroundings that I found astonishing. It wasn't subzero temperatures, record inches of snow, or the remoteness of this ultra-rural location that drew the biggest dissimilarities to the life I had left behind in South Florida; it was the subtleties. It was the fact that I had a sense of community here. I had a circle of people with whom I lived that I actually cared about. And they cared about me. In Miami, when a coworker asked how I was doing, they expected nothing more than a cursory "Fine, thanks," and would be put off by anything more. The best and worst times of my life had been defined publicly as "Fine, thanks."

Here in Green Haven, when acquaintances asked why I had never married, it was not the accusatory tone that I had become weary of in Miami. It was asked out of real caring and wanting to know my story. As quirky as it was, Green Haven was starting to feel more like home to me than anything I had ever known. Maybe it's just a good place for misfits, I thought as I pulled myself out of the Duster and signaled to Cal that I would be a minute as I walked toward the Lobster Trappe. The Vickersons' Cadillac sports a bumper sticker that reads "Some of us are here because we're not all there," which sums it up completely. Certainly the regulars at the café were quite a collection of oddballs. And I couldn't help but wonder if mavericks gravitated here, or if the place had made them that way. Classic chicken or egg, I thought. And something that didn't need resolving. Either way, I knew that Green Haven was a place that embraced more than tolerated people like me who are less mainstream—whatever the hell that means, I thought as I knocked and let myself into the Vickersons'. It had taken me over forty years, but I was learning that home is a feeling, not a place. And I had actually succeeded in starting life over in spite of the naysayers of my past who warned that I could not do so simply by saying "Goodbye and good riddance."

Knocking twice on the door with the back of my left hand, I twisted the knob and flung it open with my right, and barged into the landlord's knickknack-filled home. The place was a virtual menagerie of nautical novelties, souvenirs, and small collections displayed in what Mrs. V liked to call "Salty Chic." It was immediately clear that I had caught the Vickersons in mid-celebration of something. Mr. V did a fairly dramatic fist pump while his wife danced around gleefully. Their mood was so joyful that I couldn't help but laugh. "Oh Janey! You just missed the best phone call of our lives!" shouted Mrs. V.

"Publishers' Clearing House?" I asked playfully.

"No," Mrs. V said, nearly out of breath. She clasped her hands together and placed them tightly under her chin. "Wally's coming to live with us!"

"My brother?"

TWO

My vocabulary falls short in describing the flood of feelings following the news that my brother was soon to be out of his home in Florida for lack of federal funding. And the thought of moving him to Maine to join our makeshift family was just plain confusing. I was stunned, and trying to process, and very much aware that Cal was waiting for me in his truck. Rather than a long, heated discussion of pros and cons and other options, I opted for flight. At an embarrassingly heightened level of selfishness, I quickly and silently mulled the many ways that having Wally around could throw a wrench in my game plan, thus stunting the development of my new life. I took a breath, and asked the Vickersons to do me the favor of delivering my car to South Haven. For now, avoidance of the topic of my brother was my only strategy. I'm a pro-active kind of gal. I realized that I would have plenty of time in my own head to sift through the emotions for nuggets of reasonable reaction and action while snapping pictures of the fire scene and riding boats back and forth. I would do the right thing for Wally. I just needed a little time to figure out what that was.

I bolted up the stairs to my apartment and grabbed my camera bag, which was always stored fully loaded for assignments, consciously and woefully leaving behind my fully loaded gun belt and bag of tricks that accompany me when the job requires a badge. Although the state of Maine had legalized carrying a concealed weapon, I never felt compelled to. Green Haven was sleepy with a capital *S*. Even the drug busts were nonviolent, and very unlike the automatic weaponry wielded by the foe I had battled in Miami. I slung the camera case over my shoulder, and hustled to Cal's truck, where he sat patiently waiting and smoking a cigarette. I slammed the truck's door behind me just as Cal flipped his cigarette butt out of his open window and into a mound of snow.

We rode in silence. Silence was comfortable with Cal. I had come to know him as a man of few words. If he had something to say, he said it. If not, he didn't feel the need to fill the void with babble. And I had not been a recipient of the gift of gab either. I knew from my time spent working aboard boats as a younger woman that conversing over the noise of a diesel engine took effort. It limits small talk in a big way. As Cal had spent most of his preretirement life fishing, the trait of only speaking when you had something that *needed* to be heard was ingrained. On the other hand, I had always enjoyed conversation with my friend when and if it had been warranted. And as I had no desire to chat about this morning's "family" revelations (Acadia or Wally), I reveled in the ten minutes of solitude while feeling a paradoxical closeness to Cal.

Our silent ride was broken by the squeak of the truck's brakes as we skidded and came to a stop on Green Haven's commercial dock. The dock's parking area was freshly plowed, and the ramp was cleanly shoveled, to the delight of my overworked ribs and back. This, as I had learned, was the only functioning dock in the winter months. A number of private floats that jut from various points and coves had been put to bed like perennials, and would bloom again in the spring. Cal's boat, *Sea Pigeon*, was tethered to a float that was connected to the dock by a long, wooden ramp. The tide had the boat's dock lines stretched tight, giving *Sea Pigeon* the appearance of a dog anxious to run, but held at the end of a leash.

Someone had generously peppered the ramp with rock salt, making the low-tide descent at the steep angle less frightening. The float was so narrow that a slip at the bottom or misstep would likely result in an unintentional polar bear plunge. I gripped the hand railings at either side of the ramp as I made my way down, recalling all of the sobering statistics of hypothermia I had learned so many years ago. Even the relatively warm waters of South Florida could disable a healthy person who is partially submerged in frighteningly few hours. And northern waters in the winter cut survival time to minutes. I shivered at the thought, and accepted Cal's hand when offered to help me step over *Sea Pigeon*'s wash rail and onto her deck.

I stepped into the boat's tiny wheelhouse, moving far to the port side. Cal pulled open a hatch in the deck, exposing the engine and allowing a small bit of relatively warm air to rise into the otherwise icy structure. Crouching low to reach, Cal pulled a dipstick from the yellow Caterpillar engine, wiped it on a paper towel, dunked it back into the base, then pulled and inspected it again. Satisfied, he pushed the dipstick into place, flipped a battery switch into the "on" position, and closed the hatch. At the helm, Cal twisted the key in the ignition and pushed a black rubber button to start the engine. The starter clicked once or twice before catching, then the diesel cranked right up, sending a plume of white exhaust that billowed around the transom before dissipating into the sea smoke that whirled across the surface of the harbor and beyond. Cal unplugged an extension cord that I assumed had powered some source of heat for the engine compartment, coiled it neatly and tossed it onto the float, where the other end was still connected to an electrical box secured to an upright length of pressure-treated six-by-six on the float. Cal cast off a line at midship while I stepped to the transom. When I got a nod from Cal, I unwrapped the stern line from a cleat, freeing *Sea Pigeon* from the float. And away we went, through lily pads of ice that bobbed in our wake.

I had admired the beauty of "sea smoke," fog that forms on the surface of the water when the air moving over it is colder than the water itself, many times from the distance of my apartment's picture window. This was my first experience from within it. Cal called this Artic sea smoke "vapor," which I suppose it is, technically. Miami never had fog of any type. The sea smoke was interesting to me in that it was so different from the dungeonlike fog I had learned of this past summer. This morning, the sea smoke was wispy, and spiraled in columns that appeared to tiptoe on the surface like steam over a hot cup of coffee. It was alive, and nothing like the dense, motionless "pea soup" fog that smothered Green Haven for days on end in

June. I braced a leg as Cal rounded a channel marker and headed into the bay.

The absence of lobster pot buoys was remarkable in comparison to their in-your-face presence during the shedder season. The last time I had been aboard *Sea Pigeon,* Cal had his hands full navigating the obstacle course the lobster buoys marked. But that had been September—high season for the inshore fishermen whose dooryards were now bursting at their seams with traps and gear waiting patiently for spring so they could go out and play. A few local Green Haven guys had federal permits that allowed them to fish federal waters, which meant they could chase the lobsters offshore in the winter months. Everyone else sat and waited. Winter was opportunity to repair traps, paint buoys, splice line, support the high school's basketball and chess teams, drink, and make babies. There was a reason for the café's birthday special that ran the month of November—or so I had been told.

The bay was calm, and the drone of the diesel comforting. We passed close by a small nut of an island whose shoreline was ringed with thick slabs of pale-colored ice; chunks of white chocolate bark resting haphazardly on jagged ledges. The top of a seaweed-covered outcropping barely above water supported a community of seals. Their backs arched, pushing bellies into ledge and pointing noses and tails toward the sky, giving them the appearance of giant, black, crayon-drawn smiles. As we approached, the seals relaxed their meditative poses and slithered single file into the sea and disappeared. Like inky kernels of corn bursting in hot oil, the seals' heads popped through the surface randomly, catching corners of my periphery. My eyes darted in an attempt to keep up.

When Cal pushed the throttle up slightly, I turned and looked forward, over the bow. And there she was—majestic and mysterious—Acadia Island. The sun was now directly over the top of the highest of four peaks that linked midway to the shore, melding into a dark green mass that stopped abruptly at the base layer of stark, gray granite. The closer we got, the more shape the granite took. Sheer cliffs and rugged ledges imposed a formidable first impression, I thought. Hard and cold, like its inhabitants in my mother's stories.

A sharp turn to port led us to the opening of an inner harbor where things looked less menacing, peaceful even. A lush coating of snow blanketed large areas broken only by houses that appeared to have been placed on top of the white cover. Estates with boathouses and barns, outbuildings and garages were all buttoned up with no signs of activity. When Cal pulled the throttle back to an idle, I asked, "Where do the *people* live?"

After a thoughtful drag on a cigarette, Cal said, "Anyone here this time of year would be in the low-rent district. Bet they can't even *smell* the ocean." Of course that made sense, I thought as a dock came into view from behind a point of land. "There's the town landing," Cal said as he motioned with his head. "And that's where you'll board the ferry to come back off." Cal swung *Sea Pigeon* around a winter stick that marked a mooring, which I had learned replaced the usual ball for flotation in the winter months when the moorings were not used by seasonal boaters. Apparently ice had the ability to latch on to a mooring ball and drag it off. Shifting plates of ice headed offshore to deeper water often deposited the shanghaied moorings along the way, often over their heads and never to be seen again. The plastic winter sticks that were weighted on one end so that they remained vertical in the water did not allow ice to grab them, but rather it slid off leaving the mooring in place and marked where it could be rigged with the ball after ice season. Several winter sticks and two mooring balls with skiffs tethered to them indicated that there were two boats fishing from Acadia Island this winter. "Probably scalloping," Cal answered my unasked question about the moorings holding skiffs.

Cal threw the boat into reverse, and then quickly out of gear as we nudged the float gently and came to a stop. I stepped over the rail and onto the float. "Thanks for the ride. And I'll see you at the café in the morning. Bring me a bill."

"You sure you don't need me to wait?" Cal asked.

"No, I want to have the day to be thorough," I replied, knowing that I would have time to be thorough as well as nosy if I could gather any courage to poke around on personal business.

"Yup." Cal handed a grease-stained paper bag to me. I knew the bag contained the muffins I had assumed were for his wife. "Don't expect to find lunch." I hadn't given any thought to food, so was most appreciative of Cal's thoughtfulness. I stood and watched as *Sea Pigeon* chugged away from the float, out of the harbor, and beyond my line of vision. As I hustled up the ramp to the dock, I heard Cal push the throttle up to a full cruise, and knew he'd be back in Green Haven in about forty minutes.

At the top of the ramp, the roadway from the dock to the parking area was inclined and narrow. The one-lane passageway had been plowed many times, creating what could be mistaken as a snowboarder's half pipe. The snow was banked so high on either side of the dock, it eclipsed my view other than straight ahead or back. Ahead was the parking lot for which I was bound, and behind was the end of the dock from where I had come. There was a healthy layer of crystal clear ice coating every surface, causing me to squint in the sun's reflection. If it hadn't been sanded, I would have had trouble walking. I exited the semi snow tube and found myself in an open lot from where I could see the road that Mr. Dubois had mentioned in his instructions. I recalled his directions: turn right, half a mile on the right, yellow cape.

I enjoyed the short walk. I passed a few homes that were obviously summer residences, as their driveways had not been cleared of snow, and there were no footprints to be found. The first and only sign of life was at the yellow cape. An older-model red Jeep Cherokee sat in a plowed drive, and smoke puffed from the home's chimney. I made my way to the front door and knocked. "Come in," yelled a woman's voice from within the house. I let myself in, closing the door behind me. The house was toasty warm and fresh-baked goods smelled heavenly. The interior was rustic, but very clean and had a prominence of a woman's touch with things like curtains and braided rugs. As I wiped my boots on a welcome mat, a chubby bleached blonde appeared in the adjacent doorway. She had a phone pressed to her ear. She greeted me with wide eyes under arched brows, shrugged, and motioned me to follow her, which I did. She led me to the kitchen and pointed to a chair at the table. Placing my camera bag (which now also held my lunch) on the floor, I unzipped my coat and sat while she talked to what became obvious was a message machine on the other end.

"My name is Joan Proctor, and I am trying to reach Mr. Kohl. Will you please have him call two, zero, seven, three, three, five, five, five, three, seven? Thank you." She pushed a button on the phone, exhaled a frustrated sigh, and turned to me. "Hi there. Can I help you?" she asked pleasantly with a thick Down East accent.

"Hi, Mrs. Proctor. I'm Jane from the insurance company, here to take pictures of the house that had the fire." This was met with a look of surprise. I was embarrassed that she seemed to not be expecting me. "My boss said that you or your husband might drive me to the site and back to catch the ferry when I'm done taking a look."

"Oh, I am so sorry. It's just, well, I was . . ." she stuttered, clearly taken off guard. "Well, ummm, it's just that I assumed a man would be here. No offense. Not that I *wanted* a man over a woman. I know that women can do anything, it's just that, well, you know."

"Yes," I lied, "I can imagine your surprise. I'll have to advise my boss to give people a heads-up in the future." Maybe my mother was right about this place, I thought. What a jerk. "Are you able to take me to the Kohls', Mrs. Proctor?"

"Oh, I am so sorry. I must sound like an idiot. Call me Joan. I just assumed that you were one of those Jehovah Witnesses. They come out here every few months trying to convert us. And with so few folks around in the winter, I'm tempted to convert just for the company!"

My opinion of Mrs. Proctor lightened.

"Of course, I will be happy to chauffer you around our island," she smiled. "But first I have to make a couple more calls. And I'll try not to rattle on about nothing. My husband, his name is Clark, well, he warns everyone about me. He's still at the Kohls' house, I guess. Says it's a goner. What a shame. Just good that nobody got hurt." She took a breath and slid an open notebook closer to herself. "We haven't been able to reach the Kohls to tell them of the disaster at their house. They will be so upset!"

She began dialing again, reading the number from a notebook on the table. "My biscuits!" She grabbed a pot holder with her right hand, and opened the oven door with her left while clutching the phone under her chin. She placed the hot baking sheet filled with golden brown biscuits on top of the range and joined me at the table. She left another message, identical to the first, and mashed the hang-up button on the phone with some force. "I'm almost out of numbers," she fretted. "These people are nonexistent unless they want something from us. If Mrs. K needed beds changed or a meal prepared, I had better jump to the phone on the first ring," she complained. "Mr. Kohl woke us up one night to fix a squeaky screen door. Can you believe that? Who the hell uses the screen door after eight o'clock? City folks!" She dialed again, listened optimistically, frowned and hung up. "But when the call is going in the other direction, nobody's home! Let's have a biscuit. Best you've ever had, guaranteed. My mother's recipe with Bakewell Cream." She placed a biscuit on a plate and put it down in front of me, and did the same with one for herself. Not one to refuse food, I cut the biscuit in half, and covered it with butter that she pushed my way after slicing and slathering hers. The first bite melted in my mouth.

This was not merely a vehicle for sausage gravy. This was simply the best—as advertised by its creator.

While I savored the buttery treat, I listened to Joan. She was clearly delighted to have someone to talk to. She actually mentioned that she hadn't been "off island" since July, and that had been only for a dental appointment—annual cleaning, to be precise. She was starving for conversation (her words, not mine), and was suffering from acute cabin fever (again, her words). I listened to her leave messages. I listened to her while she told me about the Kohls and how the loss of their house was a loss of income for her and her husband as caretakers. I listened to her as she lamented changes the island had withstood, and some she worried that it would not. I listened all the way through a second biscuit, when she finally got a live voice on the other end of the phone. I listened to Joan as *she* listened. And all the while that I listened, I wondered whether including my family name when I introduced myself would have brought any reaction. With all the information spewing from Joan so quickly, it was likely that she could sum up the history of the Bunkers between bites of biscuit.

When Joan put the phone down, she shared that Mr. Kohl was traveling on business and unreachable, and that nobody knew the whereabouts of Mrs. Kohl. The couple always went their separate ways, and did not feel they needed to leave itineraries with anyone. "All I know is that he is out of the country, and that she is somewhere between here and Philly. She flew out of here just yesterday. Maybe she left the kettle on or the iron plugged in or something . . ." Footsteps overhead interrupted

Joan's surmising. She pointed at the ceiling and said, "Daughter Trudy. Home from law school. Georgetown."

"Oh, nice," I said. "Do you think we can leave soon? I really have to spend some time taking pictures before the boat leaves."

"Of course! Let me wash these dishes real quick, and we'll go. It's only a ten-minute ride." Footsteps coming down stairs grew closer. A young woman, I supposed Trudy, walked into the kitchen. She wore a T-shirt that at first glance appeared to be in Chinese characters, but actually spelled "Fuck You" in English. Her hair looked like it had just been pulled from a pillow. Static electricity fanned a few individual strands up and waving at the ceiling like sea anemone in tidal current. She was a thin version of her mother, minus the bleached hair. "Good morning, sleepyhead," Joan said softly. "This is Jane."

"Hi. The biscuits smell amazing. I'm starving." I couldn't help but point out the total lack of a Maine accent when Joan's was the most pronounced I had ever heard.

"Yes," Joan answered. "Trudy has denounced her heritage since going away to college. She has totally dropped any sign of being from Maine."

"Like a bad habit," the daughter added. Trudy took one look at me with my camera bag now on my shoulder, and said, "You must be here to document the freak show."

Before I could respond, her mother reprimanded, "Come on, Trude. That's not fair, or nice. There was a terrible fire last night, dear. The Kohls' house. It's not good. Your father and I are very upset. Jane is here for the insurance company."

"Oh, what a drag," Trudy mumbled. She clearly could not

have cared less. She pulled a cup from a cupboard and poured a cup of coffee. "Figures the insurance company is here before the fire is extinguished."

"Trudy Proctor! That is rude. Don't mind her, Jane. She's flippant when she's upset." I sensed that this was a common exchange between mother and daughter, and was not at all taken aback by it.

"Oh yeah," Trudy sighed and rolled her eyes. "I can assure you that I am one hundred percent distraught over this. It could truly not have *happened* to a *better* person than Midge Kohl." She cradled the cup of coffee in both hands, and stood tapping one foot, looking as if she were impatient about us being there, and was waiting for us to leave. It seemed to me that Trudy had something to do that she didn't want witnessed. But it could have just as easily been her poor attitude and nothing more. My training for profiling had included many courses on behavior, and I was educated to know that people of Trudy's age were normally conflicted. Brimming with confidence and edgy with self-doubt; I sensed emotions and identity roiling beneath the young woman's cool exterior.

Joan dried the dishes, bundled up for the cold, and kissed her daughter on the forehead. We climbed into the Jeep, and off we went—finally, I thought, I would accomplish my mission. The road, Joan explained, was one continuous loop that circumnavigated the island. She apologized for the rough ride, as I hung on to the "oh shit" handle over the passenger-side window.

"This place is going to hell in a handbasket," she said mournfully. "We thought the plant would be a good way to secure lobster prices and some good jobs. It was to be our salvation.

34

The whole idea seems to be backfiring. Christ, they don't even fill the craters in the road anymore," she complained as she slowed down to carefully straddle a major pothole.

I asked for some explanation, more out of politeness than interest. She explained that some summer residents had financed the construction of a lobster cooking and packaging plant as a way to create some year-round jobs and maintain a steady price to lobster fishermen for their product. Processing plants and value-added lobster products (the most popular of which was lobster mac and cheese, which was quite a contradiction, I thought) were popping up all over the coast of Maine, but this one was special as the only island-based plant. And the Acadia Lobster Products (ALP) brand was quickly recognized for its quality and story. "But," Joan continued, "the story isn't one that we are particularly proud of as it turns out."

"What's the story?" I asked, wondering how much farther we would have to go. I resisted looking at my watch. Joan seemed relieved to have someone to talk to who knew nothing of the situation. I understood the inclination to spill emotions to total strangers who couldn't judge beyond what they were told. Not that Joan was overly emotional. But it was clear that she was unhappy with recent changes to her island, and that her family's identity as Acadians had, in her opinion, been tainted by those changes.

She explained that the idea of the plant had been unanimously supported by both summer and permanent residents as a solution to the dwindling year-round population. Well-paying, full-time jobs would be a way for young islanders to make their homes and lives and families right here. Generations of kids had left to find work and never returned; the result was a relatively aged populace. The problem with the ALP solution that nobody foresaw was that there were not enough residents to fill the positions created by the plant to get it off the ground. The folks who had financed the construction of the facility were uptight about getting a return on their investments, so they rushed to a solution that not everyone was happy with. Workers were imported from the mainland. A boardinghouse was built to house twenty of them.

I didn't understand what the issue was until Joan shared that the workers had all come to Acadia through a program that gave felons released from prison a fresh start, some of whom were registered sex offenders. "I know that everyone deserves a second chance," Joan said. "But some of these folks are on their third and fourth chances. The few Islanders with young children have either already moved to the mainland or are thinking about it. And quite a number of summer people have put their places on the market. Real estate values have tanked."

Joan slowed the Jeep to a crawl and rolled her window down as we passed an enormous estate. She stopped and pointed at the main house, which was obviously occupied, with a plowed drive and lights on in windows. "The Sterns sold this place for a third of its value. Bailed out. Like rats from a sinking ship. And their ancestors founded Acadia!" Shaking her head in disgust that she had likely shared with many, she closed the window and continued driving.

"Who lives there now?" I asked.

"Perverts. Five of them," Joan stated bluntly. "The investors in the plant bought up houses as they came on the market. The ex-cons weren't thriving together at the boardinghouse, so the owners have separated the sex offenders from the crooks. And the violent criminals are living on the east side—quite posh. The only two women in the program are roomies in what used to be the Bragg Cottage."

"Wow. Sounds like the ex-cons lucked out with this program," I said.

"Yup. They are making a great wage—way above the minimum and unlimited overtime during peak season." Joan sighed. "But maybe not for long. They have demanded so much that the investors are having second thoughts and may pull out. If that happens, the ex-cons will have to move off-island for jobs."

The smell of smoke penetrated the Jeep before the fire scene came into view. The majority of my experience in fire investigation had to do with meth labs that had exploded; those odors were complex and noxious. But any house fire had a number of smells associated with the burning of building materials, age of the structure, and various contents. As we crested a slight hill, what remained of the Kohls' place appeared, still smoldering. Two external walls were still standing, but the roof had collapsed in a charred heap that covered quite an expanse.

"It was a big place, wasn't it?" I thought out loud as Joan pulled the Jeep to a stop, expecting no reply and getting none. "Okay, thanks so much for the ride. I'll need about an hour or so, then I'll have to get back to the dock." Joan agreed, apologized for babbling, and promised to "chew my other ear off" on the return trip.

As I climbed out of the Jeep, a truck rumbled down the hill, pulling in beside us. Joan spoke quieter now. "Don't get me wrong. This place isn't as bad as I may have made it sound. It's paradise, really," she said with an apologetic tone. "At least we don't have a drug problem like the mainland. And we wouldn't live anywhere else." Windows went down and Joan introduced me as "the insurance lady" to her husband, who explained that he had just returned the fire truck to its garage. His clothes were black with soot and laced with small holes where sparks had landed. His beard appeared to have been singed. A twinkle in his blue eyes double-crossed his otherwise fatigued appearance. I extended my arm to shake hands and Clark gave me his left awkwardly, holding up his right that was wrapped in filthy gauze. "Battle wound." He turned to his wife and added, "Nothing to worry about." The couple discussed how best to retrieve the Kohls' car from the airstrip, and finally decided that I might help them. They explained that the airstrip was right on the way to the dock where I needed to be in two hours, and also where the Kohls liked their car to be while they were away, as weather was often an issue with flying, making the boat a must. Of course I was happy to assist. I couldn't help but notice that Joan was not talkative in the presence of her husband, but figured that was normal. Without many people to converse with all winter, they must surely have hashed everything over ad nauseam. Joan left to get lunch for Clark, and he promised to be right behind her after showing me what was what regarding the fire.

"How can I help you, umm, what was your name?" he asked, clearly embarrassed that he had forgotten, although he had never been told my name.

Decision time whether or not to give him my family name

was short. "Jane Bunker." Clark looked confused for a second. He stood and took a long look into my eyes as if he were trying to remember something. My instinct was to nip any curiosity in the bud. I was here on insurance company business. Business first, I silently reminded myself. "I'm here to take pictures that will demonstrate the degree of damage as well as anything that might tell the story of how the fire started, you know, to rule out arson."

I followed as Clark led me through the snow on a path beaten down by footsteps. His broad shoulders said hard, physical work, while a slight slump said tired. Closer to what remained of the dwelling, acrid smoke lingered, hovering just above the remainder of a stone foundation. I could hear a vague sizzling and an occasional, faint *pop*.

"At first I assumed that Mrs. Kohl left the teakettle on. But while we were fighting the fire, I noticed a gas line busted by a frost heave. The propane must have settled and may have been ignited by the pilot on the water heater. Just a guess, though."

I didn't know whether to ask for a definition of a frost heave or give him my condolences on the loss of the fight to the fire. As if reading my mind, he continued. "I know. Everything went wrong. This place is isolated, so the fire really got ripping before anyone noticed. Then the fire truck wouldn't start. The garage isn't heated, and, well, it was awful cold last night."

"When and how were you made aware of the fire?" I asked my routine question.

"Well, I was asleep and heard the church bell. That's the Island's alarm system for any emergency. We all, well, there's only six of us left, we meet at the garage to learn what the emergency is. By the time I got there, they were already jumping the truck batteries. And I guess that would have been about ten o'clock. One of the guys had to drive by the Kohls' to get to the garage, so knew exactly where we needed to be. But the damned truck was so hard to get started. She's cold-blooded, and hasn't been run since the Fourth of July parade. Anyhow, by the time we got here, we didn't have a prayer of a chance."

"Yes, I can see that," I said as I attached a lens to my camera and began snapping pictures. "Can't do much with just one truck."

"And with the frigid temps, we had freezing issues. Once we got here, we were quite a while getting water pumping," he explained while following me around the perimeter of the scene. "Well, if you're all set, I'll go grab lunch and come back for you."

I thanked Clark and agreed to be ready in an hour. I am usually a good judge of character, and thought that Clark and Joan were solid people. Clark had been up all night fighting a fire for absentee home owners, and for what? I had written this place off as a total loss from my first glance. Now all I needed was pictures, and my job here would be done. I bolstered myself to question Clark about the Bunkers while I mindlessly snapped photographs of charcoal. I was certain that Clark had recognized my name. Good thing he's fatigued to a point of numbness, I thought. I wanted to have the conversation on my terms, not his.

The corner of the two remaining exterior walls held a stone chimney; strong and stark like the foundation bordering the mess. I immediately thought of the Three Little Pigs as I snapped pictures of the unharmed stone structure that stood in rebellion to all that had folded to the flames. I found a gap in the foundation where a doorway must have been, and stepped carefully toward the rubble, putting arms out for balance on the icy path. Quite an anomaly, I thought, to have freezing conditions this close to a fire so hot that it gobbled up a house. Recalling that the wind had been out of the northeast, I realized that the fire must have started on the northeast portion of the house and quickly spread, heat and all, to the southwest. That accounted for the ice on this side of the structure as well as the only remaining walls. Everything downwind of the trigger point had been destroyed. And it had been extremely windy in Green Haven last night. Must have been worse here, I thought. The break in the propane line could have been anywhere. If Clark was right that the water heater had ignited the fuel, it would probably have been located on the upwind side of the blaze. I should get pictures of the broken line as well as the water heater—if I could find them.

Looking down to find sure footing, I noticed a few spots of blood that had been iced over in the snow. The snow had diffused the blood to dark pink splotches. Judging from the small amount of blood, I surmised that Clark had been honest about his injury—nothing to worry about. There mustn't be much for medical services here, I thought. Residents are probably very good at taking care of themselves and each other. As I searched for the propane lines and water heating tank, I continued to snap pictures.

I let my mind wander to Wally, and was immediately struck with pangs of guilt. How could I be so selfish, worrying about how my brother could intrude in my life? Wally had always enriched, never detracted from anything. And I had planned for him to visit Maine this summer anyway. I would have to do some research for assisted-living situations when I got ashore, I thought. I climbed over a pile of smoldering ash and charred wood that still had flickering embers. At least the fire had been contained by the snow, and could not spread beyond this single dwelling, I thought.

I found what appeared to be a metal tank, still standing upright and partially covered by debris that had fallen onto it. If I moved some of the debris, I could get a few good pictures, I thought. I kicked smoking ruins of what may have been a wall aside with the toe of a boot and put the camera to my eye. Zooming in close, I could now see a small plate on the tank. I wiped the plate clean with the cuff of my shirt and snapped more pictures. I would look up the information from the plate online when I got home to include in my report for Mr. Dubois. Just a few more pictures and I'd be . . .

"What?" I lowered the camera from my eye and kneeled down to get a closer look. I took a breath and swallowed hard. A badly bloated and blistered hand nestled in the carbonized fragments of wood. The presence of remains of jewelry led me to conclude that I had found the errant Mrs. Kohl.

THREE

Statistics from the Forensics of Fire course completed so many years ago came racing back. *The average house fire burns at 1000 degrees Fahrenheit. Gold melts at 2000 degrees. Diamonds liquefy at 6000.* Jewelry is nearly always intact in the aftermath of fire, especially the good stuff. Judging from the size of what I presumed was a diamond on the badly scorched finger, the victim, whom I assumed was Mrs. Kohl, had lavish taste in accessories. This rock was beyond bling. In contrast, the remains of a dark red plastic loop had fused around the exposed wrist. The cooling process had left it brittle. I broke off a one-inch section and placed it in my camera bag out of sheer curiosity. I couldn't help but wonder what political cause Mrs. Kohl supported strongly enough to wear an awareness bracelet on the same wrist that sported a multicarat gem, and assumed that it was not one promoting fire safety. A thin gold chain with a half-heart pendant was in relatively good shape, I thought as I flipped the pendant over and read the inscription: "To the Moon." I concluded the obvious. The matching pendant must be owned by Mr. Kohl. This thought worked to ground me in the sadness of this accident. Someone had died needlessly. Someone who had been loved. The pendant must have gotten very hot, as it had left a burn on the victim's neck that could have been mistaken as a birthmark had there not been a pendant of the same distinct shape of the heart split in two. I reached for my cell. No signal—no surprise. Clark would be back soon, I knew. Until then, I would do my thing.

Any part of Mrs. Kohl that might have been spared by the blaze and crushing impact of the structural failure was now beneath the crumbling, sooty wall and ceiling that had collapsed upon her. I needed to dig her out, I thought as I shifted from insurance to sheriff. *Nearly 80 percent of fire deaths are the result of smoke inhalation*, so it was likely that Mrs. Kohl had succumbed to smoke and toxic fumes prior to heat and flames wreaking havoc. It was evident that she had not died in her sleep, as the corpse's location was in what may have been the utility area; surrounded by remains of a water heater and burned-out appliances. Clark Proctor may have nailed it with his theory of a gas leak ignited by the pilot flame of the water heater, I thought. Probably Mrs. Kohl made the mistake of trying to extinguish the fire rather than fleeing and summoning help, I surmised. I continued to toss lengths of blackened wood, asphalt shingles, and unidentified material aside, removing pieces of debris from the heap that entombed all but the left hand until all that remained was what appeared to be fire retardant dry wall.

Back in the day when gruesome was a daily occurrence, I was known for my strong stomach, but braced myself nonetheless for the sight and smell of what I was about to uncover. I lifted the edge of the wall to peek underneath. There was enough integrity remaining in this small section of the wall to allow me to pick it up on edge and off of the corpse without crumbling, exposing the thoroughly burned body. Recollections from my days spent with Elayne Pope, a forensics scientist at the University of West Florida, hit me with the smell of roast pork that wafted in my face as I let the wall fall on its flip side and away from Mrs. Kohl.

Pope had done amazing work burning cadavers in different conditions and situations to improve the breadth of knowledge and thus success in forensic investigation of death by fire. Other than the tutorial with Pope, most of the burn victims with whom I had dealt were within the cases of my DEA work; addicts who had blown their own faces and hands off in the midst of mixing a fix. This burn exceeded my past experience.

As I expected, the head, having little overlying soft tissue, was reduced to charred skull and jaw. Only sockets remained of the eyes. Both feet and legs were gone from below the knee—*limbs burn like branches of a tree.* And the entire right arm was gone to the armpit. The torso could be described as nothing more than carcass. I shook my head with the realization that I had actually been trained to unravel scenes as these. *Most fat is stored in the thighs and torso. Extreme heat splits skin, exposing fat that fuels the flames. Clothing works to wick the fat, resulting in a very thorough burn.* I was torn between appreciation for this knowledge and wishing I didn't have it. The left arm, left side of the neck, and left breast were relatively well preserved, I thought, considering the extent of the . . . dare I say "damage"? Sadly, once living beings cease to live, they are things to me. Before my drug enforcement gig, I spent years responding to automobile accidents; many of which resulted in corpses more horrific than victims of serial killers. I had to steel myself, or suffer from the nightmares, daymares, and PTSD that drive many officers to drink, or worse. I became hardened to it, tough and uncompassionate. That's why I have never been the officer or investigator asked to inform loved ones of their newly deceased. "No bedside manner" is how my superiors put it early in my career.

I wished I had something with which to cover the corpse out of respect for Clark Proctor and anyone else who might happen upon the scene. But there was nothing other than my own coat. And I wasn't about to part with that in these temperatures. The focus of my camera lens was now the cadaver. Mr. Dubois would be alarmed to learn that one of his favorite clients had been consumed along with her property. Death in a house fire complicated the investigation as well as the paperwork. I assumed this would mean more trips to Acadia for me, since there was no fire marshal or formal investigators. I had learned in my few cases based out of Green Haven that I would not have much support or help from anyone who had the requisite expertise or experience. I would head up, and facilitate, and do the leg work, ground work, follow-up work, and closing work of whatever Mr. Dubois would require to finalize the insurance claim. And I had done everything but perform autopsies on behalf of the Hancock County Sheriff's Department. If there was an opportunity to get the corpse in a body bag and off on the next boat with me, that would be ideal, I thought. My work here would be done. I wouldn't return until I had both time and inclination to do some personal, firsthand genealogical research.

I made my way back to the perimeter of the fire, slowly and carefully stepping over and around the rubble of the building, which seemed to clutch the last of dying, orange, glowing embers. Beams and framing pieces reduced to fragile spindles looked as though they might give way to any applied weight. In striking juxtaposition, the corner of a slate sink jutted from another pile of rubble and feathery ash. No more meals in this place, I thought. I wondered if Joan Proctor had reached Mr. Kohl. I hoped not. Better now for the officials to break the sad news of his wife's death. I wasn't sure who that would be. But it wouldn't be me.

Sensing that time was running short, I thought it best to walk toward the main road and away from the lingering smoke and various noxious fumes, and intercept Clark when he arrived. As I took baby steps over the icy rim formed by the overspray from the fire hose, I again noticed the splotches of blood. May as well, I thought as I dug through my camera bag for an empty container into which to scrape a sample of the blood. This was more a precaution and covering my own butt than it related to any investigative process. It was highly unlikely that the blood would ever be analyzed for DNA, so I wasn't particularly careful about contamination. I shook crumbs out of a plastic sandwich bag. My jackknife was the right tool for cutting through the thin layer of ice and gouging out enough for a fine specimen of the blood-soaked snow beneath. Zipping the bag closed and dropping it into my camera bag, I headed to the road just as the Jeep Cherokee came into view.

Joan was at the wheel. When she stopped, I opened the door, and climbed in. Joan immediately started jabbering about how Clark was so exhausted that he had to shower and get some sleep, and he was glad to have met me and . . . I pulled the door closed and put my hand on Joan's wrist, silently asking for her attention. She obediently placed the Jeep in park and looked at me with the same raised eyebrows I met when I entered her home earlier. "A woman has died in the fire. I assume it's Midge Kohl," I stated unemotionally.

A look of horror and hands flying up to cover a gaping mouth were accompanied by a loud wailing, "Oh, God. No. Oh no." I asked what typically is done when someone dies on Acadia. Joan trembled and began crying. Not one to console, I waited. She made attempts to speak between jagged breaths, but words were stolen by the need to catch the next inhale. I repeated the question. Her breathing slowly returned to normal and the crying subsided to sniffling. "Well, oh my! Well, when Clark's dad passed away, we took him off wrapped in a sleeping bag on a stretcher. The county ambulance met the mail boat at the dock, and took him to the hospital where he was pronounced dead. But that was different. He was old." Now tears streamed down Joan's cheeks again. Her hands shook violently as she sobbed. "We didn't even know she was here!" I waited for the hysteria to subside so that I could ask another question.

I really wished that Clark had come to pick me up. Men are usually much more together and less emotional when faced with dead bodies, I thought and immediately regretted the sexist in me. The same sexism that I admonished in Joan's stammering surprise this morning with the fact that I was doing what she

obviously counted as a man's job, was now reinforced by her ste-
reotypical reaction to news that someone was dead. I had a sudden urge to slap her face to bring her around, but resisted; doing
so would feed the stereotype another heap of fuel.

Joan gasped for a breath, and I jumped in the free space. "We
need a body bag, or sleeping bag, or something to wrap the remains in so that we can get them . . . umm, her to the boat. And
I need to use a phone." She pulled herself together, I assume
assisted by my calm and task-oriented order. "We don't want to
leave Mrs. Kohl out in the elements any longer," I said, using a
little psychology. "She needs to be handled by us, with the
respect that she deserves," I continued. It was a conscious effort
to refer to the corpse with the feminine pronoun.

Joan found a paper towel jammed between the seats that
looked as if it had been used to wipe the Jeep's dipstick, and used
it to dry her eyes and blow her nose. She nodded as I spoke, and
pointed to a sailboat on the opposite side of the road. "How
about a tarp? Will that work? It's a custom winter wrap made
special for the Kohls' boat—*BLISSFUL RETURNS*. Would
that be okay?"

"Perfect. Let's go," I said. She slammed the Jeep into gear
and stepped on the gas pedal like a woman on a mission, which
she was. She jammed the Jeep into four-wheel drive, and was
able to pull right up to the tarped boat that sat peacefully in its
beefy wooden cradle. The dark green tarp had been made in
three pieces. I figured that the bow section would be more than
large enough, and the easiest to handle. Utilizing my trusty
pocketknife again, I cut the lines securing the tarpaulin to the
cradle, and Joan pulled it away from the bowsprit until it lay at

her feet with an avalanche of snow that had accumulated in the last storm. I cupped my hands and exhaled into them, trying to warm them up a bit. My toes were numb. I hadn't thought of it until now, but the burned-out house held a lot of heat, and I had been quite comfortable until now. I was anxious to get back to the smoldering wreckage and grabbed the tarp. Working together, we shoved the tarp in through the Jeep's hatchback, and slogged our way through the snow, across the road, and back to what remained of the Kohls' dwelling.

"Maybe I should go get Clark," Joan said, her voice now flat. I explained that we didn't have time, and that it was best out of respect for Mrs. Kohl to not permit anyone else to see her in such a state. Joan agreed, mentioning how vain Mrs. Kohl had always been. "Why, she wouldn't be caught dead without full makeup. Oh, sorry. Poor choice of words."

I dragged the tarp behind me as I made my way back to the edge of the burned-out foundation. Entering through the same doorway I had before, I was straddling a fallen beam when the tarp caught on something, halting my progress. I didn't want to sound insensitive, so I didn't mention to Joan that my biggest concern was missing the boat—literally. I had to get home tonight to sift through the options for having my brother live in Green Haven. I needed to get off this island with or without the corpse. I yanked the tarp to no avail. Joan was lagging behind, and seemingly unwilling to lend a hand.

"Hey, grab the other end, will ya?" I yelled. Joan snapped out of the trance she appeared to be in and freed the end of the tarp, holding it like the train on a debutante's ball gown as she shuffled through the mess. She appeared to be in shock. I hated myself for being so cool about what we were doing, but years of dead bodies had formed calluses where Joan had raw emotion. I wished I could do this myself, sparing this nice woman the trauma of seeing what would cause her to be awakened by her own screams for many nights to come.

Joan stood over the body and stared in disbelief. She inhaled and wrinkled her nose. She squinted her eyes as if tolerating great pain. She stiffened as if paralyzed. I wanted to tell her that we needed to hustle, but instead allowed her a minute. She sniffed the air again, and turned her gaze at me, ready to pose a question. Knowing what she would ask, I said:

"Roast pork."

Joan's complexion turned from pale to green as she swallowed whatever had risen in her throat. She placed a hand over bulging cheeks and fought the gag reflex. "Go ahead. Puke and get it over with," I said, crassly. Joan was clearly very familiar with the house's layout. She scurried over to a once-white porcelain toilet, and threw up loudly and violently while I stretched the tarp out alongside the remains of Mrs. Kohl. I glanced over just in time to see Joan wipe her mouth on her coat sleeve.

Joan was quick to gather herself and joined me over the body with a vengeance. Her horror had now become rage. She was really pissed at me, and offered no pretenses about it. I understood her reaction as I had seen it many times before. "I can't fuckin' believe this," she mumbled. "Now what?"

I instructed Joan to help me move the corpse onto the tarp, which she did. Once we arranged the corpse into position, we proceeded to drape both ends of the tarp over the body, then roll tightly, as she commented, "Like a fuckin' burrito." We each grabbed an end of the roll and lifted to carry it to the Jeep. It was heavy, which didn't escape comment from Joan.

"Jesus Christ! Of all the people to have to be lugged, it had to be fat-ass Midge Kohl . . . I knew I should have sent Clark to get you." We struggled, but made it over and around all of the debris piles and over the edge of the stone foundation. "And he told me who you are," she continued, back to her verbose self. "Insurance, my ass. Fuckin' Nancy Drew." I was relieved that all Clark knew of my past was my occupation. But that relief was short-lived. "Just when we thought we'd seen the last of the Bunkers, along comes long-lost Jane. And look at this mess!" She was clearly implying that my presence had somehow caused the horror that she had been enlisted to deal with. No matter, I thought. I'd just let her rant. She didn't even know what she was saying, and likely would not remember most of it by the next morning. Shock affects different people differently, I knew. I wouldn't take anything personally.

We placed the corpse on the ground behind the Jeep long enough to open the tailgate. We lifted together, swung the package back and forth counting out loud, and flung it into the back of the Jeep on the third swing. Slamming the tailgate closed, Joan reached up with a high five for me. "Yeah, that's what I'm talking about. Nicely done." Clearly delirious, I thought. She'd come full circle soon and be back to the sobbing and shaking. I hoped I'd be aboard the boat by then.

Joan continued to talk—mostly about nothing—as she drove slowly, cautiously avoiding the larger bumps. I knew without her saying so that she was deliberately giving the corpse a nice, gentle ride, which seemed ridiculous on so many levels, but spoke to her genuine caring personality in spite of her outbursts. She reminded me that we needed to retrieve the Kohls' car from the airport, which again made no sense to me. But I was happy to assist her on this rather than remind her that Mrs. Kohl would not be needing it. I looked at my cell phone. Still no service.

"Unless you have Down East Premium, you might as well forget about the phone until we get back to the west side," Joan advised. She then went into a detailed history of cell service on Acadia, which took us all the way to a tiny airstrip in the middle of a thickly wooded area. I wondered why Mrs. Kohl's vehicle would be here, as she clearly had not left the island. There were no cars in sight.

Joan came to her senses and said, "Maybe it's at ALP. We have to pass right by there to get back to the dock. Mr. Kohl refuses to fly, so we like to leave the car at the dock for him," she explained. Now Joan was thinking and speculating. It's natural to try to make sense of things, I knew.

"Clark must have assumed someone had given Mrs. Kohl a lift to the airport or dock, and moved her car from the house. We are constantly moving their vehicle around. They never travel together," she explained. "Or she could have left her car at ALP intentionally and gotten a ride home from someone. Or, well, the possibilities are endless. We usually refer to their car as Waldo. Where's Waldo is a weekly game for us as their care-takers. I would feel better if we knew where the car was. And we should get it to the dock for Mr. Kohl. As soon as he gets the bad news, he'll be heading this way, I'm certain of it. And he is as particular about things as she is, or was . . ." A tear formed in the corner of her eye, and she wiped it away with the back of her hand.

I was relieved that Joan was talking sense now. She seemed to have her wits about her. Not knowing her for more than this very brief period, it seemed she could handle crisis better than the majority of people I had come across in my life in similar situations. I wondered if her ability to quickly transit the stages of this traumatic event was part of the human fabric of Acadia Island. With no law enforcement or trained firefighters, or fire marshal, or medical professionals, or . . . well, there was purportedly nobody here equipped to deal with matters professionally, so I imagined that everyone dealt with everything in their own "island way." I wondered what she knew about the Bunkers that gave her the attitude. I would certainly learn more about that. All in good time, I thought as Joan wheeled the Jeep around and up to a large metal building with signage marking it as "Acadia Lobster Products."

There were about a dozen vehicles in the area marked "Employee Parking," which really surprised me, as we had seen zero activity all day. A forklift zipped around to the loading dock and a door magically opened, displaying a pallet of colorfully designed boxes. I couldn't read the print from the distance.

"Today is frozen tails. The main plant is cooking, processing, and packaging. The product is then taken over there," she pointed to a second, smaller building, "where it's frozen and eventually shipped." We passed another building with a double loading dock. "This is where the live product is shipped from. Most of it is going to China." It was good to know that this part of Acadia was up and running and very much alive. Just in front of what

I assumed was the main entrance, I noticed a woman with what looked like a picket sign. I estimated the temperature to be in the teens. And the protester was all alone, which made it even weirder. As we got a bit closer, I recognized the bundled-up gal as Trudy, Joan and Clark's daughter. Joan had her blinders on, I thought as she consciously ignored my questioning stare through the driver's-side window as we passed Trudy, who marched back and forth before the entryway. I nearly laughed at the thought of this college girl trying to change the world— here on Acadia Island.

Joan rattled on about the miracle of high-tech freight boxes designed to keep lobsters alive, and how these special boxes were the biggest contributor to higher and consistent lobster prices. She was clearly embarrassed by her daughter, and was trying to distract me from looking at her. Joan certainly didn't need to worry about Trudy inciting any riots, I thought. She'd be lucky to get a second look.

"Phew," Joan signed. "There's the Kohls' Range Rover. The key should be under the floor mat. Follow me to the dock. You'll just make the boat." I jumped out of the Jeep and into the Range Rover, found the key under the mat, and was out of the parking area closely behind the Jeep, which sped quickly by Trudy. I glanced over and saw that her sign read "Lobsters Feel Pain!" Wow, I thought, Trudy really had her hands full protesting killing lobsters in a place where the only income is derived from doing so. Ballsy kid, I thought with a chuckle.

As soon as Trudy was out of sight, Joan began creeping along, driving barely over a crawl. I tried to be patient. Flipping open the top of my bag in the passenger seat, I dug for my phone.

No service. The time was 2:45. I had about fifteen minutes to get myself and the cadaver aboard the boat before it left. I was disappointed to have no time to insist on finding a phone to make a few calls. I wanted to give Mr. Dubois a heads-up, and call the sheriff to make arrangements for someone to collect the corpse. My landlords are welcoming, but this might be pushing their limits, I thought with a chuckle. Just then, music rang out from within the vehicle, loud and clear. A custom ringtone that I recognized as "Don't Worry, Be Happy" played as I followed the tune to a cubbyhole in the center console between the bucket seats.

I fumbled for the phone, and finally grasped it just as the music stopped. Missed call. I waited to see if the caller would leave a message. Nope. I'm fairly certain that I would *not* have answered the phone if I *had* found it in time, though. There is something very intriguing and mysterious about the phone of a deceased person. Realizing that I could now place calls with this phone, I dialed 411 and got directory assistance to text me a number for the Hancock County Sheriff's Department. Mrs. Kohl's phone beeped, and I opened the text message to the number. How fortunate for me that Mrs. Kohl used Down East Premium, and that she had no locks on her phone. Old school, I thought. But not in her choice of phones. This one was the latest and greatest of technology, and far superior to mine. I was immediately connected to Hancock County Sheriff's Department, where I spoke to Deloris, the dispatcher. She took the message for the sheriff, and promised to make all arrangements to relieve me from my duty of escorting the corpse as soon as the boat touched the dock in South Haven.

Before I could call Mr. Dubois, I was in the parking area above the dock. I could see a boat at the float, and knew that it was my ride ashore. Joan motioned for me to park, which I did, leaving the ignition key under the floor mat where I had found it. Joan backed the Jeep down the narrow, icy way to the top of the ramp where she hopped out and ran down and aboard the boat. By the time I reached the ramp, she was headed back up with two men closely behind, one of whom carried a back-board. I was relieved to see that there were no passengers coming and going on this particular trip. Word would spread quickly enough—it always does in a small, close-knit commu-nity. Joan introduced the men as the captain and mate of the boat and explained that they would help with Mrs. Kohl. The men may have been father and son, I thought. I filled them in on my conversation with Hancock County, assuring them that we would be met on the other end, and the corpse would no longer be our responsibility. As they loaded Mrs. Kohl onto the backboard, the mate admitted to being "creeped out" by dead bodies, to which the captain responded that it was thankfully only a forty-minute trip. I silently concurred.

There was some heated, yet low-voiced discussion of whether the rolled tarp should ride in the wheelhouse or on the deck. Joan wanted Mrs. Kohl's last boat ride to be more dignified than sharing the deck with boxes of empty milk jugs. The captain and crew were not excited about sharing their space within the cabin with a cadaver who was not even able to pay the boat fare, and one that seemingly had never been their favorite customer. A compromise was quickly reached: Mrs. Kohl was placed on the bench seat across the transom, the most coveted outdoor seating in the summer, and where the mate insisted Mr. Kohl always perched when transiting. This seemed to appease Joan, the consummate caretaker.

Before disembarking, Joan surprised me with a tight hug. "Well, Jane Bunker, we've had quite an afternoon, haven't we?" She reached in her hip pocket and pulled out a business card that she handed to me and said, "When you want to visit the island on different terms, give me a call. I'd love to show you around and answer any questions you might have." I promised to be in touch, and thanked her for her help. I attempted to say that I was sorry for her loss and offer an apology of some kind, but the mate was throwing lines, forcing Joan to step off the boat and onto the float. I glanced at her card as the boat pulled away from the float—"Beck and Call Caretaking," a phone number, and address—good to have, I thought as I slipped it into my bag. It would indeed be nice to visit Acadia Island under different circumstances.

From within the cabin, I stared absentmindedly out the back window. The captain and mate were very quiet. I supposed that my presence may have dampened any chitchat they might usually enjoy. The silence was uncomfortable, and I felt they were torn between wanting to ask questions and respecting my privacy. Or they could simply be shy, or not give a damn about me or how my day unfolded to end with a dead body. I wasn't looking at anything in particular until the lettering on the custom boat tarp came into focus. The Kohls' boat's name was somewhat obscured by the various folds, and now read, *BLIS-TURS*. That is the definition of macabre, I thought as I turned my attention to the forward cabin, and hoped nobody else would notice the sick, yet appropriate coincidence. The captain steered the boat while his mate stood beside him and watched the electronics. It appeared that they were making efforts to keep all eyes forward, lest they might catch a glimpse of what stretched across the seat in the stern, conjuring up all sorts of unsavory images. Even the best imagination couldn't do the truth justice, I thought. Grim.

When I thought we were about halfway back to South Haven, I checked my phone and was delighted to see nearly full service. I hustled out of the cabin and dialed Mr. Dubois at the Marine Insurance Consultants Company. He answered on the first ring, and asked where I was. He had already gotten word that Mr. Kohl was aware of his wife's death, which answered my question about whether the Proctors had been able to reach him. Mr. Kohl had also been in touch with the sheriff's department, insisting on a full investigation to negate any suspicion that would naturally arise when dealing with substantial life insurance policies. I told my boss that I had been very thorough, and did not find anything suspicious about the fire or the death. But I certainly understood Mr. Kohl's inclination to want to protect himself. I confirmed that I would arrive at the dock in South Haven in twenty minutes or so, and was assured that the county coroner would be there to receive the remains. I planned to be in the office the following morning to download all pictures and fill out all required paperwork so that Mr. Dubois could get together with the underwriters to work toward finalizing the claim, which was unfortunately a total loss. I also understood how insurance fraud would be a most welcome finding to certain parties. But the evidence wasn't there to substantiate foul play.

I hung up knowing that there would always be much ado about nothing when money was involved. Nobody would buy the relatively humdrum story of accidental death caused by smoke inhalation and unsuspicious fire until every other scenario had been ruled out. Somehow I had a hard time imagining Mr. Kohl grieving the death of his wife before mourning the loss of the house. In my experience, it's always about the money. That's just the way things are, I thought as I reentered the cabin and made myself comfortable again now that I was out of the biting cold.

The mate apologetically interrupted my musings. "Ma'am? I hate to ask, but I need to collect your boat fare," he said politely. "One way or round-trip?"

"One way, please. What do I owe you?"

"One way nonresident is twelve fifty. Round-trip you save a buck—twenty-four dollars," he said optimistically. I could tell that he had been programmed to take in as many round-trip tickets as possible. And the discounted fare for a round-trip ticket that I might never use hit the core of my Scottish dilemma. Save a buck now? Or waste twelve dollars in the event that I never return?

I found my wallet and handed the mate a credit card that I use for all insurance business–related expenses. "Round-trip, please."

"No plastic. Cash or check."

I handed him a twenty and said, "One way. And a receipt."

He went forward and dug through a plastic money bag, and returned with my change and a handwritten receipt. I thanked him. He sat across from me on the engine box that doubled as seating and smiled. He was young, early twenties. With fifteen minutes remaining in the trip, now was a safe time to strike up a conversation. "Is the captain your father?" I asked, intentionally steering any dialogue away from questions pertaining to myself or the bundle in the stern.

"No, he's my uncle. People ask that all the time. I guess we share a family resemblance."

"Both good-lookin'!" The captain chimed in, never taking his attention away from in front of the boat. We all laughed, and this was enough to break the ice.

"Mrs. Proctor said you found Mrs. Kohl. Is that true?" asked the mate. I confirmed that I had indeed discovered the remains while documenting the damage to the house for the Kohls' insurance company.

"How bad was it?" Although I knew the young man was asking about the condition of the corpse, I answered that the house was a total loss, adding that the island's volunteer fire department hadn't stood a chance. This did nothing to satisfy his curiosity. But he seemed reluctant to be brazen enough to come right out and ask what Mrs. Kohl looked like. "Do you think the coroner will unwrap her aboard the boat?"

"No, I am sure that the corpse will remain wrapped until it arrives at the morgue," I answered, not knowing whether this was a relief or disappointment to him.

"Oh. Uncle Skip here has transported a few dead bodies. Not me, though. This is my first unless you count ashes. Yup,

61

I have been aboard for a couple of ceremonies when ashes are spread around the bay. But not counting ashes, this is my first time with an actual dead person."

I was tempted to tell him that Mrs. Kohl wasn't far from cremation, but thought better of it. I had always been tight-lipped about details of any investigation, no matter how benign. That practice had kept me off the media's list of detectives who like to see themselves on the nightly news, which was fine by me. The mate seemed like a nice kid. Naïve to the world beyond Down East Maine, like many of the residents, young or old, that I had encountered. The mate, whose name I learned was Percy, seemed comfortable in this naïveté, with the exception of his curiosity about what lay across the stern in the tarp. And his curiosity kept nagging at him. He fidgeted and made small talk until his uncle asked him to switch the dock lines from port to starboard as South Haven came into view.

I stood and looked over the bow, and was surprised to see flashing lights, both blue and red, in the distance. "Looks like Mrs. Kohl gets the royal treatment," said the captain. Recalling the converted bread delivery van that served as Green Haven's official vehicle, I asked if an ambulance and police escort was typical of South Haven's response to situations such as this. "No. The EMTs have an old hearse they rigged for use as an ambulance. Doesn't instill much confidence in the patients," he replied. "The blue lights must be Hancock County Sheriff's Department. That's you, right?" I confirmed that I was indeed an assistant deputy sheriff, and that I left the dock this morning as an insurance adjuster, and was returning wearing my other hat.

As the captain maneuvered to the float and the mate secured

lines, I watched several onlookers strolling on the dock above and thought how my landlords would be upset to be missing the action. There would be no shortage of dinner conversation tonight, I thought. I assumed that the presence of the sheriff and a real, official ambulance from Bangor had stirred the locals up. A similar scene in Miami wouldn't get a second look. I had seen people step over a dead body on a busy sidewalk, never breaking stride or gaze, which I had never found remarkable until moving to Maine where everyone and anyone dropped everything to chase flashing lights. Quite a crowd had gathered at the top of the ramp, and the sheriff had to ask for room for the ambulance attendants to squeeze through with a stretcher. The sheriff was close behind on the ramp. I spotted the WBAM van that broadcast live every afternoon, and I silently prayed that no one would notice the cruel, coincidental lettering on the tarp. Too late for the duct tape now, I thought.

"Wow. Quite a commotion, isn't it?" I asked as the sheriff shook my hand, and then held it while I climbed from the boat to the float. We'd had one face-to-face when I was deputized in August, and had spoken on the phone on the rare occasions when he had needed me to respond to a call in Green Haven, saving him the trip down the peninsula from Ellsworth. I had gotten the impression that the sheriff was putting time in until retirement, and was not necessarily gung-ho about the job. He was a handsome guy, and looked like law enforcement—straitlaced. He had been in the position for years, and so had all the contacts and ability to pull strings when needed. I never felt that he was anything but honest and by the book, and I appreciated working under him. I sensed that he appreciated having me to do whatever needed to be done. He had been quick to ask for my opinions, and was considerate about taking advice that he knew would benefit the department, or put a feather in his cap. My record of recent drug busts spoke for itself. Although my experience in criminal investigations far exceeded his, I was a good foot soldier and needed no accolades.

The majority of my duties until very recently on behalf of Hancock County were intervening in small disputes between rowdy fishermen when the Maine Marine Patrol could not or would not respond, or looking for a wandering Alzheimer's patient. There had been two actual murders in Green Haven in the past nine months, something that shocked the locals, but made me think that people had gotten away with murder a lot, due to the lack of investigative work in the decades before I moved up here. There seemed to be an inordinate number of hunting accidents, boating mishaps, and unexplained deaths by natural causes in Green Haven and the outer islands that comprised my territory. If anyone had murder in mind, Down East Maine had been a good place to get away with it . . . until I showed up. I had asked the sheriff about cold cases, but he discouraged my curiosity, explaining that he wouldn't even know where to start.

As the tarp was placed in a body bag and loaded carefully onto the stretcher, the sheriff explained that Mr. Kohl had demanded a full investigation into the fire and his wife's death.

"Although I am not an expert in fire forensics, I do have extensive training from when my investigations overlapped with the fire crime scene teams in Florida. I didn't see anything on Acadia that suggested the need for an investigation," I said.

"There was a broken gas line caused by a frost heave, and the fire looked to have ignited at the house's hot water heater. It appeared that the victim chose to fight the fire rather than escape, and the smoke likely put her down quickly."

"Well, you are probably right. But Mr. Kohl wants no stone unturned—probably just covering his own ass. I imagine there's a pretty hefty insurance benefit for both the house and the wife," the sheriff said as we watched the stretcher go up the ramp and into the waiting ambulance, a WBAM camera rolling at close range. "And he wants everything expedited. He will pay personally for the crime lab and pathologist in Augusta. Her remains will be there in two hours," he added, looking at his watch. "Did you happen to collect any evidence from the scene at all that might be helpful? Anything at all to show that we are being thorough?" I suspected the sheriff had been ready to rubber-stamp the fire and death as accidental before Mr. Kohl called.

Remembering the blood sample and the piece of brittle plastic that had been fused around the victim's left wrist, I rummaged through my camera bag and pulled out both items. The bloody snow was all liquid now and fairly well diluted in the bottom of the baggie. The sheriff shrugged and handed me an evidence bag into which I dropped the plastic after shaking a small bit of lint off of it. "Purely going through the motions. So contamination won't be an issue," I said sheepishly.

"I'll run these to the lab myself and have them do a quick and dirty. I told Mr. Kohl that I would have preliminary findings as early as tomorrow." He mentioned how fortunate the timing was regarding my trip to Acadia for Mr. Dubois, and said that he would call me if and when any follow-up was needed. The camera crew swung their focus toward us as the ambulance door was shut in their faces. The sheriff was wise, I thought, to have "no comment" to the broad questions indicating that the media knew nothing other than what they had just seen. The sheriff and I said our goodbyes, and I watched him pull out of the parking lot behind the ambulance.

The crowd began to disperse. I was amazed that this number of people would brave the cold to see a tarp loaded into an ambulance. But I imagined that speculation was excitement and much needed to feed the usual rumor and gossip that was such a large part of the social fabric of a tiny community. Trucks and cars rolled out of the parking area slowly, seemingly reluctant to release contemplations and suppositions of what had transpired to result in the rolled tarp. And now the viewers watching WBAM from home could join in the conjecture, too.

I hustled over to my Duster, which now stood alone. While being alone was not new to me, I wondered what it would be like to have been greeted by someone on this end who wanted to see me for personal reasons. Or better yet, no reason at all. And I wondered while I drove what it would feel like to be returning home to someone (other than the octogenarians) anxiously and excitedly waiting to hear about my day, and whatever adventure I had experienced. These thoughts had been creeping into my consciousness more and more recently. I figured that these—do I dare call them yearnings?—well, I figured they were part and parcel of reaching middle age having never been married. I had come close on a couple of occasions, and that always made me feel better about my present status of no prospects. I wasn't sad.

And I easily shrugged off my fascination with a traditional family unit by reminding myself that there was no longer any such thing. And it certainly wasn't something that I had ever had.

I chuckled aloud as I wondered what Mr. and Mrs. V would be serving for dinner. Research and experimentation for their planned "All Mussel Cookbook" mandated the key ingredient, and I had consumed mussels prepared by every known method (steamed, boiled, roasted, grilled, sautéed, fried, raw, baked, stewed, and broiled) and in every conceivable combination. There had been a couple of flops—who knew that mussels with fresh mint would not cut it? For the most part, the social meals generously shared at the Vickersons' table were satisfying on all levels. And as I had not yet eaten lunch (muffins and now an unwrapped biscuit remained at the bottom of the camera bag), I was starving. And even if the experimental entrée didn't quite work, Mrs. V (who is most attentive to her digestive track) always serves whole-grain bread and green salad (to keep herself "regular"). My stomach was growling as I steered the Duster within the snowbanks demarking the parking space that I had cleared this morning, and Mr. V had kindly cleaned up with the snow blower.

As I scurried to get inside and once again out of the frigid air, I glanced up to see two faces in the Vickersons' kitchen window. Mrs. V smiled and beckoned me to come in. She seemed excited and impatient as she waved her hand vigorously. I motioned that I would be a few minutes as I wanted to toss my bag into my apartment and freshen up before dinner. As I entered the shop, I was greeted by the briny smell of hot mussels that had escaped the landlord's kitchen and added more hustle to my step as I bounded up the stairs.

The hot water pounded the back of my neck, and trickled the length of my body that had been chilled to its core. I turned the valve, increasing the temperature until I had filled the bathroom with steam. The worst part about the Maine winter was having to get out of a hot shower. The trick for me was to stay in long enough to get warmed up and at the peak of the hot water. When I lingered too long, the water turned lukewarm and spoiled the effect of the near scald that I enjoyed. Turning the water off, I braced myself for the brisk opening of the curtain and quickly wrapped myself up in a towel. Condensation on the mirror grew heavy enough to form droplets that rolled down and expired on the edge of the sink. I pulled on a pair of jeans and a sweater, towel-dried my hair, brushed my teeth, and declared my appearance "good enough."

"You just missed yourself on the news!" cried out Mrs. V as I let myself into their home. She turned the television off and dropped the remote into a reclining chair.

"I was on the news?"

"Well, sort of," Mr. V answered. "In the background. They should have interviewed you. All that lousy sheriff had to say was 'no comment.' We didn't vote for the damned liberal, did we?"

"No, and we never will, dear," Mrs. V replied gently. "The fool *never* has any comment. What does he *do*? How can he NEVER have anything to say? Luckily, we have you!" She smiled and took my hand, leading me to my usual seat at the table. "And we want the whole scoop."

"Not that I would defend the damned liberal," I said jokingly. "But there isn't much to comment on. As you know, I went to Acadia to inspect and document damage that occurred in a house fire on behalf of Mr. Dubois. Thank you, by the way, for delivering the Duster." I paused while Mr. V placed a partially filled highball glass in front of me and handed me a cocktail napkin with a bright red lobster printed on it. "In the course of walking through what remained of the dwelling, a total loss by the way, I found that one of the owners had perished in the fire." I held my Scotch up in a mini toast minus the clinking and took a sip, savoring the warmth it provided as well as the moment of relaxation. They both stared at me skeptically. Not that they didn't believe what I had reported, but they couldn't imagine there wasn't more to the story. "Unsuspicious fire and accidental death, period."

"How boring," scowled Mrs. V.

"I'll drink to that," said Mr. V as he lifted his glass.

"What? A house burns to the ground and a woman is practically incinerated, and that's boring? Tough crowd." I helped myself to what appeared to be a smoked mussel on a cracker. I popped it into my mouth and thought that Mrs. V had hit a home run with the mustard sauce, and was amazed how nicely the single malt enhanced the briny taste.

Mrs. V served a lovely dinner. Scalloped mussels were more about scallops than mussels, which suited me fine. Mussels we could eat year-round, and did. But fresh scallops were a delicacy that made the winter months tolerable, I thought as I nearly licked my plate clean. I attempted during the meal to bring up the subject of Wally. He'd been in the back of my mind all day, and I needed to understand the options. But each time I started, one of the V's would interrupt, changing the subject altogether. I recognized this as one of my tactics, and decided that my landlords had thought about it, and regretted verbalizing their invitation for Wally to move in here. I totally understood, and let it go. My schedule right now was mostly my own. So I would have plenty of time to research facilities in the area, or look into a rental that had two bedrooms. I would tackle that tomorrow, I thought as I thanked my landlords once again and bid them good night.

As I made my way to the door, the television set came back on. The landlords' nightly routine was to tune into *Wheel of Fortune* primarily to discuss what Vanna was wearing. Other than the wardrobe, I'm not sure they liked the game itself. I was fairly sleepy, and knew it was a combination of things: long day, outside in freezing weather, boat rides, and Scotch. I dragged myself up over the stairs and happily dove into bed. I slept soundly and dreamlessly.

A sliver of sunlight sneaked between the slats of the venetian blinds, hitting me square in the face. Not one to linger in bed (alone or otherwise), my feet were on the floor and moving before my eyes could focus. I tugged the tiny yellow and blue lobster buoy at the end of the cord to raise the shade covering the bay window, exposing a colorful sunrise, and was relieved to see that no fresh snow had fallen last night. Other than sending pictures to Mr. Dubois, I looked forward to a day of nothing scheduled, allowing me the freedom to dig into options for my brother. Now that I had a good night's sleep, I was very optimistically happy to consider the prospect of having Wally close by; sharing an apartment or finding an appropriate situation for him to live with a bit of assistance. I tucked my checkbook into the camera bag and headed out the door to the café. I knew I would find Cal there, and wanted to settle up with him for the boat ride yesterday.

The cowbells announced my entrance, where I found Cal perched on his usual stool at the counter. I plunked myself onto a stool beside him and said, "Good morning, Skipper." I pulled my checkbook from the bag and slapped it down on the place mat in front of me while Cal slowly lowered the newspaper he seemed engrossed in. "Time to settle up. What do I owe you?" I asked while nodding to Audrey, who held up a glass coffeepot.

"You want to start a tab?" Cal asked as he looked at me over the edge of the paper. "Assuming you'll be making a few more trips to Acadia to investigate, I'm available."

"Investigate what?" I asked. Cal folded the newspaper in half and flattened it with the palm of his hand, then pushed it over for me to read. The front-page headline was so bizarre that I read it twice, and then aloud the third time: "Fatal Fire on Acadia Deemed Suspicious."

FOUR

In a cloud of confusion, I read on. The article continued, explaining that although findings were preliminary, evidence had revealed the presence of a fuel accelerant at the scene and that authorities suspected that the house had been torched to cover up a murder.

Authorities? Accelerant found at the scene? Murder? Details were lacking. Wow, I thought, the local paper was nothing more than a tabloid. What a stretch! I would have to do some fast talking to convince Mr. and Mrs. V that I had not withheld information, and that the article had to be BS. "And this is what happens in a small town when news journalists have no news to report. They just make stuff up!" I said a bit louder than needed. Although I was well aware of how the media can twist things beyond spin, this was different. This was outright fabrication. I worried about the reactions of the residents of Acadia Island to the outlandish accusations of arson and murder.

"Thank God! Not to tread on your sacred ground, but I

couldn't stomach another story on bath salts or methadone clinics. There's nothing *new* about that anymore," Audrey interjected.

"You may not find news about cleaning up the neighborhood of drugs as sexy as charred corpses, but my intention is to find the root of the drug problem, and extract it like a bad tooth," I defended what I regarded as my life's purpose.

"So you did find a body yesterday, right?" Audrey asked as she poured steaming hot coffee into a chunky mug. "The usual?" she asked as she cleared Cal's dirty plate and silverware into a sudsy plastic bin under the counter. I answered in the affirmative, knowing that I would be served a toasted English muffin or yesterday's special, which I recalled was apricot-bran. I explained that I had a camera full of pictures that I would be delivering to my boss at the insurance consulting company this morning, documenting nothing that would indicate anything even remotely suspicious. "Come on, Janey. Dish." Audrey pleaded with me to save her from her daily, repetitive conversations on the winter weather.

I had come to know Audrey as a girl who had been born in the wrong place. At nineteen, pierced, tattooed, and sassy, she ran the show at the café, working every hour of every day that the open sign was displayed. She had confided in me about her dreams of furthering her education and moving to New York, something I suspected even she didn't believe was possible.

"Well, other than the fact that I knew you were headed to Acadia yesterday, my cousin is the captain of the ferry that brought you back to South Haven," she stated matter-of-factly. Before she could finish, the door blew open and in came Clydie, sporting a fur trapper's hat—full flaps down—giving his head the appearance of being much too big for the rest of him. The only thing that kept him from toppling over were the huge insulated boots that now anchored him to the linoleum.

"Ah ha!" He pointed a finger directly at me and headed toward the counter. "Now we can get the facts straight from the horse's mouth."

"Yeah, as opposed to the horse's other end that just made an entrance . . ." muttered Audrey as she made her way around the end of the counter, meeting Clyde in mid–dining room. "Clyde Leeman," she said sternly. "What did I tell you yesterday? You are banished this week. Get lost!"

"Come on, I'm harmless. I hear people saying that about me a lot."

"Harmless to those who do not value their own sanity," Audrey quipped. "Go on, shoo," she said as she waved a hand as if whiffing away a pesky flying insect.

"But I figured under the circumstances, I could get a special pass for today. Please?" Clyde put on his best pitiful face and begged while Audrey stood with her arms crossed tightly at her chest, leaning on her left foot while tapping her right impatiently. She motioned toward the door with her head. "When I heard about the murder suicide, I wanted to offer Miss Bunker my services," he said with what I understood as genuine concern and desire to help.

"See?" Audrey turned her attention back to the counter. "We already gained a dead person. By lunch, the body count will be at six." She took Clyde's arm and gently yet firmly twirled him around and led him back to the door. When he hesitated at the door mat, Audrey pointed at the dry-erase wall calendar under the clock on which she tracked Clyde's banishment periods in red marker. "See you next week. The FBI special agents should be here soon. So Jane will not be needing your help," she teased as she shoved him out and onto the sidewalk under great protest that could be heard through the closed door.

"I'd call him a halfwit, but that would be giving him too much credit," Audrey said as she hustled back through tables that were just starting to fill up. She took orders from a table of four, cleared a table of two, and dropped a bill to a customer at the end of the counter as she rounded it and crashed through the swinging doors that led to the kitchen. The doors were still flapping when she reappeared; arms loaded with full plates of eggs and all the fixings. She served the meals like dealing cards from a deck, and was in front of me again in a flash. Bending at the waist, she placed her elbows on the counter and cradled her chin in both hands. "I'm all ears, girlfriend."

"The newspaper's and Clydie's versions are far more interesting that mine," I said with an artificial modesty. "Yes, I did discover a corpse. The fire was indeed fatal. And that's the whole story. If there was more to it, which there is not, I couldn't and wouldn't tell you anyway. You know that, right?"

"Okay. That's it then. I'm just here to dispense the truth," she said and smiled. A shout came from the kitchen, calling Audrey to pick up. "Truth and breakfast." She spun away from the counter and toward the kitchen, leaving me to turn my attention to Cal, who was still plowing through the paper contentedly.

Audrey returned, slid a toasted and buttered English muffin onto my place mat, pulled the edge of the paper down from in front of Cal's face and asked, "Top off your coffee?"

Cal carefully folded the paper, running his hand over to crease and flatten it as he indicated that he was all set on coffee, and needed only his check. As Audrey scribbled some numbers on the pad she kept in her apron, I suggested to Cal that we should settle up for the boat ride, and indicated my checkbook on my place mat. Audrey ripped the top sheet from the pad, handed it to Cal, and hustled off to the center of the dining area to clear tables just vacated. "How does one hundred bucks sound?" Cal asked.

"More than fair," I answered.

"Do you have cash?"

"No, sorry. Can I get an invoice?" This was met with a twisted frown and scowl. "I'll take that as a no," I said and wrote the check. Although many people in Green Haven dealt in cash, I never had more than what was needed to buy breakfast and lunch. "I know, cash is king. But without an invoice, I can't get reimbursed."

"What if I invoice you?"

"I still don't have enough cash on me." I handed the check to Cal, who chuckled, shook his head, tucked the check into his wallet, and got up to leave.

"Thank you, dear. And let me know when you have to go back to Acadia. Looks like that might be sooner rather than later." I agreed, and hoped that he was teasing about the "sooner" trip back to the island. I would know more about my schedule after meeting with Mr. Dubois this morning, and assumed that both he and the sheriff would be ticked off at the newspaper but that they would both agree that the case was closed from all perspectives of insurance claims and law enforcement. My work out there was done. I could soon get back to my first love: drug busting.

Fortunately, Audrey was hopping around doing her miraculous juggling act, allowing me to eat my breakfast without any further interrogation. I left some cash on the counter and slipped out the door while she had her back to me. Before I had my coat zipped, her voice came through the door as she held it ajar. "Janey, I hear that your brother is coming to Green Haven. Wonderful! I can't wait to meet him!"

"Where did you hear that?" I asked with more than curiosity.

"That's all there is. There ain't no more," she teased in a sing-song voice. "And even if there was more, I wouldn't and couldn't tell you. You know that, right?" She mocked me playfully. I knew that Audrey would always get the last word, so I laughed and let her have it. I would be back for a late lunch, and would worm the origin of information out of her then, knowing that the root of the source had to be Mr. and Mrs. V. Not that it really mattered. Wally's move needn't be kept secret. But I did wonder how many people my landlords had blabbed to as Audrey disappeared when she pushed the door closed. I had planned to ask Audrey her opinion of housing opportunities for Wally, and knew that she had excellent insight and all of the local knowledge that I lacked. Audrey had a big heart under an exterior hardened by what I assumed had been a fairly tough upbringing. She was not a complainer or whiner. Just straightforward and brutally honest. I liked those attributes, I thought as I hustled to get behind the wheel of the Duster and out of a stiff breeze that pushed the hair on the back of my head around and into my face.

I was relieved to see that I had missed being questioned by the Old Maids as they pulled into the parking spot behind me as I pulled away. No need to go through the nonstory again, I thought as I made my way to the main road that would take me off The Peninsula and eventually to Ellsworth, where I assumed Mr. Dubois would be anxious to get my pictures and report.

As I ascended Caterpillar Hill, my cell phone gained service and came to life with a series of dings and beeps indicating that I had missed calls, texts, and voice messages. I pulled off and parked in a "scenic turnout" to better tend to my phone. I never used to be as cautious, but the roads in this area do not allow for any lapse in attention. Messages from both of my bosses to call them ASAP were not surprising, and I assumed they wanted to talk damage control in light of the bogus newspaper article. I clicked the phone closed and placed it in the seat beside me. No sense taking time to return calls. I always made a practice of not speaking to the press, so they need not worry about my being the source of misinformation. I would be in Mr. Dubois's office in twenty minutes. And I would touch base with the sheriff from the office's land line, saving my cell minutes for when I might need them.

As I pulled back onto the main road, I was nearly sideswiped by a vehicle heading off The Peninsula in a real hurry. I jumped on the brakes, watched the blur of the shiny black pickup swerve to avoid the Duster, and saw a fist curled in my direction through the passenger-side window. There was a blare of the truck's horn, and a middle finger launched at me from the back window as the truck sped away. Wow, I thought, I must not have looked before pulling out. That was close. As my heart slowed, I got up to the speed limit behind the truck, and noticed that I was losing ground rapidly. They are going dangerously fast, I thought as I accelerated to catch up. I wouldn't speed on this road in the best conditions. The Duster's speedometer was at 75, and the truck was pulling away. I cranked my window down, clamped my blue light with magnetic base to the Duster's roof, flipped on the flashers, and put chase to the truck. Although I had a regular weekly schedule for making rounds as deputy sheriff, I was never off-duty when something came up. I would pull these clowns over, and issue a verbal warning as I never carried anything with which to write a ticket. I had never been a traffic cop, and didn't intend to be one this late in my career.

The blue flashers did the trick. The truck slowed and pulled off into a snowplow turnaround spot, stopping in a position that did not allow me to pull the Duster fully out of the road, which I assumed was done purposely. I got out and approached the driver's window that he had lowered; he flicked out a cigarette butt that nearly hit me in the stomach. Loud rap music assaulted my ears. The two occupants were young men, I estimated in their mid-twenties. They were dressed in a way that told me they were making real efforts to look like thugs: baseball caps with visors askew and gold chains around their too-thin necks. They could use some time in the gym, I thought as I leaned toward the driver and took the license and registration he offered. A plastic two-liter soda bottle containing a bit of brownish sludge sat on the passenger-side floor. I had come to recognize this as evidence of "Shake and Bake," a "one pot" method of manufacturing methamphetamine. These personal meth labs were not only mobile, but also circumvented laws restricting sale of the ingredients to make meth.

There was a coat draped over a box that sat between the guys, an obvious attempt to try to hide it from me. "What's the rush, guys? You nearly plowed into me," I said sternly. No answer was always a cue that there was something going on other than speeding. "What's that under the coat?" More silence. "Step out of the truck, please." Both men stared straight ahead and sat motionless. I realized that they were scared. "Don't make me call for backup," I said. "All I have to do is radio the station, and my team will be here to place you both under arrest," I exaggerated. "And if you run, how far do you think you'll get? There's only one way off The Peninsula, and we are on it."

The driver looked at the passenger, sighed audibly, and slowly opened his door and climbed out of the truck. His jeans were slung low, showing more of his boxer shorts than most people would be comfortable with. I instructed him to stand at the tailgate, which he did. The passenger slid out and stood by the door, which remained open. I removed the coat from the box, revealing a sealed twelve-by-twelve cardboard carton upon which was printed some red and black Chinese characters. "Well, I don't happen to read Chinese, so I'll ask once more. What's in the box?"

"It's stuff we use to ship lobsters to China," answered the passenger nervously.

"You don't look like fishermen to me," I said.

"We aren't," answered the driver from behind the truck. "We are . . . well, we are shippers."

"Right. Well, I'll have to open the box and take a look." I tore open the top of the box and looked inside. The box contained several small plastic pouches that appeared to be vacuum-sealed, and bulged with an off-white powdery material. I picked up a pouch and turned it over in my hands looking for any markings. I had been making drug busts weekly, but nothing as substantial as this.

"It's not what it looks like," said the driver disgustedly. He spat tobacco juice into the snow, where it created a miniature black hole.

"Oh, I know what it looks like," I answered. "And I will take it to the lab to confirm." I lifted the box from the seat, tucked it under my arm, and picked up the soda bottle that had been rolling around on the truck's floor with discarded food wrappers. I asked the passenger for his identification, which he pulled from a chain-drive wallet that held quite a bit of cash. I asked if the information on their IDs was current. They both nodded. Grabbing the keys from the ignition, I instructed the men to get back in and out of the cold while I checked out their credentials. I placed the box and the plastic bottle in the Duster's trunk and slammed the lid closed. I climbed behind the steering wheel and copied both names, addresses, and license numbers into a page in a notebook I kept in my camera bag. I retuned their licenses and registration, and informed the men that in a few days they could call Hancock County Sheriff's Department to retrieve their "shipping supplies," if they weren't arrested first. I had been taught, since working drug cases in

Maine, that there was no sense of urgency in making arrests when locals were implicated. These were not the drug dealers of Miami who were in the States illegally and could easily hit the road and escape arrest. Most pushers and users of illicit drugs in Maine were indigenous. They had nowhere to run to, and wouldn't if they did. The Mainers I had arrested for drug-related crimes were mostly addicts who knew that the jig was up, and didn't do much to fight charges brought against them. These two guys could easily be users who were selling or transporting to support expensive and growing habits.

"Why don't you just write me a speeding ticket?" the driver asked with a voice that cracked in a near cry.

"Oh, we are way beyond that," I replied and confirmed that we would be seeing one another again very soon. "Until then, slow down." I returned to the Duster. The men were smart to let me pull back onto the road before them, and I watched in my rearview mirror as they pulled out slowly and headed in the opposite direction. I figured that now that they had been relieved of their possession, they had no destination, no schedule, and no plan other than relaying the bad news to others who might be working with them, and bracing themselves for the arrest that would surely follow. I had busted so many smugglers and dealers of fentanyl in Miami that I had lost count.

These two Mainers were low-enders, as I call them, and not at all in charge of anything. Best-case scenario is that they would lead me to someone higher up in the drug organization, I thought. And I knew all too well about chemicals coming from China. Designer drugs like W-18 and U-4700 are smuggled into the US, and have yet to be outlawed. The chemists are able to stay one step ahead of the FDA and DEA by tweaking the chemical composition of any banned substance. The box I had confiscated might certainly be found to contain a substance that is not dangerous and totally legal to possess in the US. However, when combined in certain proportions, they become the lethal injectable, ingestible, and inhalable illicit drugs that were now running rampant in Down East Maine, bolstering addiction until its users overdosed. It is unclear how many deaths can be attributed to these designer drugs as most overdoses are reported to be heroin. So the prevalence of synthetic opiates could be grossly underreported. We had the same issues in Miami, only on a much larger scale. If I could help find the party smuggling the chemicals, we could snuff synthetic opiates at the source.

The state of Maine was presently at a tipping point of sorts in reference to drugs. There was a thirty-one percent increase in overdose deaths in 2015, and the governor had just vetoed a bill that would have allowed pharmacists to dispense overdose antidotes without a prescription. Although I understood the importance of saving the lives of addicts, I sided with the governor in his opinion that making Narcan and other overdose antidotes readily available was in essence prolonging the agony for many junkies who would eventually die of overdose or other associated causes. The governor preferred addressing the root of the problem by stopping trafficking into Maine, expanding education and prevention efforts, and pushing doctors to be vigilant about tightening their prescription pads for the painkillers that so often lead to heroin use. The growing epidemic had been well timed with my arrival from Miami, I thought.

Fortunately, both of my destinations for this morning—the

sheriff's office and the home of Marine Safety Consultants—are within a few miles of one another in Ellsworth. For the sake of expedience, I dropped the box of chemicals and the mini meth lab off to the sheriff, and asked that he transport it to the lab for ID, which he graciously agreed to do. I gave him the notebook page on which I had copied the license and registration information of the men, I explained, who had almost run me off the road, which led to the confiscation of evidence. The sheriff seemed delighted that I had stumbled upon what would likely lead to another chink in the drug cartel's ambitions and intentions. Every ounce of illegal substance that we could stop from being shot into an addict's veins was definitely worth the pound of cure. The naïve people of Down East Maine were still in the stage of disbelief when learning of the record numbers of overdoses, drug-related crime, arrests, and convictions. Somehow that worked to the advantage of law enforcement, I thought. Smugglers, dealers, and users were not advanced in avoidance techniques, making my job a bit easier.

Before I left the Hancock County Sheriff Station, the sheriff confirmed that he expected preliminary findings from Mrs. Kohl's autopsy by late afternoon, and promised to call me with results. We both concurred that money offered by her husband had certainly sped up the process, as we were accustomed to waiting up to a week for "lesser" victims.

"It's not what you know, it's who you know," I commented.

"It's actually *not* who you know, but who knows *you*, that matters most," the sheriff chuckled. "Well, I expect that we'll learn nothing that we don't already know. And between the autopsy and the fire investigation, we can put this to bed right away and get on with the business of fighting crime." That sounded good to me. The only thing an autopsy would provide me was peace of mind that Mrs. Kohl had indeed succumbed to smoke inhalation. Mr. Kohl would find a bit of comfort in knowing that his wife had not suffered the excruciatingly painful death that burning alive would have been.

Entering the office of Marine Safety Consultants, I was greeted by a very happy Mr. Dubois. Not that he isn't always friendly, but today he was buoyant beyond his usual good nature. "The underwriters are very happy with us. And by us, I mean you!" Mr. Dubois exclaimed. "Believe me, we need all the good-will we can get. Insurance is getting more and more competitive, and I can't always get coverage for some of our clients who have homes on these remote outposts."

"Why would they be happy about a total loss?" I asked.

"Don't you read the paper? The fire has been deemed suspicious thanks to you!"

"But my findings support accidental fire, no arson suspected," I said.

"Really, no need to be modest, Jane. The sample of diesel fuel you sent to the lab is compelling evidence to the contrary. The Kohls heat their house with propane and wood pellets. Diesel fuel should not have been on the premises." I was perplexed, and this must have shown on my face.

Mr. Dubois noticed and asked, "You thought the sample was blood, didn't you?" I nodded silently. "It was diesel fuel. I assume that the smell was masked by smoke and fumes at the scene. That is logical. And the color, well, diesel used off-road is dyed red and not subject to road tax. So guys use it in boats, tractors, anything that requires diesel fuel but that doesn't drive on the state highways."

"Wow. That makes sense. No wonder the house was burned so thoroughly. Now the question is why, right?"

"Yes, but that's not my concern as the insurance broker. When you go back to Acadia, which I assume you will be doing pronto, you can gather whatever evidence you need to support the fact that the Kohl fire was intentionally set. I don't care why or by whom—just that it wasn't incidental or accidental is good enough for our immediate purposes. Then we can let the law authorities take it from there." Mr. Dubois was apparently quite relieved with the prospect of arson, and I suspected that the Kohls' house was insured for quite a sum that would not need to be paid out by the underwriters if foul play could be proven.

Mr. Dubois explained that he had just received the report from the lab identifying the sample of red liquid as diesel fuel, so the sheriff had not been notified. We agreed that the state fire marshal and police would naturally get involved as soon as the sheriff was in the loop. I handed Mr. Dubois the small storage card from my digital camera, and promised to do more investigating when I got back to the scene, which I imagined I would be doing wearing my deputy sheriff hat. I explained that I would be speaking with the sheriff later, and said goodbye.

Well, I thought, the Kohl fire was certainly now more interesting. The questions mounted: Who set the fire and why? Was Mrs. Kohl's death suspicious? Or was her presence in the house unknown to the arsonist? Did Mrs. Kohl set the fire herself to collect the insurance and accidentally kill herself? Did Mr. Kohl want his wife dead? Or was there an explanation for the diesel fuel that negated the incendiary theory that Mr. Dubois was pushing? Oh yes, I would be heading back to Acadia soon, I thought. I now had some real investigative work to do. I would have to wait for the autopsy report and other forensics to be complete before forming any schedule and strategy for the full investigation. And that left me with some time to look for options for Wally's living situation, which is what I planned to do while waiting to hear from the sheriff.

I had done a bit of research into housing opportunities when I first moved to Green Haven, and there were a couple of what sounded like good options for Wally. I had always been aware of the probability that my separation from Wally would trigger changes in his behavior. Anxiety, withdrawal, and even dementia can occur as a reaction to certain stressors such as separation from or loss of a key attachment figure in adults with Down syndrome. But the fact that upheaval might be worse kept me from dragging him along when my relocation became inevitable.

Once I got settled in and busy with two jobs, my quest to have my brother here in Maine fizzled. Any pangs of guilt were subdued by reasoning that I shouldn't disrupt his life just because I wanted to start a new one for myself. And this reasoning was bolstered by weekly phone calls that always found Wally thriving and surrounded by people who knew, understood, and loved him; something that I had never experienced myself. To be truthful, I had not given any serious thought to moving Wally to be nearer to me until I learned that he was soon to be homeless in Miami. And now that I understood that his present care facility relied on federal funding, I had to question the credibility of the reports from his caregivers of his happiness after I left. Funding was need-based, and calculated per resident.

Because I am a habitual list and note maker, I still had the page on which I had recorded, months ago, addresses of two assisted living facilities in Ellsworth. My thought at the time, and it had not changed, was that Ellsworth was just far enough away from Green Haven to allow Wally the independence that he needed. Again, I had to check my selfishness quotient. Although I had not looked for a place in Green Haven for my brother, I could honestly say that I was not aware of any. Had I inquired? No. And wasn't Ellsworth a good step for Wally, coming from an eighteen-hundred-mile distance away from me and shortening that to thirty? Had I considered sharing a place with him? Yes, I had. But only briefly. His independence was top priority. Or was it my privacy that topped the list? What single, middle-aged woman wants to live with her brother? Not me. I pushed all of this from my mind as I walked through the entrance of Sunset Assisted Living.

Nope, I thought, and did a quick U-turn in the lobby. Two old folks in wheelchairs was all I needed to see to know that this was not the right place. The problem with assisted living is that most of it is geared toward seniors. Not that I have anything against senior citizens, but Wally needed to be with people of all ages, as he is prone to attach himself to and emulate those with whom he spends time. This is one reason why everyone who gets to know him loves him so much, I realized. Within a few hours of being with someone, Wally imitates speech patterns, expressions, accents, attitudes, and body language. It's like having a clone of yourself without the facial features and physique. Most

people take this as a huge compliment. But a few find it annoying, and even think that Wally is mocking them. The best situation for Wally, I thought, would be that which mirrored real life:
living among people of all ages.

The next place on my short list of prospective housing for
Wally was Anderson Ridge, which came highly recommended.
I had looked online, and had made an appointment to get a tour
of the facility. If it was everything the website promised, it was
grand. I wouldn't be able to see the outside activities today, as
they were venues for seasonal sports and leisure events. But I
would tour the indoor swimming pool, art center, library, music
hall, and game room. They even had an indoor shooting range,
which I was undecided about. When I questioned the safety of
the range on the phone, I had learned that only "airsoft" guns
were allowed and that every shooter had a fully trained staff
member with them. The woman on the phone had assured me
that the rules of the range were strict. But Wally had always
been intrigued with my guns, and to my knowledge had never
fired a gun of any kind. Not even a BB gun. Although I would
prefer that he play chess or shuffleboard, I was in favor of afford-
ing him the opportunity to learn about gun safety and the basics
of target shooting.

As I pulled into the parking area for Anderson Ridge, I was
startled by the ringing of "Don't Worry, Be Happy" from within
my bag. Jesus, I thought, I had inadvertently dropped the late
Mrs. Kohl's phone into my camera bag. I let it ring and go to
voice mail, then dug it out of the bottom of my bag and placed
it in the glovebox for safe keeping. I locked the Duster and headed
for the front entrance of the main building. My possession of the

phone, although an honest mistake, haunted me a bit. I had absentmindedly dropped it into my bag after using it on the island, and would turn it in to the sheriff to return to Mr. Kohl. I should have paid more attention, I thought. Now I would be embarrassed to admit that I had it, and have to explain why. Maybe it would be better to simply return the phone to the Kohls' vehicle on my return trip to Acadia to investigate the fire, I thought.

The surroundings of Anderson Ridge were beautiful. A pristine blanket of snow on slight slopes that looked like swells on a white ocean gave the area a peaceful calm. Cross-country skiers circled the perimeter of the open fields, trekking along the edge of a thick forest of mature spruce that towered like sentinels. In the distance loomed great hills linked at their waists to one another, forming the ridge for which the facility was named. Before I opened the door under a sign that read "Visitors and Guests Welcome," my phone beeped with a new text message. I flipped the phone open and read the message from the sheriff: "Call me ASAP. Urgent." Seeing this as a reminder that I should turn off my phone for the tour, I did so, knowing that I would call the sheriff when I returned to the Duster. Experience with the sheriff to date had taught me that his sense of urgency was over the top. And after having witnessed his texting skills (or lack of), I knew that if this had been a true emergency, he would have called.

A perky and pleasant young woman greeted me inside the door. After a short chat, the tour began. I was very impressed with the facility, and knew it was right for my brother. When we sat down in her office, the woman quickly got to the business end of things. "Full residency with access to all of the wonderful staff and amenities is five thousand dollars per month," she stated.

Wow, I thought. This was way out of my reach. No private insurance, no long-term care insurance, no Medicare, no estate from which to draw a plan from, and no substantial savings or investments left me with a sinking feeling. My silence prodded the woman to continue. "There are modified plans that include access to the facility, events, and staff during weekdays, if that is better suited for your budget."

"Transportation to and from might be an issue," I said, relieved to have an excuse other than my budget.

"Is your brother a ward of the state?" she asked. "If so, there are *other* places." This was my exit sign. I thanked the woman for her time and left feeling defeated. I wanted the very best living situation and care available for Wally. But this I couldn't afford. I would have to move to plan B, I thought as I climbed back into the Duster and turned my phone back on to call the sheriff.

"Hi, Sheriff. Jane here. What's up?"

"This is very preliminary, but I just got a heads-up from the state's lead pathologist. Mrs. Kohl was dead before she was burned."

FIVE

After I caught my breath, I told the sheriff that I would be back in his office right away to discuss what he wanted me to do in light of this dramatic development. Within the past two hours, the case had changed course a full one hundred and eighty degrees. An incidental fire and accidental death had suddenly and shockingly been revealed as murder and arson. I was fuming at myself for not being more vigilant about questioning, and perhaps doing more investigating, yesterday while I was at what was now a crime scene on Acadia Island. Having made what I had always considered to be a rookie mistake—assuming that I already knew what had transpired—was now resulting in a mild case of self-loathing. I had only seen the evidence that pointed in the direction of what I *was* looking for.

At the top of my game, I would have left no stone unturned. I would have assumed the worst possible scenario. Now, because I had been too comfortable and overconfident in the theory of "nothing suspicious," I had to retrace steps. I had allowed myself to lapse into a lackadaisical attitude that I attributed to my association with the local law enforcement community as a whole. Yesterday, I had been more concerned with not missing the boat off the island than I had been in digging deep into what may have been right in front of me.

The more time that elapses after the events, the fewer witnesses and people there are who actually know something, the more people who know nothing will speculate and share theories, and the greater chance of evidence disappearing or being contaminated. And once news of murder and the arson to cover it up spreads through Acadia, the more tight-lipped residents will become, in hopes of protecting the island's reputation, I assumed. Most people would form their own theories, and have their own suspicions shaped by prior prejudices; looking at things through unbiased eyes would just get more difficult as the days went on.

As soon as I had a plan and strategy to execute, I would contact Joan and Clark Proctor. Because of their relationship with the Kohls, and the fact that they are the only people I had met on Acadia, they would be invaluable with helping to connect dots of evidence that I accumulated. As lifelong residents and caretakers for summer people, they knew everyone and understood the nuances that would be invaluable in solving the whos, hows, and whys of Mrs. Kohl's death. The Proctors would accommodate me with a ride and help with names and locations of others I would need to question, starting with who was the last person to see and speak with Mrs. Kohl, I thought. I had already established a tentative rapport with Joan, and would work to strengthen that. Although we hadn't had much time together, there's something about handling a dead body with someone that forms an odd, yet poignant bond. Joan understood the intricacies of relationships—both good and bad—inherent in a very small community. And Clark was very involved in the working community. They were exactly what I needed to help with this case. They were islanders.

I would gather what information I could through the sheriff's department. I had been granted full clearance and entry into the department's computer, which provided access to every bit of electronic information available—local, state, and federal—and had used it to research rap sheets for the many drug-related crime investigations that had filled my days. Because of my background and high security clearance, I had access to CODIS and NDIS files. And laws requiring search warrants for police searches of electronic information had not been instituted in Maine, so anything was fair game. I had learned more from suspects' and victims' social media sites than I had in the federal restricted electronic files. All of this at the tip of my fingers that itched to get surfing; I stepped on the Duster's gas pedal a little harder. Assuming that the state's pathologist would continue to expedite his work, I would be returning to Acadia Island soon. This time I would be in my element. Criminal investigation was my comfort zone. And now that it was clear that a murder had been committed, Jane Bunker would snap into action. I would ditch the camera bag, trading it for my trusty sidearm. No more Mister Nice Guy, I thought as I sped along Ellsworth's busy main thoroughfare, weaving in and out of two lanes. I was on a mission.

Upon my arrival at Hancock County Sheriff's Department,

I was greeted by the sheriff himself. He agreed that I would singlehandedly strategize, organize, and conduct the Kohl investigation as I had more experience in "such things" than anyone in the department, or even the Maine State Police. He would provide whatever assistance I needed, but assumed that would be minimal. He guaranteed full access to any information as it became available. I did not feel put upon in the least. On the contrary, I preferred working alone on cases and had made that clear from the onset of my being deputized. I explained to the sheriff that I was in possession of Mrs. Kohl's cell phone, and that I would start there. He and Deloris, the dispatcher, had spent the morning setting up a small office for me. I had resisted this space in the past, preferring to be in the field. But now that I had the need for private space with a computer, desk, file cabinet, and landline, I was appreciative of their efforts. "And Deloris will be happy to help you in any way possible," the sheriff vowed.

I wondered how much help Deloris could provide, as I knew her as a constant complainer and whiner. She meant well, but according to her, she was "misunderstood." She was extremely paranoid, which was not a bad trait to possess when working on things that needed to be kept confidential. She had aspired to be an officer in the Maine State Police. Unable to complete the required number of chin-ups to meet the physical test, she had taken the job as dispatcher for the HCSD as a default position. Upon our initial introduction several months ago, Deloris had made it clear that Maine was one of only two states that do not allow female recruits to do a modified chin-up. Of course Florida was *not* the other one. Although Deloris was fanatic about working out, she just could not gain the upper body strength needed to pull her chin to the bar ten times. Her dashed dreams were what accounted for her somewhat sour disposition, I thought.

As there was little dispatch needed, Deloris had lots of time on her hands to diagnose every problem in Hancock County without offering a single solution. And she followed every complaint with "but that's just me." This disclaimer allowed her to be quite free with berating everyone and everything in casual conversation. A badge and gun were all she ever wanted. And as they were unattainable, she lived a life unfulfilled. The prospect of helping me with a murder investigation seemed to delight her. There was no question for whom the second chair in the office was intended.

The sheriff left "to make rounds," which I had learned included a stop at Martha's Diner for a bite to eat. He would also visit the lab where he would have the box of chemicals tested and ID'd before returning to the office. The Kohl investigation would require my full attention, I thought as he reminded me of the probable drug arrest that would be imminent once we knew that the white powder in the pouches I had confiscated was indeed what we suspected. That opened the door for me to give Deloris something to do that would be helpful. I put her in charge of gathering information on the two men from whom I had taken the large stash while I began going through Midge Kohl's phone for clues. "Everything is important," I advised Deloris. "Dig deep. They had enough powder to wipe out every addict in the county!"

Deloris responded with a hearty, "Aye, aye," and took a seat in front of a laptop computer. The bottled redhead was quite an imposing figure, and not at all what one might expect to see as a dispatcher. She took pride in her figure, wearing clothes that emphasized her muscles, which I recognized as the result of her many hours spent in the gym. Deloris was so boisterously negative about all of life, that I had secretly dubbed her Dubious.

"The sheriff has not been using me to my full potential," she started. "All I do here is answer the phone and make coffee. And let me tell you, I could run this place. I have lots of training, but was sabotaged before I earned my badge. You want the dirt on these goons? I'll serve it up." She began typing with much more force than needed, which I found slightly annoying. "It's about time someone recognized my ability. The sheriff is not the best leader. And not the brightest bulb either. But that's just me." She rapped on the keyboard as I got comfortable in my chair with Mrs. Kohl's cell phone and a yellow legal pad on which to make notes. Although I needed help, I wasn't confident that Deloris was the gal for the job.

Within thirty minutes Deloris was declaring she needed to make a road trip. "Both of these losers live and work on The Peninsula. Facebook pages list employment with Empire Seafood. I'll go check with the boss at Empire and ask a few questions." I knew "The Peninsula" as the chain of islands connected by a series of bridges to Ellsworth on its eastern border. Most of what I had heard about the area was that it was notorious for fencing stolen goods. Hot outboard motors and electronics could be purchased for short cash on The Peninsula, and summer homes were not safe from winter break-ins and robberies. And what I had heard was immediately confirmed by the overzealous Deloris.

"Most of the people who call The Peninsula home are self-employed clam diggers, worm diggers, or seaweed and moss rakers. And as clams, worms, kelp, and sea moss are all found along the shore, thieving harvesters have easy access to frontal properties," Deloris said. She was certainly opinionated, I thought. "What do you say to a little visit to Empire Seafood?"

"Maybe I had better stay here and work on the Kohl case," I said. "You go ahead, though." I would be glad to be rid of her for a while, so I offered no resistance to her taking the lead in getting some firsthand scoop that could come in handy in convicting the drug runners.

"You haven't been here long enough to know about The Peninsula. But there are some very bad hombres over there. I have never met anyone east of the Sullivan Bridge who could be trusted. But that's me."

"Thank you for your insight," I said. "It's nice to have the local knowledge."

"Of course I'll need a gun," Deloris mentioned, trying to sound nonchalant.

"Yeah, I'll run that up the flagpole and let you know." I was confident that my tone dismissed the request without my words doing so. Deloris shrugged and muttered something derogatory as she donned her coat and left the office.

Alone with Mrs. Kohl's cell phone, it didn't take long for me to discern her preferred mode of communication. There were a couple of missed calls, no voice messages, and tens of thousands of text messages. Most of the contacts in her list were a combination of a first name and company name, like "Dave—Eastern Seafoods." The texts to the seafood companies were all business, mostly about orders, pricing, and shipping details.

But a few of the lengthy text threads were denoted only as a phone number with no name or other identifying info attached. And the majority of these were unpleasant exchanges. Many of the nasty notes were complaints about incomplete or late shipments of lobster products. There was one text chain that I found disturbing and of great interest. Mrs. Kohl's end of the first week of sporadic communication was a repeated, "Who is this?" Or a nonresponse, which elicited the worst from the ignored text messenger. The thread began on January 1 with "Happy New Year Lard Ass," and went downhill from there.

I scrolled through the thread and continued all the way to a long string that had been sent the day before yesterday, the day of Mrs. Kohl's murder. The tone in the messages went from anger to absolutely incoherent rages. I highlighted and forwarded specific exchanges that I found most telling to my own phone.

"Your world will come crashing in if SHIPMENTS do not stop."

"I don't know who this is, or what you want."

"But I know you. And I know what you are doing."

"Stop harassing me."

"Ha! Going to the police? We both know that will never happen."

The person texting Mrs. Kohl, from the looks of other exchanges, seemed to be completely unstable, and possibly in a serious state of deteriorating mental health. There was name calling and even some physical threatening from the mystery person. Mrs. Kohl's responses later in the thread ranged from defensive to promising to get law enforcement involved if the verbal abuse and threatening persisted.

"You are a capitalist pig. You are a complete sow."

"Can we meet and talk about your issues with me?"

"Time for talk has passed. I warned you. Dirty pig!"

"Who is this? Only a coward hides behind anonymity."

"This coward will take you to slaughter. First I'm going to make you sweat like the pig you are."

"If I take this to the cops, you'll be arrested for criminal threatening."

"Go ahead. Stinking, bitch sow!"

I wondered if Mrs. Kohl had at the very least alerted any officials—or even her husband—to what could be called harassment. I would check into that, I thought as I jotted a note on the legal pad.

I researched the cell number from which the text originated, only to find that it was a prepaid and thus not able to be pinned to an owner. I called the number and got an immediate computer-generated message about the number being no longer in service. If the nasty texts had escalated to action, then the murderer had been wise enough to throw the phone filled with evidence into the ocean, I surmised. I read through the messages again, slowly this time, searching for clues to the sender's identity. Anyone who watches crime shows on television knows enough about forensics, research, investigation, and how to evade detection. And anyone who knows how to use Google can really fine-tune their criminal activity, I knew. Hell, if terrorists can learn to build bombs using materials found at their corner neighborhood market, then any average Joe can learn how to place nontraceable calls and text messages. Law enforcement these days was mostly about staying ahead of the criminals, who often know more about new technology than the crime fighters do.

I found it noteworthy that the texts were mostly fully and properly punctuated. There were no emoticons or shortening of words. Grammatically, the messages read well, which was an odd juxtaposition with the content. I assumed the sender was educated. Some of the messages were more bullying than threatening, while others were accusatory. It was not clear exactly what enraged the texter, only that Mrs. Kohl had been warned about some activity and had not stopped and would face consequences. There seemed to be some underlying principle that had been treaded upon by Mrs. Kohl. While there was relatively little vulgarity, there were certainly some very derogatory accusations and statements.

One common term throughout the thread was "Capitalist Pig." There were a lot of accusations of cheating, and I got the sense that this was business-related rather than personal or marital. I wondered if this was a disgruntled employee. That was certainly a possibility, and one that I would check into.

"The only thing lower than a pig is a snake in the grass."

"Who are you?"

"Slither under another rock. Bite the hand that feeds you. You are completely detestable."

"Trust me. I will find out who you are."

"Trust? You are the picture of deceit. Lying, cheating pig!"

I knew that my investigation would include speaking with many of the ex-convicts working at ALP. Likely there were a number of employees at ALP who had been educated prior to being convicted of whatever crimes they had committed.

It finally became clear that some texts were copied and sent over and over again. One that was sent twice in one day and then again nearly every day was:

"Well, you have created quite a circus, haven't you? You have ruined everything I have ever cared about, and things will never return to normal."

Interestingly, this particular text never elicited a response from Mrs. Kohl. I got the sense that this was in reference to the island itself. From what I had learned from Joan Proctor, this sentiment was shared by many year-round residents and summer folk alike. Summer people who had sold their family estates for pennies on the dollar thanks to the ex-con presence would certainly be plenty angry with Midge Kohl and her group of ALP investors. And locals who had been raised on this quaint and pristine paradise would be sick about the changing population and would fear for their children among the new inhabitants, many of whom were convicted for gruesome acts of violence. Could that drive a parent to a violent and murderous rage, I wondered?

I was stuck on one text. "Your daily actions are inhumane. You are nothing but a cold-blooded killer. Your outward civility is cracking and barbarism is oozing from within." Even among all of the nasty insults, this one stuck out as different and more meaningful. But I wasn't sure why. Although the texts were incriminating, they were not helping me with a suspect list. If anything, they created a longer list than what would be useful. Employees, summer residents who sold out, year-round people who held Mrs. Kohl responsible for irreversible change, parents, customers, or business associates . . . The possibilities were plentiful at this point. I had been mulling over and through text messages for two hours when I realized that I should be looking at Mrs. Kohl's emails as well.

Fortunately, Mrs. Kohl's email on her phone was not password protected, allowing me entry into what I assumed was her only account, as it contained both business and personal correspondence. The majority of what remained in her inbox was ALP related, and was mostly complaints about a missing, late, or incomplete order. It was clear that her associates within the seafood industry only reached out when there were problems. There was no small talk, or light-hearted notes. Even the personal emails that had been sent from what I assumed were family members or friends were very detail-oriented about dates of events or notices of deaths or weddings or baby showers.

I scrolled through the contact list, and found nothing unusual or eyebrow raising. I looked through sent mail, and found the same—nothing that looked threatening in any way. I opened up the recently deleted and trash files, and found an email with an attachment that was sent to Mrs. Kohl from ihateyou@fumail.com. The phone struggled to open the attachment. I was getting antsy, so I forwarded the email to myself so I could open it on my laptop. It was taking forever to send. It finally went out with a "ding." I watched anxiously for it to appear in my inbox. Suddenly, I became aware of some hushed voices in the outer office area. I thought I had been left alone, and now wondered who was with me. Deloris would have made a grand and noisy entrance. And if the sheriff was here, who was he speaking with, and why in whispers?

I quietly closed my laptop, and slowly stood up from the chair. Walking deliberately and without making a sound, I crept to the side of the open door and peered down a short hallway to the main lobby of the department. Although I could hear a slight rustling of clothing and padded footsteps, I could not see who had come in. Whoever had entered had done so sneakily. Normally, Deloris would have greeted anyone who came through the front door. In her absence, someone had taken great liberty, I thought. I stepped into the hall as I heard a door close. I hustled to the lobby. Papers that had been stacked neatly on Deloris's desk were now strewn haphazardly. Two large file cabinet drawers had been left open. The only doors that I could not see from my office were the restrooms and the storage room. Assuming that whoever had entered did not do so to use a bathroom, I tiptoed over to the storage room door. Before I twisted the knob, I felt for my revolver and recalled that I hadn't donned my holster this morning as my mission did not require a gun.

I hesitated, and looked out the window into the parking area. Sure enough, the only vehicle other than mine was the same pickup truck that had nearly T-boned me this morning. The same vehicle occupied by the two drug addicts from whom I had confiscated a large box of illicit substance sat indiscreetly front and center. Pressing my ear closer to the door, I could hear low voices and the shuffling of cardboard boxes. The guys were here to collect their "shipment," I knew. Now that I understood who had sneaked in, and what their intention was, I flung the door open with some gusto and walked into the storage room to chase the pests away. As quickly as I entered, I found myself staring down the barrel of a .38 Special gripped in the shaky hand of the thug who had been the passenger this morning. Putting my hands up, I backed away from the gun slowly and said, "Whoa. You shippers take your work seriously."

"Don't fuck with us!" yelled the other man, who was sporting a red, puffy cheek that would soon be a huge black eye. His clothing had been tattered, and I could tell he had been roughed up a bit. "Where's the box?" he demanded as he continued to plow through boxes and containers on a shelf.

"The sheriff took it to the lab for analysis," I said.

"That's bullshit!" he yelled. "There's nothin' illegal about the chemicals, and if I don't get them back right away, there'll be hell to pay." He continued to rifle through everything in the storage area while his partner kept the gun trained on me. Both men were jittery. I assumed that the shaking was a combination of needing a fix and the fear of what would happen if they did not deliver the goods to whoever had intended to receive them, and who had likely paid dearly for them.

"It looks like someone beat you up. Is that because a lobster shipment may be held up without your box of *chemicals*?" I asked. "Why don't you just tell me who you work for? Otherwise you'll both be going down while your boss finds some other morons to run his errands."

"Look, bitch! You are on the wrong end of this equation to be asking us anything. Now, I am going to ask you once more, nicely. Where is the box?" The look on his face was utter desperation. I was not afraid of being shot. In fact, I was confident that the man with the gun was scared, and was not about to pull the trigger. The way he held the gun was with extreme unfamiliarity. He was so awkward with it that I wondered whether it was even loaded. Best to not find that out the hard way, I thought as I backed up, increasing the distance between my chest and the gun.

"You are being stupid," I said bravely to the gunman. Maybe I could reason with him. "You are going to be arrested for possession with intent to sell an illicit substance. And if you do not drop that weapon right now, you'll be charged with assault of an officer with a deadly weapon. These are felonies. You know what that means, right?"

"Don't talk to her!" the lead man screamed. "Give me the gun!" he demanded, and grabbed the pistol from his partner. "Get on your knees!" he yelled at me as he waved the gun toward my head.

"Donny, don't," pleaded the weak link. "Come on, let's get out of here."

"Are you crazy? You're not the one that's gonna pay for this. I need to get that box back, NOW!" His eyes widened and he started breathing very loudly. Sweat rings had wicked wider in the armpits of his T-shirt. He fired a shot into the ceiling, which startled his partner more than it did me. "The next one has your name on it," he said through clenched teeth as he brought the barrel down slowly from pointing up to directly at my head. "Now are you going to give me my stuff? Or am I going to kill you?"

As he started moving in closer to me, I got nervous. I could probably outmaneuver him and suffer a glancing wound at worst, I thought. I needed him to get closer to make my move and not get shot. The barrel of the gun was almost touching my blouse when I swatted it away with all of my strength. The gun skittered across the linoleum floor, coming to rest at the base of the wall. The man went for the gun, and I went for him, tackling him and pinning him to the floor with great ease. "Get the gun!" he screamed to his partner as I straddled his torso and locked my hands around his frail wrists. His partner turned to escape and ran directly into the sheriff, who now filled the doorway.

Within two minutes both men were cuffed, read their Miranda rights, and marched off to be booked and jailed to await bail and an arraignment date. Both men waved their rights to silence as they walked down the hall with the sheriff. They bickered back and forth like schoolchildren. The Hancock County Jail wasn't like what I had known as typical lockups in Florida. It was a small facility, and the warden and guards were honest family men who did not mistreat detainees. There would be no drugs or gang rapes. It was jail, period. These boys would sleep, eat, and wait. Oh, and detox. Because of the explosion in drug-related arrests recently, all authorities within Maine's criminal justice system had undergone extensive training and had ample stores of all antidotes for withdrawal from a variety of toxic substances. Hancock County even offers counseling and therapy to addicted inmates who find themselves suddenly in a drug- and alcohol-free zone. The two addicts were clearly jonesing, and would be suffering some form of DTs shortly, I knew.

I remembered the first time I faced the barrel of a gun, and how I had silently prayed. I hadn't prayed for my life to be spared, but rather for forgiveness. Since then, I had been close to meeting my maker so many times and in so many different ways that I hated myself for being so cool about it. Was I lucky? Or was I really that good at what I do? That was a question I had pondered often throughout my illustrious career. I always came down on the side of being good. After all, if I attributed my life to luck, I would have to believe that someday my luck would run out. And that would make it hard to get out of bed in the morning.

As I collected myself and headed back to my office, I found a bit of comfort in knowing that I had been right about the two addicts. The weak link would eventually talk to save his own skin, perhaps leading me to someone higher up in the organization. Getting these two out of circulation was not a feather in my cap at all. They would be replaced by two more just like them—probably already had.

Before I opened my laptop I had a sudden, gut-wrenching thought come over me. What about Deloris? She had headed out to find the addicts' boss at Empire Seafood. She was alone and unarmed. These guys played a little rougher than I had anticipated. There was no sense in my going to find her without a gun, I decided. What if her feelings about people on The Peninsula were spot on? When the sheriff returned from booking the addicts, I would let him know where Deloris was heading and why. Until then, I would continue my thorough search for clues through Mrs. Kohl's phone.

The email attachment I had forwarded to myself from Mrs. Kohl's deleted files that originated from ihateyou@fumail .com sat ready to download. The attachment appeared to be a lengthy video. I wondered what I would do with an email that came from such a vile address. Would I delete it without opening? Or would curiosity get the best of me? I hit the "open" icon under the attachment and watched.

The video's caption was "Undercover at a Lobster and Crab Slaughterhouse," and subtitles included, "PETA's groundbreaking investigation of crustacean slaughter recorded animals who were ripped apart and boiled alive." I knew little of PETA (People for the Ethical Treatment of Animals) before moving to Maine, but here, many PETA activists rallied and protested during the weeklong Lobster Festival. Protesting lobster fishing in Maine is not an easy gig. When activists start meddling with livelihoods, things can escalate quickly, making a peaceful protest a real challenge. PETA had pretty much been run out of town by an angry mob two years in a row. Maybe this video was a safer way to get their message out.

I watched the video from start to finish, twice. It was quite an exposé that featured the grimmer side of lobster processing. The narration was real conversation taped in live footage by the undercover PETA agent who was posing as a new employee-in-training at a processing plant. The trainee/agent was shaken to his core while being instructed. He kept asking if the lobsters could feel pain. The answer from a supposed manager was "Who gives a crap? Keep up!" Suddenly, the back of my neck tingled. I hadn't had that feeling in months. This was the "aha moment" I had been waiting for. Trudy Proctor. Joan and Clark's save-the-world daughter.

I scanned through the text messages again until I found the one that included the circus, and read it again. "Well, you have created quite a circus, haven't you? You have ruined everything

I have ever cared about, and things will never return to normal." Hadn't Trudy used the phrase "freak show" when I met her? And didn't her picket sign profess that lobsters felt pain? This made sense, I thought as I scribbled more notes on the legal pad. ihateyou@fumail.com may very well be the same person who had sent the hateful text messages from an untraceable cell phone. I had my first real suspect. Trudy Proctor had motive. But was she capable of murder? Maybe Mrs. Kohl's death was unintended, and then had to be covered up by the fire. Trudy certainly appeared to be exhausted when I met her. And she didn't seem upset or surprised about learning that the Kohls' house had burned to the ground. And maybe the picketing at ALP was a guise to hide the fact that she knew Mrs. Kohl was not there.

As I combed the contents of Mrs. Kohl's phone, looking for more evidence that might support or deny Trudy's involvement in the death, the sheriff returned from the jail. "Mind if I interrupt for a minute?" he asked.

"Not at all," I replied and put the phone down. "I wanted to speak with you anyway. I am concerned about Deloris. I let her go to Empire Seafood to poke around. In light of having a gun pulled on me, I am now regretting allowing her to go."

"She'll be fine," he answered with confidence.

"Really? I'm not so sure. Drug dealers who lose a large package are not kind. And they do not appreciate people nosing around their turf uninvited."

"That's what I wanted to talk with you about. The chemicals you confiscated are not illegal. They are actually used in shipping live lobster to China." I was stunned. I would not have been surprised to hear that the chemicals had not yet been added to the list of banned substances. But to hear that they actually served a legal purpose was hard to believe. "But at least we have the punks on aggravated assault with a deadly weapon. They'll never make bail."

"Wow, I did not see that coming," I said quietly. "I guess I shouldn't be worried about Deloris. What about the mini meth lab? Did the lab analyze the contents of the soda bottle?"

"Spittoon. I suspected that, the lab confirmed, and they were both in possession of chewing tobacco that is now in storage at the jail." This revelation did nothing to relieve my anxiety about having been so wrong about the two men. "Didn't you notice the Copenhagen rings on their left rear pockets?"

"I did not. I guess I was too busy wondering if my head was going to be blown off," I sniped defensively. "I'm sorry. I just don't believe that those guys are on the level. Why come wielding a gun to collect something that is not illegal and would have been released anyway?"

"The Peninsula."

"Yeah, so I have heard," I smiled. "I'm not buying it, though." Before I could update the sheriff on what I had found in Mrs. Kohl's text and email messages, the sheriff's cell phone rang loudly.

He snapped the phone out of the case he wore on his belt and answered. He listened and nodded. "Oh, yes. Yes, okay. What? Jesus. When will you have more information? Thank you, and we'll look for your formal report." The sheriff placed the phone back on his belt and sat in the chair next to me. He rubbed the back of his neck, massaging what looked like stress.

"That was Dr. Lee, the state pathologist. He's having a hard time due to the condition of the corpse."

Although I had no formal training in pathology, I had assumed that there was not enough left of Mrs. Kohl to make any definitive statement. I waited as the sheriff stared into space and shook his head. When he made eye contact with me he continued, "He is confident that the victim was dead prior to burning." The sheriff sighed, removed his phone from his belt, opened it, and stared at it as if it held answers to questions that were bubbling to the surface in both of our minds. Snapping the phone shut and clipping it back on his belt, he continued, "Dr. Lee is still working and will know more later."

Looks like I had myself a murder to solve.

SIX

"Overkill" was all I could muster in response to the sheriff's bombshell. I never imagined that Mrs. Kohl's death may have been premeditated. In light of the autopsy findings revealing that the fire had been set to hide a murder, I now had much more to consider. And the condition of the corpse might make it very difficult to prove how she was actually killed. Modern science and technology in capable hands were nothing short of miraculous. But I wasn't confident that Dr. Lee had the latest and greatest of any of the ingredients needed to pull off a conclusive finding that a decent defense attorney couldn't shatter. For now, I didn't have time to worry about the chances of getting a conviction. I had a killer to find and arrest.

I have never been much of a multitasker, so I would not attempt to straddle two cases. I would put aside my feelings about illicit drugs and The Peninsula. If I was correct about something being askew that could not be brushed away with the usual justification of happening "east of the Sullivan Bridge," there would be ample opportunity to crack that wide open after I closed the door on Mrs. Kohl's murder. The nefarious nature of the killing of Mrs. Kohl would haunt me, and that would propel me to the case's conclusion at the cost of neglecting everything and everyone else in my world. I had made a number of mistakes in the last twenty-four hours. And I was not going to make any more. My single and intense focus would be arresting the vicious killer of Mrs. Kohl.

The information that the sheriff had delivered from the state's pathologist raised one big question in my mind: Was Trudy Proctor capable of these godawful actions? As soon as Deloris returned from her road trip, I would hand her the task of researching Trudy. I needed school transcripts, medical records, all social media activity, and a list of people with whom she associates. Until Deloris could dig in, I would work on a plausible and possible time line of events that could possibly incriminate or exclude Trudy from my suspect list. Right now, with the texts, emails, and attitude, she was looking good for it.

All I knew about Trudy's schedule was that she was home from law school; Georgetown University, as I recalled. So she had to have been on Acadia Island at the time of the murder. I knew that Trudy had a dislike for Mrs. Kohl. It seemed to me that for the fire to have done such extensive damage, the house must have been burning all night—even with the help of the red-dyed diesel fuel. And the diesel must be readily available on the island, and used by anyone with a diesel-powered boat, truck, tractor, or generator. I did a Google search and was disappointed to see that some firefighting pumps are diesel powered, which would explain the presence of the fuel at the scene if the island's volunteer firemen had access to such pumps. I made a note to check that out. And what about the broken propane line? I wondered if I could examine and determine whether it had been broken by the "frost heave," as Clark Proctor assumed, or may it have been broken by the murderer to intentionally fuel the fire? That would have been difficult to do without some equipment to dig up the gas line from the frozen ground. Just a shovel would not have sufficed. Maybe the line had been broken where it entered the house, I thought. I wished I had taken a better look at that when I was there. I could sift through my pictures and hope to see something useful. I jotted that on my notepad.

Before I knew it, the sheriff was in my office saying "good night." Time had gotten away from me, I thought as I realized that I had gotten lost in Google. It had started with the fire pumps, gone to proper propane line installation, and I would now consider myself an authority of frost heaves and what havoc they can wreak. Researching had consumed my afternoon and early evening. The sheriff complained that he had also suffered the "lost in Google" syndrome, as he had been researching sodium tripolyphosphate or STPP, the chemical that I had confiscated. "It is used in lots of seafood processing and shipping," he stated. "It helps fresh product retain moisture and quality. I learned that using it to ship live lobsters is very recent technology. When live lobsters are treated with a solution of STPP, they don't lose weight on the flight to China. Shrinkage has been a huge problem in the past."

"That explains the Chinese writing on the box," I said.

"Yes, I called a friend here in town who works at a lobster

shipping house. They ship lobster in a specialized container, which is too expensive to be disposable. So rather than shipping back the empty containers for reuse, which is also cost prohibitive, they fill them with these chemicals, which are cheaper to buy in China than in the US," he said. "The two-kilo pouches are good for one thousand pounds of live lobster, which is the capacity of each individual shipping container." The sheriff yawned and looked at his wristwatch. "And the big producers get the chemicals for free from their Chinese customers, which sweetens the deal."

I filled the sheriff in on where I was with organizing and putting together a strategy for the Kohl case. I had hoped to return to Acadia Island the following morning, but knew I needed to wait for final results of the autopsy and labs. No sense getting off on the wrong course if I could have all of the information soon, I knew. I would stay and research a little more before going home, and would return to the office early in the morning.

"Besides, I'll need to wait for Deloris to get back here to switch the phones to her cell, right?" I asked, remembering that the office isn't actually manned after five p.m., and that all incoming calls go to voice mail unless it is an emergency. In the case of an emergency, the caller is prompted to hang up and dial 911, which automatically transfers to Deloris's cell phone. If Deloris doesn't pick up within three rings, the call transfers to the Maine State Police. This technology is critical in small-town law enforcement where budgets do not cover around–the-clock enforcement. Although the Staties make rounds at night, they don't understand the lay of the land like a local does, nor do they know the bad actors in the same way that childhood friends do. The sheriff can usually snuff a conflict before it gets out of hand, while the presence of State Police can sometimes add fuel to the fire. The sheriff is more likely to drive a drunk home, while the State Police are quick to fill the jail. Of course, most people planning to do harm do so after hours for all of the logical reasons.

As long as I was waiting for Deloris, the sheriff asked me to grab the phone in the event that it rang, which was unlikely as it had been extremely quiet. I agreed to do so, wished him a good night, and got back to the Kohl case. I had read every single text message and email, listened to a few benign voice messages, and scrutinized the entire contact list. I had made notes on anything that I considered pertinent or worthy of follow-up. My sense of Mrs. Kohl was that she was not very well liked, had few friends, and her business associates and customers only dealt with her because ALP produced the best-quality value-added seafood on the market. Her husband did not communicate with her. She made her employees nervous. Her real estate dealings on Acadia were sketchy. If this was her only phone and represented all communication with the world, Mrs. Kohl lacked passion. Her correspondence was void of emotion. I hadn't seen a single exclamation point or bold print or underscored word. She was neither happy nor sad. She was never excited or disappointed. I doubted that she had pleaded for her life if she had warning before her death. My image of Mrs. Kohl was one that did not allow her to put up a fight, or struggle, or scream for help, or beg for mercy, or pray for forgiveness. If her murder had been premeditated, it was one that gave the killer no satisfaction, which, I thought, explained the severe nature of the crime. Except for the fact that Mrs. Kohl had been murdered, and the way in which she had been killed, she was uninteresting. Mrs. Kohl was boring to the point of being intriguing.

It had been dark for a couple of hours when I looked up from my computer. The security lamps around the building illuminated snowflakes like confetti seen through footlights. Although it had been a snowy two months, I was not yet jaded. Except for shoveling, I got a thrill from a snowy forecast, and liked the challenge that driving roads needing to be plowed provided. I made a habit of listening to the "no school" reports when I got out of bed, and felt a tinge of vicarious excitement for the kids for whom school was canceled. Watching snowflakes flutter through a window was mesmerizing, much like gazing at flames in a fireplace. I stared, yet didn't really see anything. My mind was racing in contrast to the slow and graceful descent of feathery flakes. Like Robert Frost, whose name is most appropriate for his poem "Stopping by Woods on a Snowy Evening," I had promises to keep. And promises made to myself were the most difficult to possess.

The office phone blared, startling me from the hypnotic trance the flakes had rendered. I jumped and grabbed the receiver. "Hello, Hancock County Sheriff's Department," I answered, verbatim in content and tone that I had heard Deloris use.

"Hi. This is Jackie. Is Deloris there?"

"No, she isn't. Would you like to leave a message?"

"Well, yeah I guess. Can you please have her call home when she gets there? I am starting to get worried. She is always home by five thirty. I tried her cell," the woman said. "The roads are starting to get bad, and the car doesn't have snow tires."

"Will do. And if she shows up at home before I see her, can you ask her to check in with Jane? She has my cell. I'm getting ready to go home and don't know how to switch the phone over to night mode." I explained to Jackie that Deloris had gone to do some legwork, and that I expected her back in the office any minute now.

Although Jackie seemed delighted that her partner had finally been given an assignment worthy of her talents, she was nervous about her tardiness and noncommunication. I understood this and advised her to get used to it. If Deloris was to become the asset that I suspected she would be to the department, she had to start at the bottom of the totem pole. Jackie confirmed that Deloris had already occupied the bottom rung. After all, she had manned the office as dispatch, secretary, and errand girl for six years! She had been to the Academy, and passed all with flying colors "except the chin-ups"—which kept her from a badge and placement in the Maine State Police. "How much upper body strength do you need to pull a trigger?" And I suspected this attitude had a lot to do with the fact that Deloris had not been issued a gun. We hung up.

Jackie's call had me looking at the clock and calculating how many hours had passed since Deloris had headed east, full of the gung-ho that I recognized from many experiences with the almost-made-its who feel they have to prove the system wrong. Deloris had left her post here at the office at just after noon, and it was now 6:15. It should have taken forty-five minutes to drive from Ellsworth to Empire Seafood, I learned as I Googled the business's address. I estimated an hour, given the road conditions, and allowed thirty minutes for a quick lunch. She really should have been back by now, I thought. All she was doing was verifying employment for the two guys that we had since arrested on subsequent and unrelated charges. I tried her cell, and got no answer. I assumed the cell coverage was inadequate, and decided to give her another call in thirty minutes if she did not surface before then.

Thirty minutes passed, and still no answer. I didn't want to alarm Jackie, so decided to not call to tell her that her partner had not returned to the office. Instead, I would have to drive to The Peninsula and find Deloris. She was very likely off the road in a snowbank and waiting for a tow. In the past, I had found wayward partners in bars drowning sorrows, or hotel rooms working on extramarital affairs. I doubted this was the issue with Deloris. No bars or hotels open in Down East Maine this time of year, coupled with the fact that there were not likely to be many lesbians looking to lead her astray, left me assuming that she was overdue for innocent reasons. Jackie's concern about the absence of snow tires was a good one. The Duster was useless without them. And Deloris drove a compact Hyundai that she was oddly proud to tell me was manufactured in Egypt. I had wondered what Egyptians knew about driving in snow.

I gathered my things, shut down my laptop, and locked my office door. Stopping in the lobby, I checked the top of Deloris's desk, and was relieved to find instructions on how to switch the phone over to night mode. I was impressed with the degree of organization Deloris practiced. Everything was labeled and filed under obvious headings. Deloris could be a real asset to me, I thought as I turned out lights and locked the main door behind me. The weakness in my operation was the paperwork end. If I could enlist Deloris to help, we would make an excellent team. I knew that Deloris desired more hands-on investigation, and an arrest with a shootout would be considered a bonus.

I chuckled to myself; Deloris would be disappointed to have missed my disarming of and diving tackle onto the junkie. I brushed an inch of snow from the Duster's windshield and climbed behind the wheel. I would have to allow her some involvement to appease her. Maybe I could discuss theories and bounce ideas off of her. She struck me as having a quick mind and being a quick study—she probably retained everything she had been taught at the Academy. She knew more about Maine law than I did. And she had the most valuable attribute of any successful law enforcement officer: common sense. By the time I reached the first causeway, I had come full circle with my opinion of Deloris. Well, here's hoping, I thought. Everyone deserves a chance.

When I drove across the second causeway that connected Little Berry Island to Great Berry Island, I noticed that there were no tire tracks in the freshly fallen snow, so I assumed that Deloris had not come through in the last hour. Nor had anyone else. I pulled over onto the narrow shoulder to look at the map I had printed out. There was no way to go wrong. After the first bridge, I was to take a right at every opportunity and land in the small village of Champlain. Champlain was at the very end of The Peninsula, and Empire Seafood is located at the head of a large wharf there. I continued, and drove below the posted speed limit as the road twisted and turned wildly around coves and between houses. I wished I had come in daylight.

The first streetlamp marked Champlain's western border with a sign that read "Welcome to Champlain," but that had been partially defaced by someone with spray paint to add "Now Leave." Probably school kids entertaining themselves, I thought as I poked along the road, which was so narrow that I wondered what I would do if I met an oncoming vehicle. It was now 7:45, and may as well have been midnight for the lack of activity. Houses were either completely dark, or lit by television screens that I could see through windows facing the road. I dawdled along, passing closed signs on the Post Office and General Store. I passed the Champlain Congregational Church with a sign lettered with a pithy message in line with those that I had come to know as signature, quintessential, Maine religion: "1 Cross + 3 Nails = 4 Given."

A short, dark stretch of road gave way to a well-lit and full parking area hemmed by a number of warehouse-style buildings and a dock. The driveway was gated, but open. I entered and circumnavigated the lot, looking for a Hyundai, which I found parked in front of what appeared to be the office building. Deloris's car was covered with two inches of snow, while those around it were clean, indicating that she had been here since the last shift left and the present shift began. I regretted allowing Deloris to come here. I found an empty parking spot and pulled in. Some of the buildings were dark. I would start in what I assumed was the processing plant, which appeared to be alive with a full second shift. I proceeded on foot.

When I entered the processing plant, I was impressed with the cleanliness and amount of stainless steel. There was no fishy smell whatsoever. All workstations were manned by people dressed in white protective suits and white booties. Most of the workers appeared to be Latino, I thought as I wandered looking for a tall redhead among the hair nets. The workers were lined up on either side of two long tables where they picked crabs.

"Hello, can I help you?" A man's voice called from behind me. I turned around to a pleasant-looking young man who wore a blue shirt with "Manager" embroidered above the chest pocket.

"Yes. I'm from the Hancock County Sheriff's Department," I showed him my badge. "I'm looking for a woman. Her name is Deloris and her car is in your lot. Have you seen her?"

"The majority of our second shift are hired through a sub-contractor. Most of them don't speak English or drive here. I can look through the contracts and see if there is a Deloris," he offered. "What does she do?"

"Oh, no. She doesn't work here. She works for the police department, and came to Empire to verify employment of two guys we are investigating. She was overdue getting back to the office, so I decided to come find her. I take it cell phones don't work here." I looked at mine—no service. Tension pulled at the back of my neck. I was afraid of what may have happened to Deloris.

I gave the manager the abbreviated account of the day, starting with this morning's episode with the two men and ending with their arrest. I mentioned the chemicals that I had mistakenly thought were drugs. He said that he didn't know of the two men or any chemicals that they may have been transporting. He shrugged and said, "But I only run the second shift. Maybe they're legit. Don't know. We only process at night. Shipping is in the morning." My stress level doubled as he spoke.

"I need to look around. I need access to all buildings. Deloris's car is in the lot. She must be here somewhere." My nerves exposed themselves as beads of sweat popped out on my forehead. The manager handed me a master key from his pocket, and explained that he would stay on the job unless I needed his help. I asked permission to speak with some of the people working the line. He agreed, but warned me that I wouldn't get far unless I spoke Spanish. I confirmed that I did, thanked him, and started hustling through the plant.

The laborers I attempted to question were hesitant to look up from their work of picking crabmeat. I learned that they were doing piece work, so the more pounds produced, the higher their compensation. Their fingers flew. No one had seen a tall, redheaded, white Caucasian. They had started their shift at five o'clock. I searched the break room and both restrooms. No Deloris. I searched coolers and freezers. No Deloris. I searched the packaging and supplies storage room. No Deloris. I searched the manager's office. No Deloris. She was not in the plant. I headed outside and into the next building.

The entryway was dark and damp. I could hear the humming of machinery and the sound of circulating water. I fumbled along a wall with my right hand and found a row of light switches and flipped them on. Fluorescent lights flickered and came on dimly at first, revealing the biggest wet storage tank system I had ever seen. Series of fiberglass tanks linked by miles of hoses and pipes that circulated salt water ran the length and width of the enormous room. Two large compressors aerated the tanks through perforated PVC pipes that lined their bottoms. The tanks were full of live product; mostly lobster and a few tanks with crabs. I walked the room from end to end looking in every tank. I shouted out several times for Deloris and got no answer. There was a certain creep factor involved in being alone in a room with so many crawling creatures, all of which seemed to be following me around the room with their buggy, black eyes. I quickly exited and, swelling with doubts, hustled to the office building.

I found lights, turned them on, and called out several times for Deloris. I searched every office, closet, and restroom. Every door I swung open was accompanied by a flutter of anxiety with what I might find. There was no sign of her. Why had I allowed her to come here alone? I hustled out and ran to the warehouse, where lights revealed mountainous stacks of pallets and shipping boxes and containers of many different sizes. I called out, and, much to my relief, heard a muffled cry from behind a door at the far end of the warehouse. I ran to the door and was again relieved to find that the master key opened it right up. I flipped on a light and found Deloris in a heap on the floor surrounded by bits of dusty plaster. "Are you all right?" I asked as I ran to her.

"No. I think I have broken bones in both feet. Thank God you're here! I have been yelling for help for hours." She broke into tears.

"What happened? Who did this to you?"

"I did it to myself," she whimpered. "No one here would

125

admit to knowing the two men. I didn't want to leave without some sort of lead, so thought I would look for evidence of drugs. I was up there," she pointed straight up to a jagged hole in a very high ceiling. She had apparently fallen through the upper level and onto the cement floor where she now sat. Around her were scattered fragments of ceiling that had come down with her. "I sneaked up a back staircase that led to the attic. I found more packaging supplies. I guess the floor is old and couldn't support my weight. I caught a beam, and held on for as long as I could, dangling there, knowing that a fall from that height would not be good."

I looked around for something with which to drag her to the door, as her feet and possibly ankles were badly broken. I found a large piece of corrugated cardboard and helped Deloris onto it. "I tried to pull myself back up through the hole, but didn't have the upper body strength." She cried harder. I understood this to be a long-awaited confession regarding her inability to pass muster in the mandatory physical test required of all Maine law enforcement officers.

I tried to move Deloris with the cardboard to the door. It was not an easy task. The floor was damp, and the corrugations in the cardboard acted like suction cups. "I'll run for help," I said.

"No, please. I am so embarrassed. Please. I'll crawl."

"Okay, but don't ask how *I* managed to pass the upper body strength test," I teased, trying to lighten the mood. It worked. Deloris rolled her eyes and giggled. "This will never go beyond the two of us, right?" I asked.

"My lips are sealed," she called out to me as I ran to bring the Duster closer to the door. I was glad that she wanted to keep this hushed, as I was feeling somewhat responsible. Deloris crawled over the threshold, down two steps, and into the snow where I placed the cardboard for her. She rolled back onto the makeshift sled, and I easily pushed her to the waiting car.

She was in a great deal of pain, but more concerned with how she had "screwed up," and how to explain her injuries in a way that would not humiliate her. I told her not to worry, and that we would think of an explanation on the way back to Ellsworth, where we would get to the hospital's emergency room for treatment ASAP.

Once Deloris was loaded and as comfortable as I could make her, I returned the master key to the plant manager and thanked him for his help. I lied and said that I had found out that Deloris had had car trouble and that she'd hitched a ride home without telling anyone. I assured him that someone would retrieve the broken Hyundai soon. It was break time, and the employees huddled around a table in their break room, eating prepackaged junk food from the vending machine. They chatted in an accent I couldn't place. As I passed the open door to exit the plant a man waved and spoke in Spanish.

"*Te veremos pronto, estoy seguro.*" There was something in his tone that indicated that he knew something that I didn't. But maybe I was reading too much into it, I thought as I got back to the Duster. I had missed the mark so badly on this whole thing that I had to be careful not to grasp at any little crumb to re-deem myself. Best to just let it go, and stay focused on the Kohl case. And now that Deloris would likely be incapacitated,

I hoped she would be eager to help with researching and documenting.

The snow had stopped falling. It hadn't amounted to more than a couple of inches, which did not require plowing, but did make the roads "greasy," as the locals liked to say. Deloris was in agony, nodding off and coming to, in and out of a pain-induced shock akin to a high-on-opiate state. The outgoing side of Champlain's welcome sign had also been altered with spray paint to include "Don't" before the "Come Again."

As we made our way from Champlain Village to Great Berry Island, headlights came upon us very quickly from behind. The vehicle had intense high beams that the driver neglected to dim, nearly blinding me with the reflection from the rearview mirror. I slowed to allow the impatient driver who was now tailgating an opportunity to pass. Instead of passing, the vehicle, which I could now tell was a pickup truck, nudged my rear fender. I sped up to put some distance between us. But the driver quickly caught up, and I received another bump; this one a bit harder, causing the Duster to careen off the snowbank on my right and bounce back into the road. There was no place to pull over. And I was hesitant to do so, since I didn't have my gun. I had always prided myself in my ability to out-drive the best of 'em in normal conditions. But the icy, unfamiliar roads had me at a disadvantage.

The truck's driver continued to menace my travel by blaring the horn and tapping my rear bumper. I was extremely nervous when I crossed the causeway between Great and Little Berry Islands, as there was nowhere to go, no shoulder onto which I could be forced, just frigid saltwater. And Deloris was in no condition to either fight or take flight. My only option was to keep driving and hope to keep the Duster on the narrow road. The truck's high beams lit up choppy seas that lapped either side of the one-lane road that twisted and turned between Little Berry Island and the road to Ellsworth. I was pushing the Duster as fast as I dared, and feared sliding off into the ocean. There was no time to fumble for my cell phone, and Deloris was out of it. I had a feeling that if I stopped and confronted the driver, I would be facing the barrel of a loaded gun for the second time today. I had the clichéd white knuckles, and my heart was pounding. I didn't dare stop at the intersection of The Peninsula Road and Ellsworth Road, so I skidded around the corner as fast as I could, nearly losing control and just missing a ditch where we would have been a captive audience for the bastard behind us.

The Duster fishtailed back and forth wildly as I fought the urge to scream. As I regained control of the Duster, I watched the truck stop and do a three-point turn in the intersection; heading back down The Peninsula. My heart slowed to normal and I relaxed my grip on the steering wheel. I assumed that the escort was the locals' way of saying goodbye and good riddance. I didn't discourage easily. It would take more than aggravated road rage to keep me from returning to the formidable Peninsula. But my return trip would be on my own terms, and would have to wait until Mrs. Kohl's murderer was behind bars.

I had many years of experience with the most unsavory neighborhoods in Miami where most law enforcement officers would not enter. Liberty City was the worst. The residents of Liberty City worked very hard to maintain their bad reputation. The distinction they held for the highest crime rate was indeed earned, and they liked it that way. When the cops are scared, the bad guys triumph. Hoodlums can do whatever they want without fear of being arrested. I sensed that The Peninsula enjoyed a similar dynamic, making it the perfect place to conduct illegal activity. The remote nature of the outer islands, like Acadia, kept the police at bay. Places like The Peninsula were readily accessible, so they had to use fear and intimidation to keep law-abiding citizens quiet and out of the way. The driver of the truck that had just harassed me would no doubt be boasting about his exploits by now, I thought as I entered the lot for emergency room parking at Ellsworth Medical Center. And anyone who didn't cotton to the terrorizing of innocents had better shut up, or risk becoming the target of abuse themselves.

I shook Deloris awake and said, "I am going to get some help and a wheelchair." She nodded and winced in pain. When I returned with both, she was on her cell with Jackie, apologizing and explaining that she had fallen through a ceiling. There was no mention of dangling from a beam without strength enough to pull herself back up and avoid falling.

"I was being chased by men with guns! When I crashed through the floor and landed below, they left me for dead. I crawled back to the main road where I was able to flag down Jane," she lied to save her own ego. I would go along with that, I thought. No harm. "Yes, I am going to be fine. Come to the hospital, and I'll send Jane home." I took that as my cue to leave, and did so after Deloris promised to call me with a list of her damages and schedule for treatment and return back to the department.

It was 11:30—well beyond my new Maine bedtime. I yawned, stretched, and walked around the Duster to inspect the rear end that had been hit several times. Except for minor dents and scratches, there wasn't much to see. The trunk still opened and closed. The entire length of the passenger side was scraped and dented. I would not get it repaired, I thought as I once again climbed behind the wheel and started for home. I had minimal insurance on the car, and didn't want my premium to go up. I would rather drive a battered vehicle than spend the money. Besides, the Duster was so old, fixing it up would be like putting the proverbial lipstick on a pig, I thought. Maybe the scratches and dents would add to my car's character. This last thought made me realize how exhausted I was. I called the sheriff at his home and filled him in on all that had transpired. He said that he would head to the hospital and stay with Deloris until she could be examined and injuries were diagnosed and treated. We agreed to regroup early in the morning.

I climbed the stairs to my apartment slowly. There was a sheet of paper on the outside of my door on which the Vickersons had written a series of time-stamped notes. I tore the note from the door and took it in with me to read from the comfort of an overstuffed chair. I kicked off my boots, and read. It appeared that Mrs. and Mr. V had taken turns trudging up to leave notes. The first one had been written at 6:00 this evening, and there was one left at every thirty-minute interval until 10:30. The comments and questions ranged from one word to full paragraphs, depending on who was writing.

Mr. V was a man of few words, so he preferred bullets to his wife's creative, literary prowess. The gist of the notations was primarily the question, where was I? Dinner was ready at 7:30. The mussel soufflé was marvelous. There were leftovers if I hadn't eaten. They were concerned at 8:00. Worried at 8:30. Suspicious at 9:00. Theorizing at 9:30. Mad at 10:00. And hoped to see me in the morning at 10:30. I laughed as I got ready for bed. Henry and Alice Vickerson had become the parents I never had. I knew they would be very good to Wally as well. I had been distracted from my search for an appropriate home for him, but would resume when things quieted down. I knew time was getting short to make arrangements.

The bed was cold. I shivered and pulled the blankets under my chin tightly. Just as I was drifting off, I heard the tune "Don't Worry, Be Happy." I thought it might be a dream, and ignored it. It started again and stopped. Who would be calling a dead person's phone, I wondered? And who would be calling so late? I sprung out of bed and dug through my bag to retrieve Mrs. Kohl's phone. There were five missed calls, all from the same number and all placed after ten this evening. I dialed the number from which the missed calls had come using my house phone. I had a suspicion, and thought I recognized the voice as it answered with a hesitant, "Hello?"

"Trudy?"

"Yes. Who's this?"

SEVEN

The phone went dead. She had hung up on me, which was not surprising. Evidence was mounting, and what had originally been a hunch had developed to a strong possibility for Trudy being responsible for Mrs. Kohl's death. I surmised that Trudy was now getting nervous in the wake of this morning's newspaper article declaring arson, and needed to find Mrs. Kohl's phone to destroy all incriminating correspondence. It appeared that she had been calling it and listening for the ring, as she had not left any messages. She was too late in her phone search, I thought smugly as I turned it off and tucked it away for safe keeping. I could try calling her again, but that might be counterproductive, I thought. At this point, Trudy only knew that Mrs. Kohl's phone had been unanswered. She didn't know where it was or who had it, if anyone. She had no idea that the autopsy indicated foul play. I doubted that she had heard enough of my voice last night to recognize it as mine. And she only knew me as an insurance investigator. She had no clue that I would be conducting an investigation into the murder that I was confident she had committed. I had investigated many murders that had never been solved. Cold cases were frustrating and extremely upsetting, especially when the killer is known but can't be proven. Trudy was an amateur. This case would be a cakewalk. But first I needed some sleep.

Waking before daylight, I had slept soundly and was feeling refreshed. I had a lot to do before heading out to Acadia Island. I also understood the importance of getting back to the island soon. Time spent here in Green Haven increased the time for tracks to be covered, alibis to be created, evidence to be destroyed, and stories to be perfected. I would arrange a boat ride with Cal. The mail boat was too public, I thought. I would not alert the Proctors of my trip until the last possible minute. Forewarned is forearmed. It would be to the benefit of the investigation, I thought, to catch them off guard, and not allow them time to concoct justification for the evidence I already had. My gut was that Joan and Clark would not believe that their daughter could be capable of murder. They would defend her in spite of any evidence I could gather. That's what parents do. I would be walking a tenuous line, needing their help and support as the only connection I had with the Island, and my only transportation once I landed ashore there. We would not part as friends, I knew, as I had intentions of having enough evidence to arrest Trudy and bring her back to Green Haven with me on my return trip. Once in custody and at the station, I could likely get her confession quickly and without most of the brutal tactics sometimes employed to force hardened criminals to talk. I did not anticipate questioning Trudy in her own environment, as that would be too comfortable for her.

I needed to slow my cart down and let the horse take the lead, I realized. The first thing I needed to do was to obtain a search warrant for the Proctors' home and vehicles. I could easily do so by calling the on-duty judge at the Hancock County Courthouse or asking the sheriff to obtain the warrant for me. I had been issued search warrants over the phone before without problems. But knowing the lack of service on Acadia, it would be wise to get the warrant lined up prior to boarding a boat. Once I had Trudy's phone and other electronic devices, I would have reasonable cause for her arrest simply from the history showing that she had called Mrs. Kohl's phone several times last night. I would either make a warrantless arrest, or detain Trudy for forty-eight hours, giving me time to find probable cause to justify the formal charges. I dialed the sheriff's office number. He was an early bird.

The sheriff had been at the hospital with Deloris and Jackie until quite late. Deloris had been X-rayed and CT-scanned. Results showed both of her heels had been broken by the impact of her fall. One heel was in need of only a cast, but the other required surgery, in which the orthopedist had used screws to piece the badly fractured calcaneus together, the sheriff reported. She would go home today, he said. And she was already complaining about missing work. The sheriff had agreed to allow Deloris to transfer all incoming calls to her home phone where she could dispatch. And he also agreed to speak with me about getting Deloris involved in some way from home in whatever I had going on. "Our girl will need physical therapy for several months. She'll go stir crazy if we don't give her projects to work on," he said.

"Yes, but how much can she do from home?" I asked. "I was looking forward to having her assist in the Kohl investigation, but now she can't do any legwork."

"You will be surprised. There's a lot you don't know about Deloris. She had a career in computer science before she decided to join the enforcement team. She's a Tier Three analyst," he boasted. I knew this as the top of the line in computer forensic support, and was impressed. I had never gotten certification, and knew how valuable her skills would be to me in the cyber aspect of the Kohl case. Deloris would be able to seize evidence and do forensic analyses and data recovery in the likely event that the killer had sabotaged any electronic link to evidence. I was excited to think of the work I could get done with my own, personal, digital investigative analyst, or DIVA, as the tech junkies were referred to.

On the topic of the search warrant, the sheriff lamented the fact that Deloris was not back in action, as she was apparently the go-to gal for just about everything that the sheriff needed done. He agreed to get the warrant himself and deliver it to me so I could get moving on the search and arrest if justified, or detainment if more time was needed to gather probable cause to arrest Trudy Proctor. And in light of the distance and travel factor to and from Acadia Island, I knew that I would need every last second to get her to the station, allow her to obtain counsel, and interrogate until she confessed. The sheriff agreed to meet me in Green Haven with the search warrant later that morning.

I would find Cal at the café and hire him to take me back to Acadia.

I never imagined that I would consider twenty-seven degrees "warm." But relative to the daily temperatures I had endured so far this February, this morning was "nice." I unzipped my coat as I walked from the Duster to the café. The sun, just above the horizon, cast a long shadow along the sidewalk, which had apparently been cleared for the first time this month. I could smell the coffee and hot, greasy, home-fried potatoes as I passed the kitchen's outside ventilation duct. I realized I had acclimated to the winter weather, noticing that I didn't even have a hat on this morning. My blood had thickened, as I was promised it would, back when all I could do was complain and shiver. And that wasn't the only thing that had thickened. My waistline had expanded nearly a whole size. That was due to the café, I knew. I had consumed far too many muffins. My breakfasts in Miami usually consisted of Cuban coffee and a piece of fruit. I had been craving fresh fruit all winter here in Green Haven, where a strawberry is quite exotic. I'd do anything for a mango, lychee, or avocado, I thought as I entered and was greeted by Audrey's usual "Hi, girlfriend!" I waved to Audrey and acknowledged the presence of Marlena and Marilyn as I passed the table where they enjoyed plates full of eggs and pancakes. The figures of both gals were probably a result of their daily breakfasts, I thought. I wondered if I would take the same shape with another ten years. I hoped not.

Cal was in his usual position, perched on his usual stool at the counter and hiding behind his usual newspaper. When I took the stool beside him, he slowly and deliberately creased the paper and dropped it beside his place mat. He took the glasses from his head, folded them, and tucked them into the pocket of a blue button-up collared shirt. "Don't let me interrupt your reading," I said as I pulled my coat off my shoulders and tucked it between my legs and the cushioned stool top to keep the sleeves from hitting the floor.

"Okay" was all Cal said as he donned his reading glasses, picked up the paper, and turned to the sports page. Audrey splashed coffee into a mug and set it in front of me. I pretended to look at the menu printed on the place mat. I had memorized it long ago, and knew that I would end up with an English muffin.

"What's up, Janey? Anything fun going on today? Any dead bodies on your schedule?" Audrey teased.

"Well, I came in to grab a bite to eat and to ask Cal for a ride back to Acadia."

"I can help with the bite to eat," she said. "Whatcha havin'?"

"Do you have any fruit?" I asked optimistically.

"Oh no. You're on the fruit kick again." She rolled her eyes. "The only fruits here are Marlena and Marilyn. But that's not what you have in mind, is it?" She spoke loudly enough for the mentioned gals to turn their attention from their breakfasts and wait for my response.

"I'm just checking. I thought you might have something with which to make a fruit cup. I'm craving a piece of fresh fruit."

"Welcome to Down East Maine!" Audrey laughed. "This is the end of the road for the produce truck. I'll see what we have, but don't get your hopes up." The last time Audrey had made the effort to serve me fruit, she had placed a banana on a plate.

And the time before that, it was an orange that I had to peel myself. The only other sign of fruit that I had seen served in the café since November was a maraschino cherry used to enhance the sliced orange garnish on a slab of grilled ham. July and August were all about blueberries. They were included in most orders in one form or another. And September and October featured apples. And that was it for the local fruit scene, I had learned. I had assumed that if I kept asking for fruit, Audrey would eventually procure a melon or something. I realized how mistaken I was when she appeared with a bowl of canned fruit cocktail and served it to me.

"There you go! The date on the can says it's expired. But not that long ago."

"Great," I said in a tone that I hoped she would take as less than enthusiastic. "I'll have an English muffin, too."

"Whoa! Really going all out this morning, girlfriend. Did you get a promotion?" And off she hustled to serve breakfast and insults to other customers, leaving me to speak with Cal.

I pushed the bowl of what I suspected could be rancid fruit to the side and cleared my throat. "I'm ready to interrupt now."

"When do you want to go?" Cal asked, lowering but not putting the paper down.

Lowering my voice to a whisper, I said, "I am just waiting for a search warrant. I hope to meet the sheriff at the dock as soon as possible."

"Meet you aboard *Sea Pigeon* in an hour?" Cal suggested. I agreed that one hour should work, and was relieved that Cal had not asked questions. I couldn't risk anyone overhearing that I was bound to Acadia Island with a search warrant. Word traveled too quickly here. I knew that news of foul play in the death of Mrs. Kohl had not yet bled into the café, otherwise Audrey would have been all over me with questions and theories.

Audrey returned with a toasted English muffin and a pot of coffee with which she topped off my mug. She said that she had questions if I had time to chat. I confirmed that I had no time, wishing to avoid her disappointment. She ridiculed my tight-lipped adherence to protocol when she asked about the Kohl investigation. "Oh, fine. Then I won't tell you about the perfect place I found for Wally." And she quickly disappeared through the swinging doors and into the kitchen where everyone could hear her barking orders at this month's short-order cook. I had learned that the cooks who worked with Audrey were given a thirty-day trial, at the end of which they tended to leave on their own accord, or be fired. I waited for Audrey to burst back through the doors. I had dropped the ball yesterday, due to work, on re-searching accommodations for my brother. I really wanted to hear what Audrey was talking about.

As I ate my breakfast, Audrey breezed back and forth several times, making eye contact only. She knew I wanted to speak with her, and was having fun avoiding me. After Audrey had cleared their dishes and handed them a slip, Marlena and Marilyn approached. "Audrey mentioned that you might be looking to rent a room for your kid brother," Marlena began. "We have an efficiency that is quite exceptional."

"What I need is quite *affordable*." I took a deep breath and continued. "Thank you so much, but I can't imagine what rents are like in Green Haven in the summer." Now Audrey was within earshot, and clearly tuned in on our conversation. "I'm sure your apartment is very nice, though."

"We'd like it if you would come and look at it," Marilyn chimed in. "It's really a sweet place, and we would be open to working something out within your budget to get someone in there year-round."

Now Audrey swooped in. "Yeah, Janey, you can work *something* out with these girls. Wouldn't I like to be a fly on the wall," she continued. "Or maybe not."

"You are so rude!" Both women whispered harshly. Cal wisely saw this as his cue to exit, and confirmed that he would warm up the boat and wait for me at the dock.

"Hey, just trying to be helpful." Audrey was delighted to have embarrassed the women. "Am I not the one who suggested that you speak with Janey? And Janey, didn't I just tell you that I had found the perfect *situation* for you? Oh, I mean your brother of course."

I now faced the women, intentionally putting my back to Audrey. "Okay. I have a pretty intense schedule for the next couple of days. But I would love to see your place."

"Oh, now this could be interesting," Audrey said gleefully. "The cheapest, oh excuse me, the most *frugal* person in town possibly renting from the two most . . . shall we say *entrepreneurial*?" she asked as she tapped my shoulder. "Watch out, Janey! They sell tickets for the tour of their house."

"Don't you have tables to wait on?" I asked.

"Yes. And I will leave the *three* of you to negotiate terms. Ta ta." And off she went, lightly prancing around the café, clearly tickled with herself. The women agreed to show me their efficiency at my earliest convenience. I placed some money on the counter and followed them to the door. "Don't do anything I wouldn't dooooo," Audrey advised in her singsong, teasing voice that we were all too well acquainted with.

"She is such a smart-ass," Marilyn said to Marlena, who held the door for her. "If there was any other option for breakfast . . ." We all laughed, knowing that we shared a deep affection for Audrey in spite of her compulsion to be the wise guy. She never meant any harm, even though some of her comments could be hurtful if taken in the vein in which they were not intended. "I am looking forward to the end of Clyde Leeman's banishment," she said and smiled.

As we walked to our respective vehicles, the gals filled me in on the "sordid details" of their rental unit, which they said had never been rented nor lived in. It had been built as a mother-in-law apartment by the previous owners of the property, and was attached to the main house by a breezeway with doors on each end. It was one bedroom, a galley-style kitchen, a full bath, and a sitting room that included a large flat-screen television and "the best view in Green Haven." I admitted that it sounded like an ideal spot for Wally, and mentioned that I couldn't afford the rates of the facilities in Ellsworth. I was happy to have another option. Marilyn said that they were confident we could figure out something that would work for all of us, as they really wanted someone to live in the unit, which had been empty since construction. "Of course your brother will have to look after the cats for us," sighed Marlena as we parted ways.

"I think Wally would enjoy that," I said as I waved and climbed into the Duster. As I drove, I put the thought of

Wally's residence on hold, knowing that I needed to concentrate on the urgent matter of getting to Acadia, making an arrest, and returning with the killer before sunset. I knew this schedule was optimistic. I stopped on top of Hutchins Hill, which the locals referred to as "the phone booth" for its amazing cell reception regardless of wireless carrier. I called the sheriff and learned that he was en route to Green Haven, and expected to arrive in twenty minutes with the signed search warrant in hand. I gave him instructions to Cal's boat, and agreed to meet him there for a quick handoff before cast-off.

Twenty minutes was just enough time to run home and leave a note for the Vickersons. They would no doubt be very upset if I left without a trace, as they liked to know my whereabouts at all times, claiming that this information was for my own safety, and not at all to satisfy their curiosity. I pulled in, and left the car running while I bolted up to my apartment and found the note they had left me the night before.

In the interest of time, rather than finding a new sheet of paper, I simply answered their note from last night—line by line. Dinner was ready at 7:30. *Sorry I missed it!* The mussel soufflé was marvelous. *I am sure it was!* There were leftovers if I hadn't eaten. *I grabbed a bite in Ellsworth.* They were concerned at 8:00. *Everything is fine.* Worried at 8:30. *I am really sorry that I worried you.* Suspicious at 9:00. *I had to work late.* Theorizing at 9:30. *I always appreciate your concern, and will call you the next time I am out late.* Mad at 10:00. *You have every right to be angry.* And hoped to see me in the morning at 10:30. *I am off to Acadia Island this morning and will see you this evening. Official sheriff's office business. Lots to tell you.* I added this last tidbit to soothe their hurt feelings and feed their imaginations. I would, and always did, confide in my landlords, like I imagined I would do with parents if I had ever had any worthy of confidence. I never told them anything that would be harmful if blabbed, but just enough to let them feel that they were in the know, and thus had a leg up on the rest of the busybodies.

I checked the contents of my bag with the list I kept glued to its inside flap. Satisfied that I had what I needed, or actually items that I would not need (like a box of ammunition for my weapon, fingerprint kit, handcuffs, a canister of tear gas, a Taser with a full charge, a handheld VHF radio with a full charge, a signaling mirror, a jackknife, a compass, a headlamp, a twenty-foot length of paracord, a cell phone charger, a box of wooden matches, and a package of peanut butter crackers), I taped the note on the Vickersons' door and headed to the dock where I found the sheriff and Cal waiting patiently on the float next to *Sea Pigeon*. I had decided against calling the Proctors on Acadia Island for a ride or assistance in any way once I arrived. Doing so would have been a heads-up in the wrong direction, I thought. I could walk the short distance to their home, and go from there to ALP where I would investigate and confiscate as needed. I was thankful for the relatively warm weather.

The sheriff handed me the search warrant, and said that he would be checking on Deloris and would get her set up to work from home as soon as was reasonable following her discharge from the hospital. Until then, I was to call his personal cell phone if I needed or wanted to contact him. I agreed to call him at noon with a status report, and stepped over the wash rail and onto the deck of the boat. The sheriff quickly cast the bow and stern lines and wished me luck as Cal put the engine in gear and pulled away from the float. It was interesting, I thought, that nearly everyone with whom I had come in contact with since moving to Green Haven knew how to move around boats and docks. They all knew how to handle lines, get in and out of dinghies, row, run outboard motors, tie knots . . . Even those with no real firsthand experience aboard commercial boats had knowledge of nautical things and spoke the language. I guessed it was part of the birthright of the locals. The sheriff, I had learned, grew up working the stern of his father's lobster boat. And daily conversation at the café included details of who was offshore, whose boat needed what for repairs, launching dates, lobster prices, etc. It was nice, I thought, that the entire community understood and appreciated the heritage and tradition of the fabric of their town, and specifically what lobster fishing meant to the local economy.

Before I knew it, we were rounding a high headland on our port side and entering Acadia Island's inner harbor. I felt a slight rush of excitement and anticipation for what might transpire here today. If all went well, I would be heading back to Green Haven with my prime suspect and enough evidence to get a confession or conviction in the absence of one. The *Sea Pigeon* nudged the dock gently and Cal reached to wrap a line around a cleat. "Want me to wait here for you?" he asked.

"I wish it would be that easy," I answered. "But I'd like for you to come back for me later. I want to avoid public transportation today as I intend to return to Green Haven with a suspect, and don't need the rumors to fly prematurely."

Cal understood and was happy to leave and return at 2:45

that afternoon. If for some reason he wasn't there, I could jump on the mail boat at 3:00 and call the sheriff from the dock in South Haven for a ride to the department, where we could question or process Trudy Proctor depending upon how things progressed between now and 2:45. I hopped onto the float, and watched as the *Sea Pigeon* scooted around the shore and out of sight. I took a deep breath and started up the ramp and toward what I knew would be an eventful day.

At approximately 8:30 a.m., I rapped on the Proctors' front door with authority. The door opened and Joan invited me in. She asked me to join her in the kitchen, but I remained just inside the door. She was not surprised to see me again after the newspaper article stating that the Kohls' house had been intentionally torched. It was obvious to me that she had no knowledge of the autopsy that indicated that Mrs. Kohl had been murdered, and that her body had been placed in the house and burned in an attempt to mislead all. I wondered whether she reasoned the death of Mrs. Kohl was accidental or incidental in light of the arson finding.

"Yes, I am back to do some investigating into the arson case. I have a search warrant and will need access to Mrs. Kohl's car and office, assuming she kept one at ALP." I figured that would be the best place to start. No sense forcing my own hand and stunting the growth of any information I might get freely from the talkative Joan. "I'll also need to take another look around the fire scene," I added as Joan got her coat. "When I was here the other day, I wasn't looking at this as a crime."

"I am happy to help. I'll drive you to the plant, and introduce you to the general manager, who *might* cooperate with you on that end," Joan said calmly. "The place gives me the creeps with all the ex-convicts who have done who knows what. I wouldn't put it past any one of them to burn a house down. Some of them are convicted arsonists, you know." Although I hadn't yet looked at rap sheets, I was not surprised to learn that arsonists would be eligible for this relocation opportunity. I reminded myself that I was looking for a murderer. And it was unlikely that someone capable of first-degree murder would have been released and allowed this opportunity to start fresh. I followed Joan out to the driveway and climbed into the passenger side as she continued. "The Kohls' Range Rover is back at ALP again, stored until summer. The town tows vehicles that are left at the dock too long. Too hard to plow around them. I'm sure Mr. Kohl would allow you the use of it to carry out the investigation. I know he's anxious to get to the bottom of who set their house on fire, and the unfortunate death of his wife," she suggested. Something in her tone made me take notice. Of what, I wasn't sure. "He is still out of the country. Can you believe it? Well, their relationship was a strange one."

The bumpy ride in the Jeep was quick. Now that she was not driving a hearse, Joan was not shy about the gas pedal. She chatted until we opened the door to the main entrance of ALP. Before I stepped in, I took a long look around the parking area and surrounding grounds, and asked, "No protesters today?"

"She's still sleeping," Joan answered quietly, as if embarrassed. I nodded and followed Joan through a short corridor and into a large room that bustled with workers who appeared to be quite content with their tasks. "Prepping, cooking, cooling, picking, and packing," Joan said, pointing an index finger at a different workstation with each word until she had covered the entire room. "We all attended the grand opening and got the nickel tour. At that time we didn't know that we were getting a boatload of rejects and perverts," she confided. "And now they outnumber us!" The place smelled of disinfectant and sanitizing agents that one would naturally associate with seafood processing. "I feel filthy when I leave this place," Joan noted as she stepped around a shallow puddle. The plant was very clean, so it was clear that Joan's feeling had nothing to do with dirt or grime.

A man in uniform approached and introduced himself as Manny; he asked how he could help us. Joan quickly said, "This is *Detective* Jane Bunker. She has come from the mainland to find and arrest whoever torched your boss's house, and obviously felt that this was the most logical place to start."

If Manny was insulted, he didn't let on. A long silence followed. Joan turned to me and said, "You know where the key to the Range Rover is. I'll be at the house if you need anything. Otherwise, I'll see you at the dock. You are leaving on the late boat, right?"

"I made other arrangements. But I will be back at your place later. I need to speak with your husband and daughter," I said.

"Okay," she said with a questioning look. "Clark is working at the Kohls', starting to clean up the mess. You'll see him over there, I'm sure."

I thanked Joan and she disappeared. I suspected that she would run home and jump in a hot shower. The fact that her husband may be inadvertently disturbing the crime scene in the name of cleaning up at the Kohls' house made me nervous. I didn't need much time at the plant, though.

"Manny, thank you for your cooperation. I need access to Mrs. Kohl's office," I stated. Manny motioned for me to follow behind him, which I did. I tried to chat, but got nothing more than a nod or a shrug from my guide. I asked who was in charge. Manny indicated that he was until one of the absentee owners arrived. Manny knew how to receive orders, process, pack, and ship both live and value-added product, so he could run the show until payday, when he assumed the plant would shut down if there were no checks available. Apparently Mrs. Kohl had been solely responsible for payroll. And nobody wants to work for nothing. So if checks were not received on Friday, everyone would walk off the job—forcing a closure until things were rectified.

Manny parted thick plastic strips that formed a doorway, allowing me to pass through before him and into a walk-in cooler. He led me through the cooler to the other end, and through another plastic barrier where we stepped into a "boot dip mat" to disinfect our shoes before entering the next area, which was full of a briny-smelling steam. Half a dozen employees tended to the cooking, never looking up from their jobs. Ex-cons knew to avoid eye contact, and could no doubt sniff out law enforcement even through the strong aromas of steamed shellfish and chemical cleaning agents. We transited the room filled with giant, stainless-steel vats heated by large propane burners, stepped into another boot disinfecting pool, through a stainless-steel door and into a corridor. There were four doors, all marked with block letters: OFFICE, RESTROOM, STORAGE, and EXIT.

Manny said that with the exception of the storage room that

had a combination lock on it, the other three doors were un-locked, and he excused himself to return to work. I asked him to please unlock the storage area, which he did. I asked if he was aware of anyone who might want to do harm to Mrs. Kohl.

"It could have been any of us," he replied as he turned to leave.

This was not at all helpful. What I was hoping for was some eyewitness account of a bad scene between Trudy and the de-ceased. Surely they had words and confrontation if the texts were any indication. Trudy's picketing on the sacred ground of Mrs. Kohl's pet project here at ALP must have led to some-thing. Oh well. I already had enough evidence to detain Trudy for questioning. I couldn't expect help from people who had probably learned the hard way not to be snitches. •

I couldn't help but wonder what felony Manny had been convicted of. I had been around many ex-cons, and had learned that although the stigma attached was unfair in some cases, most suffered from mental anguish and emotional trauma known as institutionalized personality disorders. Must make for an interesting work environment. Most ex-felons' psyches are a complicated mess resulting from the usual deprivations of imprisonment, chronic helplessness in the face of authority, and antisocial defenses stemming from dealing with the predatory inmate milieu. It's no wonder there is such a high rate of recidi-vism, especially with addictions, I thought. And what an oppor-tunity for a second chance these employees of ALP have here on Acadia, I thought as I opened the door marked STORAGE.

I switched on the fluorescent lights. The room was filled with various items, all neatly organized on labeled shelves. The floor under the shelves was lined with canisters of refrigerants used to charge compressors for coolers and freezers. There were gauges, leak detectors, thermometers, special compressor oils, spare bearings, and other miscellaneous items used to maintain refrigeration systems. There were rolls of bubble wrap, broken-down boxes, and tape guns. There were many rolls of colored plastic tape, all organized by color and width, and boxes of clear plastic bags of several sizes marked in pounds and ounces that I assumed were used to package seafood product. There were pumps, hoses, and filters for the live tanks. And there were boxes with Chinese characters on them—identical to the one I had confiscated from the two thugs. One of the boxes had a tape gun resting on top of it. A closer inspection revealed that all of the boxes had been opened and resealed using a clear tape rather than the original brown carton tape that the supplier had used. Maybe ALP was reusing the boxes after the chemicals were emptied out, I thought. I cut open one of the boxes, revealing the same vacuum-packed pouches of white powder that I now understood was used to enhance the quality of seafood shipped to China and reduce shrinkage in weight attributed to water loss. Satisfied that all was on the up and up, I moved to Mrs. Kohl's office. I made a mental note of how strange it seemed that the storage area was kept locked while Mrs. Kohl's office was wide open.

The office was small and ordinary in every sense of the word. With the exception of having no file cabinets, Mrs. Kohl's place of work was just that—a place to work. Similar to her electronic correspondence, her space was void of personality. After dusting the laptop computer for fingerprints, I unplugged it and tucked it in my bag. This would be great for Deloris as she rehabbed her heels, I thought. I dusted the outside of the desk drawers, then looked through them carefully. There wasn't much in the way of paperwork, which was not at all meaningful in this day of electronic records. I found some paper clips, ink pens, and Wite-Out. There were empty file folders. Strange to find things to do with paper, and no paper itself, I thought. There was quite a large inventory of printer paper, and some ink cartridges stacked neatly beside a color printer, but no copies or printouts of any kind. No thumb drives laying around indicated to me that someone may have beaten me to the office and grabbed everything that may have contained evidence. Either that, or Mrs. Kohl kept everything on her laptop.

I opened the door to a small coat closet. There was a long wool winter coat on a wooden hanger. I patted down the length of the coat, feeling a sizable, soft lump. I rifled through the pockets and found a miniature rag doll wearing a PETA button. The doll was hastily made from an off-white ladies' knee sock, and quite primitive with eyes drawn in black ink. The button's pin had been pushed through the doll's chest and the point exited through its back. This was it. My heart raced with excitement as I bagged and tagged the doll that I assumed was intended to send a message to the owner of the coat, whom I assumed was the late Mrs. Kohl. If I could tie the email account from which the PETA video and other hate mail had come from to Trudy Proctor, her fate was sealed, I thought.

The only other personal items in the closet were a pair of

ladies' shoes. The shoes were what I would refer to as sensible, which meant they were ugly and comfortable. I thought they looked big, and upon inspection learned that they were in fact a size eleven double E. Knowing that the average woman's shoe size worldwide is an eight and a half, I assumed that Mrs. Kohl was of above average size. The extra width could be due to being overweight, I thought.

I did a very quick check in the restroom, and found nothing of interest. I shut off all lights and closed all doors, locking the storage room. No need to set up the crime scene tape, I thought. Someone had already been here. And I had what I needed. Now I would drive to the Kohls' house and sift through the rubble for anything that I may have missed in my cursory investigation. I would be examining the scene through a different lens now that arson had been confirmed, I thought as I made my way back through the lobster cooking area and to the processing floor, where I found Manny doing quality control on packaged lobster tails with a small digital scale. I thanked him for his help, which we both knew was a stretch.

The Range Rover was parked in a back lot by itself. I found the key under the mat and headed toward the Kohls' house. Stopping on a hill where I had strong cell reception, I realized that it was nearly noon. Time to check in with the sheriff as promised, I thought as I dialed his cell number. "I hope you come home with a suspect or a strong lead at the very least" was his greeting.

"I have more evidence that points to Trudy Proctor. And I have Mrs. Kohl's computer, which I hope Deloris can tackle. I'm heading to the Kohls' house now to look around, and will be back at Green Haven with my prime suspect at three-thirty. Can you meet me at the dock?" I asked.

"Oh, I will be there," the sheriff said. "Did you get the text I forwarded from Dr. Lee?" He asked. "When news gets out of the autopsy findings, all hell will break loose. Be diligent with Miss Proctor. We can't afford any mistakes."

"Dr. Lee works fast! I'll check my texts when I can. For now, can you give me the abbreviated version of his report?"

"Salt water in the one remaining and severely damaged lung indicates drowning as the cause of death. Here's the catch: It appears that Mrs. Kohl drowned in scalding water. He also found immersion burns on the left arm."

Mrs. Kohl had been boiled to death—like a lobster.

EIGHT

Heinous is a word that I have seldom used to describe crime. It's a word that I do not take lightly, and save for the most wicked of the worst, unspeakable criminal activities. I had investigated murder by many odious methods including but not limited to beating, bullets, bludgeoning, butchering, battering, and burning. But this, if the pathology was correct, would be my first boiling.

As I digested the news of the autopsy, I pondered how the new information might help or hinder my case against Trudy. If the murder weapon was indeed a vat of boiling water, ALP was the most likely place the murder could have been committed. Where else would one find a volume of scalding water large enough into which an adult human could be submerged? And my prior visit taught me that ALP was not big on security. The exterior door at the main entrance had not been locked. And there had been no passcodes or swipe cards needed to access interior areas. I could not rule out anyone as a suspect on grounds of accessibility to the crime scene, I realized. I remained parked on the hill and waited patiently for the text of the autopsy report to come in from the sheriff. My pulse quickened when a series of alerts dinged from my phone, indicating that Dr. Lee had sent a number of short texts.

Although other aspects of the autopsy paled in comparison to the boiling, another key finding reported by Dr. Lee was the presence of something close in chemical composition to sodium tripolyphosphate (STPP) in the water found in Mrs. Kohl's lung. Dr. Lee had reasoned that as STPP was used in seafood processing, he was not alarmed by its presence in water that was intended for the cooking of lobster. I recalled from recent research that STPP was also similar chemically to one of the ingredients used in illegal designer drugs such as U-4700. But there was no reason for me to factor drug use into the equation when seafood processing fit so perfectly. The autopsy also reported skin slippage indicative of scalding, and some second- and third-degree burns characterized by charring as a result of direct contact with flames. No surprises there, I thought as I drove slowly toward the Kohls' house, or what was left of it. It seemed clear that Mrs. Kohl had been boiled to death and the arson was a failed cover-up attempt by the killer.

ALP had now become crime scene one, and with the amount of disinfectant cleaning and sterilizing agents, I was sure there would be no trace of evidence in the plant itself. But I would have to revisit the cooking area to judge the degree of possibility that Trudy or someone else may not have acted alone. Mrs. Kohl was not a small woman. Trudy may have needed help, I surmised. If so, there was a much better chance of someone cracking and confessing under the pressure. I needed to find out the hours of operation of the processing end of ALP to determine if the killer would have had access to a large vat of boiling water with or without witnesses. Then there was the question of motive.

If Trudy really is the militant guardian of lobster life, perhaps she rationalized that killing Mrs. Kohl was an eye-for-an-eye type of justice. It was twisted, but some animal rights activists could be pretty radical, and college-aged kids can easily be recruited by groups with similar beliefs and converted to extremism. The texts, emailed video taken of the ALP processing line, protesting at the front door, the doll with the PETA pin, and Trudy's nonchalance at learning that the Kohls' house had burned to the ground all supported my theory. And boiling Mrs. Kohl in the way that she had killed so many innocent and defenseless lobsters would be considered poetic justice in the mind of a confused and impressionable girl who was desperately trying to prove herself to whatever cultish organization to which she aspired to be ordained. I figured I should look into Trudy's background and early life, and as the Kohls' burned-out house came into view, I decided to move Trudy Proctor's history to the top of the priority list of digging details for Deloris.

It was immediately obvious that Clark Proctor had done some clean-up at the scene of the fire. Although nobody was here now, there were new tracks in the fresh snow—both footprints and belt tracks made by a large piece of equipment, probably a bulldozer or backhoe. The only wall of the house that had been left standing after the fire was now bulldozed flat. There was a pile of other debris that had been stacked as neatly as was possible, given the contents of the pile. The footprints were all made by one person, and appeared to be a man's size twelve with an intricate and aggressive tread, like the sole of a work boot.

I found the beginning of the prints next to where the large tracks stopped, where the driver had jumped out of the machine. I followed the prints around the piles of rubble and throughout the house's foundation. It appeared that the man, I assumed Clark, had worked hard to make the property as picked up and organized as possible, and suspected that this was part of his duties as the Kohls' caretaker. I found a pile of metal drawers and the remains of a small file cabinet. The drawers still contained burned up bits of ink pens, a metal ruler, and some small fragments of melted plastic with USB flash drive plugs. Although I suspected the flash drives were totally destroyed, I bagged and tagged them. This would account for the lack of evidence at Mrs. Kohl's office, I thought. One of the drive units that hadn't totally melted had been labeled "AIPIA." That would be another task for Deloris, I thought, and wondered what the acronym stood for—Acadia Island something . . . Maybe Joan Proctor knew. I would have to ask her—before I accused her daughter of murder.

I carefully inspected the propane gas line where it penetrated the foundation. It was broken off on the inside of the foundation, indicating that it had been broken with the intention of helping to fuel the fire. The broken gas line had been used to throw off the fire investigation, making it appear that Mother Nature had been the culprit by sending a frozen piece of earth bulging up and snapping the copper pipe. But if a frost heave was actually responsible, the pipe would have been broken on the outside of the house. Diesel fuel was the primary accelerant, and propane was a bonus. It seemed likely that most residents of Acadia not only had access to diesel, but they also had use for it, making diesel more of a fact than evidence that could incriminate.

Making my last lap around the footprints, and finding nothing more to add to the evidence, I started back to the Kohls' vehicle. Suddenly shots rang out.

Bang! Bang!

I instinctively hit the ground and rolled behind a stack of charred boards. Jesus! I had been caught off guard. The shots had come from the edge of the woods on the property's northern border, and the bullets had whizzed closely over my head. I drew my gun. I waited for more shots. The silence made me nervous. Two more shots boomed out, and it sounded like the shooter had moved in closer. I forced my breathing back to normal and slowly moved from a prone position on my back to a low crouch. I peeked quickly over the pile. I saw nothing. I stood, pointing my gun toward where the shots had come from; straining to see color or movement among the trees. I saw a flash of bright red out of the corner of my eye, and quickly swung the sights of my gun toward it. I waited, and saw nothing more. I walked sideways to the car, keeping my gun pointed toward the woods. I was a sitting duck; all alone in a wide open space with nothing substantial behind which to take cover. Once behind the Range Rover, I breathed a sigh of relief and climbed behind the wheel to compose myself. Had someone taken potshots at me? If so, I assumed they were meant as a warning. Otherwise, I would have been hit. Residents of rural Maine exercise their second amendment right vehemently. If the shots had been intended to scare me off, I wondered what I had gotten close to that forced the hand of the shooter. ALP? The fire scene? Trudy? I set my gun on the seat beside me and put the Range Rover into four-wheel drive. I needed to get to the edge of the woods within the protection of the vehicle, I thought.

The Range Rover crept slowly but surely through and over the snow-covered clearing. I thought about the gunfire, and how narrowly the shots had missed me. If there were as many people who disliked Midge Kohl as I was being led to believe, and "island justice" prevailed as I had learned about from Cal and others, then anyone would be compelled to scare me off. I had never been the type to run scared. Islanders did not like law enforcement; they took care of problems in their own way. And if someone died, well, that's just the way it was. If someone like Midge Kohl had been murdered, I could expect to get no help in the investigation. Worse yet, my investigation could even be sabotaged. The Range Rover bogged down into a deep drift of snow. The wheels spun freely. I was stuck. The snow was deep in this spot. If I had to get out and walk, I would be fully exposed to the shooter. I certainly couldn't run the zigzag, random shot avoidance pattern I had always practiced.

I tried backing up, and got about two feet before the tires were spinning again. I had very little experience driving in snow, but had driven in soft sand while in hot pursuit of a criminal. I dropped the Rover into the lowest gear, and applied the smallest amount of pressure to the gas pedal that I could. Luckily, the vehicle responded. I steered toward a flat-looking area, made it out of the drift, and tried a different route to the woods. I heard myself exhale in relief.

I thought about how vulnerable I was, just by being on the island itself. There was no way off, except by boat. Everyone here knew the lay of the land far better than I did. If someone wanted me dead, they could toss my body into the ocean to be eaten by the crabs. Other law enforcement officers would not venture out to investigate, I knew. And if a fisherman happened to pull up my remains, they knew to practice catch-and-release rather than put themselves in the line of fire. So, the question was: Why hadn't Midge Kohl's body been thrown into the ocean? If the house hadn't been burned, there would have been no fire investigation. There would be no corpse, no autopsy, and no murder. It seemed that her killer had acted out of rage, and without careful planning. I wondered about the possibility of Midge Kohl having been killed prior to boiling, and knew that Dr. Lee would have no way of proving that. Salt water in the lungs and cause of death being consistent with that of drowning meant that Mrs. Kohl may had been submerged in the vat of water for as *little* as four minutes.

I realized that if the shots fired had been those of warning and intimidation, I needed to find out who had fired them without getting shot. I could not allow myself to get panicky. I must be onto something incriminating, elsewise, why the intimidation? The lack of solid leads and majority opinion that *everyone* had motive pulsed courage into my shaken psyche. I had to now investigate the shots. It was urgent. The Range Rover was moving so slowly! I was anxious and considered trying to go faster. But each time I depressed the accelerator, the beast bogged down rather than surging ahead. The minutes it took to reach the woods seemed like an eternity.

When I reached the location where trees kept me from driving any farther, I parked the Rover, shoved my cell phone into my coat pocket, and got out with my gun drawn. I trudged into the forest through knee-deep snow until I came to an area that had been packed down by snowshoes. The snowshoe tracks were of two different and distinct patterns; evidence of two people having been here. Two bright yellow twenty-gauge shotgun shell casings had landed on the trail. I picked them up as delicately as I could and stuck them in my pocket. The walking was easier on the snowshoe path, and I assumed that I would gain ground quickly on whoever had fired at me. Moving as quietly as I could, I stopped every twenty seconds to listen for any sign of the shooter, who might be just out of my range of sight.

The tracks seemed to be heading back toward the road, I thought. I saw a flash of bright red darting between trees. I stepped behind a large spruce, and peeked around to watch. I caught glimpses of what appeared to be a man. Where was his accomplice? The man slowly worked his way to the edge of the trees, where I could see that he was standing over something as if inspecting. The man had a shotgun slung over his shoulder. He stood and straightened up with his hands on his lower back as if stretching after exerting himself.

After a minute or so, the man bent over and grasped something and started dragging it toward a small clearing between the road and woods. A sudden pang of angst hit me in the stomach as I realized that the second set of tracks could have been made by what was now being so difficultly towed through the snow!

While he worked, I moved closer, keeping trees between me and the man. I was now able to see the road. The man struggled and stopped to rest again. I heard a very loud vehicle approaching. An old beat-up pickup truck appeared from the other side of the bend, stopping on the corner. It looked like the truck had been pieced together with parts from several vehicles. The driver got out of the truck and hiked through the snowy clearing, joining the man in the red coat. Was this a third party? I ducked into a thick stand of spruce trees, pushing branches aside to open my view. I snapped a few pictures with my phone, but I was too far away to hear what they were saying. The men looked around, and satisfied that they were alone, worked together to drag whoever had been shot. Once they were behind the tailgate of the truck, my view was partially obstructed by the truck itself. What I did see left me breathless. The men quickly hefted their victim into the back of the truck, climbed into the cab, did a three-point turn in the middle of the road, and drove away.

As soon as the truck was out of sight, I hustled back to the snowshoe path and followed it to an area that was totally blood soaked. I took a deep breath and exhaled audibly. The blood pattern and number of tracks all on top of one another indicated that there had been quite a struggle. The path beyond the circular area was streaked with blood. There was no mistake. A dead body had been dragged, obscuring parts of the snowshoe tracks and leaving a trail of blood that got thinner as I followed it. I bent over for a closer look, and found a few hairs in the blood. My heart raced with the knowledge that whoever had fired the shots, had connected with at least one target, and may have me in their sights next. I needed to move quickly. The killer must know that he had missed me. Or was I simply in such close proximity to the shots that I mistakenly assumed they had been meant for me? Either way, I couldn't risk the truck beating me to the Range Rover, I thought as I began sprinting along the path.

I ran the distance back to the far end of the beaten path, and traced my own steps through the deep snow back to the Rover. Back within the safety of the Range Rover, I caught my breath and gathered my thoughts before leaving the edge of the forest. I had always had an innate sense of knowing when I was being watched. Now, I felt very much alone. As I added things up, I realized that the killers had not seen me, and that I had been overly paranoid. Better than dead, I thought. Now what?

I really needed backup if I wanted to chase down men with shotguns on their own turf who seemed to have no issue with firing lethal shots. And unless murder was a common occurrence on Acadia Island, what I had just witnessed must be directly related to Mrs. Kohl's demise. This case had snowballed, I thought as I looked at my cell phone—no service. If I wanted to stick to my game plan, I didn't have time to pursue the truck. It might be a while before anyone would miss someone enough to become suspicious and report them missing. Even though my gut said that this shooting was directly connected to the murder of Mrs. Kohl, I had to abort the chase and get back to business.

I reluctantly resolved that by now, the shooters could have discarded the body and the murder weapon. I glanced at the time, and refocused my priorities.

Cal was scheduled to pick me up at three, and I needed to question the Proctors and get Trudy off the island before anyone got wind of the fact that I was on to her. If Trudy had accomplices, which I was now gaining confidence that she must, they might try to shut her up—for good. If the killing had been a conspiracy, the college kid who was naïve enough to leave cyber evidence would be the weak link. Now Trudy Proctor was not only a suspect, but perhaps needed to be placed in protective custody.

The slow drive through the snow and back onto the road tested my patience. I gripped the steering wheel so tight that my hands grew white and started to get numb. Back on the main road I drove for a few miles, noting two plowed drives that the truck could have taken, and finally knew that I was at a huge and distinct disadvantage regarding investigating this new twist. I again reminded myself that my priority was getting to the bottom of Mrs. Kohl's murder. And I needed to get a move on.

Just before reaching the Proctors' driveway, my phone beeped with a voice message. It was the sheriff. The lab had identified the plastic that had melted and was embedded in Mrs. Kohl's wrist (that I had mistakenly assumed was an awareness bracelet) as "poly bag tape." According to the message, this was a specialized tape used to seal poly bags that are commonly used in food-processing operations. I had seen many rolls of this tape in the storage area to ALP! The sheriff suggested that Mrs. Kohl's wrists had been bound with the tape prior to boiling—"sort of like a large lobster band," he said, referring to the rubber bands that are used to keep lobsters' claws closed so they can't clamp onto someone while handling, or injure other lobsters once captured and in a crate. I cringed at the image. Trudy certainly had not acted alone. It would take more than a 120-pound girl to overpower and bind the hands of a much larger and stronger woman, and get her into a pot of boiling water. Whoever had helped, and possibly planned the murder, might now be looking to cover more tracks. Mrs. Kohl's hands must have been bound prior to being killed. Why bother after she was dead and couldn't put up a fight? The plot was certainly thickening, I thought as I pulled into the Proctors' driveway behind their Jeep Cherokee. I had to get Trudy off Acadia Island without spilling any details—or any more blood.

It was 1:30 p.m. when I knocked on the Proctors' front door. Joan and Clark were at the kitchen table eating a late lunch and listening to a marine weather forecast. "Come in, Jane," Joan called out. "Want a bowl of chowder? It's supposed to get nasty out there."

"No, thank you," I said, knowing that being served lunch was not part of my future with this family. And today's activities hadn't done much in the way of producing an appetite. "But I will sit with you. I have questions, and hope you can help."

"Certainly! Did you round up any suspects at the plant? You'll probably leave with a full boat," she added as she dumped oyster crackers into a bowl of creamy-looking, delicious-smelling steaming chowder. "Fresh halibut. You sure you won't have any?"

I thanked her and turned down the invitation again. "Clark, what can you tell me about the fire that I don't already know? Who first discovered it? Who alerted you? That sort of thing," I tried to make it sound like routine questioning, so he wouldn't clam up.

He replied that he heard the church bell and drove to the fire department, where others gathered quickly. But no one had asked who rang the bell in the chaos of getting the truck and pumps running. "Once the bell is rung, the girls start the phone chain to let everyone know there's an emergency. But I have no idea who rang the bell. Is that important?" he asked.

"Well, it's protocol to find out who reported a fire, especially in the case of arson," I answered. "And it would be helpful to know who last saw or spoke with Mrs. Kohl. Any thoughts on that?"

"We wouldn't have any idea, would we, dear," Clark said, including his wife in his answer. He blew on a spoonful of chowder to cool it before slurping. He swallowed and smacked his lips in satisfaction. "But I would bet it was one of her employees. She spent most of her time at ALP. Not much of a socialite. Other than me and Joan, nobody was allowed in her home."

"And we were only over there for caretaking," Joan qualified this for her husband. "You know, snow removal, cleaning, lawn mowing. Stuff like that."

"And never without a schedule set by Mrs. Kohl. She did not welcome surprise visitors. She sent us a schedule of duties she wanted performed and a detailed schedule of when she expected them done. She was a stickler. Printed out our schedules weekly—one for me and one for Joan. We always joked about punching the clock when on Mrs. Kohl's time."

"Did anyone else receive printed work schedules," I asked.

"Not that I know of," answered Joan. "She relied on us to hire anything done that needed doing that we couldn't do ourselves. She didn't care who did it, as long as it got done on her schedule. She liked her privacy, and expected us to protect and respect it."

"Did she have security cameras or an alarm system at the house?"

"No. She was adamant about *not* having them. We suggested getting them when the convicts started moving in," Joan replied. "But the Kohls thought being on Acadia meant not having to lock doors. And it *used* to."

"Is your daughter home? I need to ask her some questions, too. I noticed she was outside the plant when we were there the other day. Maybe she saw or heard something."

"She's in her bedroom. But she doesn't know anything," Joan answered. "If she did, she would have told us." A voice squawked on the VHF radio. Joan answered, "Come in, Skip."

"Hi, Joan. Weather report is lousy. Supposed to get brutal cold and blow forty-five out of the northeast. I'm canceling the late trip this afternoon. Can you spread the word?" My heart sank as I realized that the incoming weather might cause Cal to cancel as well, leaving me on Acadia without a way off—with my suspect and at least another killer and accomplice—until the next morning.

"Will do. See you in the morning?" She asked of the voice in the radio that I realized belonged to the captain of the mail boat.

"Roger that!"

Joan placed the radio in the middle of the table. She looked at me and said, "Well, I guess you are stranded until tomorrow. We have a spare room and lots of chowder."

"Oh, thank you. But I have a ride coming for me at three. Would you please ask Trudy to come down and speak with me? It's important that I cover all the bases, and I am running short on time." Joan reluctantly got up from the table and went up the stairs, leaving me alone with her husband, who was intent on his lunch. "Do you know who drives a rusted-out, green pickup with a gray hood and one orange door? And no muffler?"

"That describes half of the vehicles out here." He laughed. "But sounds like it might be Roy Knight. He's the only real local employed at the plant, other than me. He helps with maintenance. What did he do?"

"Oh nothing really," I lied. "I heard the truck before I saw it, that's all. Interesting paint job."

"One hundred percent custom," was all he said, before polishing off his bowl of chowder and excusing himself to get back to work. He yelled up the stairs to Joan, pulled on a coat, and headed out. "Have a safe ride back ashore," he said flatly. As he shut the door behind him, Joan and Trudy appeared at the bottom of the stairs. Trudy once again looked like she had just crawled out of bed.

I stood and extended a hand to Trudy. "Hi, Trudy. We met the other day. I'm Deputy Sheriff Jane Bunker, here on behalf of the Hancock County Sheriff's Department." Pushing by me, and ignoring my hand, she plunked herself in a chair and yawned. "I am not going to beat around the bush. I am here investigating the death of Midge Kohl, and have reason to believe that you might be involved in some way." She looked at me defiantly, grabbed a handful of oyster crackers, and started popping them into her mouth one at a time. I could not tell her that I was concerned for her safety, as doing so might end up tipping off the others who were involved. Better that they think Trudy is taking the fall for them, I thought.

"Are you for real?" she asked. "I have no intention of helping you. I couldn't care less about Midge Kohl. And I have nothing more to say." Her mother looked stricken, and was unusually quiet.

"I have a warrant to search your house. I would like to start in Trudy's bedroom," I said.

"Yeah, knock yourself out," Trudy said rudely.

Trudy followed me up the stairs to an open door. The room was a bit disheveled. I knew it was her bedroom when I saw a poster that asked "Would you eat your dog?" I unplugged the laptop computer and cell phone, putting the phone in my coat pocket and computer under my arm. I found a box of PETA propaganda pins, identical to the one that was stuck through the voodoo doll in Mrs. Kohl's coat pocket. And I found a single sock that I assumed was the mate to the one the doll had been made with.

"Really? You are taking my sock? This is a joke," Trudy said with a laugh that seemed a little nervous. "I refuse to help you. I won't answer a single question."

"Well, silence is one of your rights," I said. "But this will be easier with your cooperation." Although I had enough evidence to place her under arrest, I decided to not do so in her parents' home. I recited the Miranda warning and, instead, informed Trudy that I was taking her ashore with me for questioning. She shrugged and sighed.

"You are arresting her?" Joan asked. "For what? She is allowed to peacefully protest!"

Trudy pushed her wrists toward me as if offering them for handcuffs. She smiled awkwardly, which threw me off a bit. Strange gal, I thought. "No, I don't need to cuff you if you are coming along without resisting. Why don't you pack a bag." Trudy rolled her eyes, seemingly disappointed about not being handcuffed.

"You are not taking my daughter out in this weather! Didn't you just hear that the mail boat has canceled?" Joan cried. "Do we need to get an attorney?"

"That would be a good idea," I answered honestly. "I can detain Trudy for questioning for up to forty-eight hours without charging her."

"Charging her for what? I need to get Clark. He will be so upset!" Joan seemed paralyzed. She did not want to leave Trudy here with me. And she wanted to go find her husband. She sat and put her head on the table next to half a bowl of chowder and cried. When Trudy came down the stairs with a backpack, Joan started again. "Trudy, you are not leaving this house! And that's final!"

"Mother, this is none of your business. I will call you from jail. I am going to jail, right?" she asked optimistically. "And

I do not need a lawyer." She was so anxious to be arrested and thrown in jail that *she* led *me* to the Range Rover. Her mother was distraught, which was not a surprise. "This is actually pretty stupid," Trudy muttered as we entered the parking lot at the dock. "What a waste of taxpayers' dollars. What exactly am I suspected of doing? Do you think I play with matches?"

I was relieved to find Cal aboard *Sea Pigeon* at the float. I parked the Rover, packed everything tightly into my bag, and asked Trudy to follow me to the boat, which she did, maintaining her right to silence. The wind had picked up, and the temperature had dropped significantly. I handed my bag to Cal and climbed aboard right behind Trudy. We stepped into the heated cabin and out of the wind. Cal said, "The forecast is calling for thirty-five knots out of the northeast. You sure you want to do this? It's gonna be sloppy."

"I'm good to go if you are," I answered, knowing that Cal would never take unnecessary risks, and that he had been on the water all of his life. I trusted his judgment implicitly.

"We can handle thirty-five all right. But we will be pounding into it the whole way. It'll be uncomfortable, not dangerous. Hope you don't get seasick," he directed to Trudy, who gave him a disgusted look. Cal cast off the single line he had secured to the float, and off we went. I was relieved to be officially off the island with my suspect in custody. I sat next to Trudy on a bench seat on the port side of the small cabin and started making a mental list of things to do when we hit Green Haven. Still without cell service, I knew that my list would start with calling the sheriff as soon as we were within range. Trudy sure was a cool customer, I thought. Most people capable of premeditated murder are not easily shaken, I knew. As soon as I had her in the interrogation seat, I knew she would crack. She was tough right now, but that would change after a few hours of questions and no food or sleep. She would be singing like the proverbial bird before sunrise tomorrow morning, I thought.

Sea Pigeon slipped through the calm water of Acadia Island's inner harbor as smoothly as a fish. I struggled with the fact that I had witnessed a killing that would likely be a link to the murder of Mrs. Kohl, and regretted that I couldn't stay on Acadia to investigate further and make the connection. I had pictures that would hopefully reveal who I had seen drag a corpse through the snow and place it in a truck. I still believed that the first two shots had been fired in hopes of distracting or scaring me away so that the killer could proceed with a plan without being caught. I must have struck a nerve at some point in my travels today. I would have to bring backup with me on my next trip. By then, I would have a firm understanding of the whole scenario. Trudy was the key to that, I knew.

When we rounded the headland and entered the bay, *Sea Pigeon* bucked slightly with each wave that met her directly on her stem. Within five minutes, we were taking spray that quickly formed ice on the forward windows, and Cal had to pull the throttle back a little. When the wind increased from a whisper to a whistle, Cal said, "Well, we've got the full thirty-five." I stood and clenched the dash with both hands to steady myself in the wheelhouse, which was starting to bounce. When I looked at Trudy, she was staring at her feet. I watched as her face grew pale and sweaty. I asked if she needed some air. She shook her head and threw daggers with her eyes.

At sunset, the wind and tide worked against each other, making steep waves that slammed the *Sea Pigeon*'s bow and sent green water over the housetop. Cal pulled the throttle back to just above an idle. He was now navigating with the electronics due to the thick ice that obliterated the view through the windshield windows. As the wind increased from a howl to a screech, Trudy's complexion went from pale to green.

"It must be blowing fifty. Damned weatherman," Cal said. Trudy placed a hand over her mouth. Her cheeks bulged. I grabbed a trash can and placed it between her feet. She used it loudly. At this juncture, I was thankful that I had not eaten any fish chowder. Every time the boat went up on a sea, my feet left the deck briefly. I softened my knees to absorb the violent pounding and was working hard to remain upright. *Sea Pigeon* was getting pummeled by waves that crashed high on her bow and cascaded over the housetop and down her wash rails. We were thrashing wildly. Yet the bullying sea was not the greatest concern; the ice was. When a vessel "makes ice," it tends to get very top heavy as the ice forms only above the waterline. I knew this not firsthand, but from reading, as my sea time had been in warmer climes. Cal asked me to take the wheel while he opened the door and stuck his head out to inspect the rigging for ice. "Just keep her bow into the wind," he said calmly. The wind helped the door close with gusto, startling Trudy from her trancelike state to hysteria. Trudy was no longer playing Joe Cool. Cal looked at me and shrugged as he took the wheel again. "We're halfway home. She's loaded up with ice. No good. I'll tuck up in the lee of Squirrel Island and wait it out. We'll be comfortable there."

I agreed, even though I understood that Cal wasn't asking my opinion. It was the right thing to do, and the only sensible option. We wallowed, pounded, shook, and shimmied for another fifteen minutes, then slowly got out of the wind. I wondered how this turn of events might affect my interrogation and ability to prosecute. Would this violent weather and our presence in it be considered a form of excessive force, or a violation of Trudy's rights? Could the decision to leave Acadia arguably be police brutality through psychological intimidation? None of that would matter if I could just get Trudy to confess. But would her confession be deemed coerced because of the storm and her seasickness? There was nothing I could do about that now, I thought.

Although it was a dark, moonless evening, I could see that we were very close to the shore of what Cal had called Squirrel Island when I looked at the radar screen. Cal switched on the weather channel on his VHF radio, and we all listened intensely for an updated forecast. When it came, it was bad. The low pressure system that was upon us had stalled and was intensifying. Cal quickly set the anchor and worked at deicing the *Sea Pigeon* with the handle of his deck broom. I sat and stared at Trudy, who stared back while we listened to the thump, thump, thump of broom against soft saltwater ice. "Feeling okay?" I asked.

"Never been better." Trudy stretched out on the bench seat and used her coat as a pillow. I didn't dislike many people. But I found Trudy entirely distasteful. I had apprehended many criminals whose actions were despicable. But there had always been something, even if very tiny, that I could appreciate or sympathize with without losing sight of my goal to have them convicted and punished appropriately in the name of serving justice. Perhaps some microscopic idiosyncrasy would surface, giving me reason to not hate Trudy so intensely, I thought as she filed her fingernails with an emery board. "What I did on my winter vacation . . ." Trudy said. When she brushed the fingernail dust from her shirt into the air that I was breathing, I thought I might lose it. I bit my tongue.

Trudy pretended to sleep when Cal reentered the wheelhouse. Cal confirmed that the anchor was holding us in position, and that we would remain here until the wind dropped out, which might be daylight. Cal then radioed ashore and got someone who agreed to call his wife, who would be instructed to call the sheriff to alert all concerned parties as to our plight. I asked that Cal relay specific instructions to inform Joan and Clark Proctor. "They will be worried," I said. At this, Trudy sat up and started flossing her teeth. "Or not," I muttered under my breath. Wow, I thought, this girl had an uncanny ability to irk me.

Time passed slowly. Even the second hand on my watch seemed to be dragging its feet between ticks. I avoided looking at my cell phone after I saw that service was not available. Trudy asked what time it was every five minutes, and then calculated how many hours and minutes remained in her detainment before being released. Other than that, we were silent until Cal announced that he needed a cigarette, and left the wheelhouse. I joined him in the cockpit for a minute, just to get a breath of air and some distance from my annoying suspect. I knew Cal would not ask questions, nor would he offer an opinion or advice. He was good that way. It was brutally cold, and the wind buffeted by the island screamed over our heads like a flock of vultures waiting to feed. Twenty minutes away from Green Haven, and twenty minutes from Acadia Island; I thought this was what Purgatory must look like.

When I reentered the wheelhouse, I was horrified to see Trudy posing for and snapping selfies with the cell phone that I had confiscated from her bedroom. "Did you take that phone from my bag?"

"Yes. It's mine."

"Stealing or tampering with evidence is a criminal offense. You have learned about obstruction of justice, haven't you?"

"Yes. I learned about that in the same class in which I was taught about false arrest."

"You are not under arrest. Yet."

"Mind if I tape-record this conversation?" Trudy asked as she tapped the screen of her phone, I assumed setting it up to record.

"Knock yourself out," I said, mocking her with her own words, and quietly optimistic about a pending conversation.

"Time?"

"Eight forty-five p.m., February fourteen."

"Forty-one hours and fifty-three minutes remaining until my release," Trudy said smugly. "I need to use the bathroom. And I would like a glass of water."

I had an unopened bottle of water in my bag, which I gladly handed to Trudy just as Cal came in from having a smoke. "Cal, do you have a head down forward?" I asked, referring to the possibility of a marine toilet in the forepeak of the boat.

"Nope. I have a clean bucket though." Cal opened the door, reached out, and untied a short piece of line, retrieving a white, plastic, five-gallon bucket. "You can take it down forward for some privacy."

"I have to use that?" Trudy was skeptical.

"*That* is better than what you'll have in jail," I responded honestly. "Take it below and use it in private, or take it on deck where I will escort you."

Trudy grabbed the bail of the bucket and headed toward the companionway steps that led to a tiny compartment in the bow of the boat. "Gender neutral?" she asked as she descended the first step.

"All inclusive," I answered as I handed her a few tissues from a pack I had in my coat pocket.

Within two minutes Trudy stuck her head up into the wheelhouse and asked, "Now what?" Cal informed her that she should toss the contents of the bucket over the rail and secure the bucket. "Throw it in the water? With Dickless Tracy here? She'll add that to my rap sheet . . ." I was amused with the reference, surprised that Trudy would know of Dick Tracy at her age. Cal thought better of his suggestion to throw the sewage overboard, and asked that Trudy leave the bucket below for the time being, which she was quick to do. "Time?"

"Eight fifty-one." This was followed by an updated accounting of time remaining in custody, and on and on it went until midnight. I watched condensation on the inside of the windows form drops that rolled down the glass and splashed on the sills. Cal flipped the VHF radio to the weather channel, where the automated forecast had just been updated. The computerized voice held no more good news than it did inflection. If the forecast was accurate, we would be sitting on anchor behind Squirrel Island for at least another twelve hours. Trudy asked about food. Cal produced a box of crackers and a jar of peanut butter from a cubby in the forward console. Trudy looked dismayed at the offering and closed her eyes again. "Let me guess," I said. "Nut allergy, right?" Trudy ignored this, and spread out on the bench, leaving no room for me to sit down. Cal offered me his seat. I politely refused, since Cal was nearly thirty years older than me and needed the seat more than I did. When my legs tired, I squatted with my back against the door.

At two a.m., the wind shifted slightly, swooping around the end of Squirrel Island and rolling the *Sea Pigeon* in the long swell it produced. Trudy sat upright and grabbed the trash can that Cal had emptied over the side while she was feigning sleep. After a bout with dry heaves, Trudy had had enough. She stood up shakily and said,

"Okay, okay. If I answer your questions, will you take me home? I thought I was going to jail for a night or two, not being tortured with your company. No offense, Captain," she added for my benefit. "You are not the one making me sick."

"Are you waiving your right to silence and to an attorney?" I asked. "And you understand that anything you say can be used to prosecute you?"

"Yes, I understand my rights." Cal nervously got up and headed toward the door. "No, please stay," Trudy pleaded. Cal turned to me with a questioning look. I nodded that it was fine for him to remain, and was relieved that it had been at Trudy's request. She knew enough about the law to make her a tricky one, I thought. And the last thing I needed was for Trudy to be let off the hook on a technicality. I started the recording function on my cell phone and began.

"Do you know Roy Knight?" I asked about the man whom I was convinced had shot at me, and killed someone else. Trudy's face grew red and the tears started. She tried to control her breathing, and swallowed sobs before they could escape. She opened her mouth to speak, and her voice cracked. She took slow, deep breaths, exhaling through pursed lips. "Take your time," I advised. "You need to tell me what happened. I have pictures and other evidence. I know you did not act alone, and you do not have to go down alone," I said. "I will get to the bottom of this. And the more help I get from you, the better the outcome will be for you."

"But I *did* act alone," Trudy sniffled. "At least it started out that way. I just wanted everyone to get what they deserved. Then everything got out of control."

I waited silently for more. Cal's eyes had grown wide. I was sure that his experience with interrogations, statements, and confessions was from television shows. But instead of what is seen in a police drama, my best information is gained through patience, not screaming and badgering and repeating accusatory questions.

"I just got caught up in it. I never intended for things to go so far. My life is over," she said quietly.

NINE

Trudy's tough exterior had cracked like an eggshell, exposing a soft, gooey inside. Now that she had broken down, I needed a written statement, I thought as she sobbed with her head in her hands. Once I had her signed, detailed statement, I would return to Acadia Island with the sheriff and arrest Roy Knight and whoever else Trudy might implicate. The first step was to get Trudy to Hancock County Sheriff's Department, where I would encourage her to accept legal counsel prior to saying anything more. Once she had an attorney working on her behalf, I would feel better about raking her over the coals and getting a full, legal confession. As the communication of our location and situation had been broadcast over the VHF radio, I suspected that all residents of Acadia were now aware that Trudy had been apprehended. As it turns out, I thought, there is no better protective custody than being stranded at sea with weather conditions that prohibit anyone from venturing offshore to find you.

Trudy needed food and sleep, I thought as I watched her hands shake. I considered asking her to ID Roy Knight's accomplice. Whom had I seen helping with the shooting victim and driving the getaway truck? As soon as the accomplice was arrested, he would turn on Roy just as Trudy was turning on them both, I assumed. None of this could happen from behind Squirrel Island. As long as we were aboard the *Sea Pigeon* waiting for a weather window to open, everything was on hold, except for covering tracks and destroying evidence on Acadia. I prayed for the wind to drop out.

Once Trudy gained some composure, I informed her that I was placing her under arrest for the murder of Midge Kohl. The word "murder" acted like kryptonite on the defeated girl's shattered psyche. She sat bolt upright. Her bleary eyes turned to sharp, fiery holes that flickered around the wheelhouse. Tears dried like beads of water in a hot skillet. I was glad that both Trudy and I had recorded all that had transpired to this juncture, as I was certain that her tune was about to change. "I hated that pig. But I didn't kill her," she said coldly.

"Oh God!" Cal sprang from his post at the door. "Don't use that word on my boat!" He was in Trudy's face, wagging an index finger back and forth. "Don't ever say that again. Terrible, bad luck . . ." Cal was very upset.

"What word? Hate? Sorry, man," Trudy apologized.

"No. The three-letter word. The word for the curly-tailed animal. It's wicked bad luck. Now you've done it," Cal admonished Trudy for committing what is a cardinal sin aboard any boat.

"Hey, I said I'm sorry. How was I supposed to know that pig

is forbidden?" Trudy took some evil joy in saying pig again in spite of Cal's warning. She smirked as Cal trembled. "Wow. What a basket case. I'd like to know how things could get worse than being stuck here with the two of you and being accused of murder." Trudy was now regaining her hateful cockiness. I advised Trudy to remain silent, and knew that there would be no more questioning until we got ashore and could do so in a more appropriate setting (and one that would not get my case thrown out of court). The DA would not look kindly on what had transpired so far, I knew. Trudy slumped in a corner and closed her eyes while Cal tuned the radio to the weather channel again.

"There's just some things you don't do or say aboard a boat," Cal insisted to me. I had never seen Cal upset. I totally understood how intensely old-time mariners held and obeyed superstitions like the use of the word "pig." "She's already killed one person, and now she's gunning for us!" Cal was absolutely exasperated. Trudy snickered, rubbing salt in the open wound. "She'll pay for that. We all will." Cal snapped at me as if I were somehow responsible for Trudy's behavior. Cal paced back and forth nervously waiting for something to happen as a result of Trudy's noncompliance to what he held as the gospel.

Cal and I listened to the endless loop of weather statistics and forecasts for several zones up and down the coast "From Eastport to the Merrimack River and out to twenty-five nautical miles from shore . . ." without much change. At four a.m., the weather service updated the automated system, and the update was slightly improved according to Cal, who was still seething from his passenger's comments and attitude. We couldn't tell from where we were anchored, but the wind had apparently shifted to a more easterly direction, and had dropped out a bit. The forecast continued, adding that more wind was expected by noon and there would likely be warnings issued for "moderate to heavy freezing spray."

Cal explained to me his opinion that we had better run for the small window of opportunity to get ashore, or remain here for another twelve hours. He seemed delighted to note that we would be running "side to it," or in the trough of the waves, making for an uncomfortable ride from Squirrel Island to Green Haven.

"And if she didn't like the pounding, the roll will really get her. Better have the trash can handy." Trudy responded with a groan of anticipation as Cal went on deck to haul the anchor and secure it before leaving the leeward side of our shelter of Squirrel Island. I couldn't help but think that Cal's decision to leave our sheltered position was at least partly based on his wanting to punish Trudy for treading on his beliefs. Although I knew that Cal would never intentionally put us in real danger, I also knew that Mother Nature had a mind of her own and didn't often listen to the weather forecast.

Sure enough, Cal was right about everything. This was a good (and likely our only) opportunity to make a break for it. "If we don't go now, we will have to wait another twelve hours," Cal said anxiously as he ran *Sea Pigeon* around the sheltered end of Squirrel Island and into a choppy, confused sea that resulted from a changing wind direction. The long swells from the northeast were now competing with an easterly wind that blew the tops off the waves, beating them down slightly. The easterly wind didn't have the same biting cold that the northerly did. No ice formed. It was still pitch dark.

"Six miles of open sea, then we'll be in the lee of the mainland and things will settle down," Cal stated as he worked to keep his boat on course while the seas mounted, rocking and rolling *Sea Pigeon* rail to rail. Trudy was even more miserable than she had been when pounding into the waves. The rolling motion hit her hard, just as Cal had predicted. She was violently ill. I tried to get her to take a few sips of water, which she refused. Suddenly *Sea Pigeon* was smashed by a wave broadside, jarring Trudy from the bench seat to the floor where she rolled around helplessly like a rag doll in a washing machine. The trash can and contents now sloshed back and forth across the floor with each roll of the boat. Trudy was entirely soiled with the bile from her own stomach. The stench was overwhelming. I couldn't offer Trudy help as I couldn't release my grasp of the handrail that was keeping me on my feet.

After rolling around the floor like a marble, Trudy finally came to rest with her back against the port side of the wheelhouse, where she braced her feet against the base of the settee. She hung her head between her bent knees and exhaled a low, weak moan. Every wave that struck our starboard side sounded like a clap of thunder. Cal fought the wheel, and steadied the boat as she fell into a giant trough, then rolled off the backside of a wave, nearly rolling us over. "We should be at the dock by five forty-five," Cal advised. I suspected this would be the longest thirty minutes of Trudy's life—up to this point, that is. She would surely have some longer ones in the future. We'd see how

Little Miss Tough Guy responded to a night in a jail cell and real interrogation.

I carefully made my way to the deck outside to use my cell phone. I found a dry, warm spot on the port side of the boat where I ducked behind the exhaust system and I called the sheriff, who had been anxiously waiting to hear from me. I advised him of our ETA in Green Haven. He promised to meet us there and take charge of my suspect. We agreed on a plan. I would go home for a shower and clean clothes, grab a bite to eat, and drive to the station, where I would lead the questioning of Trudy. The Proctors had retained an attorney to be present at all times, according to the sheriff. I warned the sheriff that he would have his hands full with Miss Proctor, and filled him in on what she had said so far and that I had recorded all.

I slowly made my way back across the deck and into the wheelhouse, lunging and grabbing anything that I could hold on to, timing my moves with the wildly rolling *Sea Pigeon*. A wave slapped the starboard gunnel, sending spray that soaked my backside before I could shut the door. Trudy was incapacitated, otherwise she would have been elated to see me dripping with salt water. My suspect had assumed the fetal position between the stanchions that supported the end of the settee. I could see the calm water ahead of us, and knew that our ride would flatten out and that Trudy would recover when her feet hit terra firma. Cal's focus was on steering *Sea Pigeon* up, over, and down the waves and troughs that had grown in height. I watched a bead of sweat roll from his temple to the corner of his earlobe, and was thankful that this would soon be over for our captain.

We rounded Sewall Point and entered Green Haven Harbor, where the wind was unable to torture us. Trudy crawled out from under the settee and stood to look out the windows. It was dark, but a crease of sunlight nudged the black curtain on the eastern horizon. We were silent as Cal navigated through dots on the radar screen that I knew were boats on moorings. A streetlamp at the end of a dock marked the floats where Cal berthed *Sea Pigeon*. Cal gently landed the boat on the float and tied her up at the stern and bow. I was comforted by the sight of the sheriff on the dock under the light. He would relieve me from my charge of tending to Trudy while I regrouped. I gathered my bag and explained to Trudy that she would go with the sheriff to the station where she could get a shower, food, and a nap before I would meet her there to get her statement. She extended her wrists out to me to be cuffed. I explained that handcuffs were not necessary. She insisted, so I obliged her and helped her over the wash rail and onto the float. I led Trudy to the sheriff, who looked a bit surprised to see her cuffed. I shrugged and helped Trudy into the backseat of the sheriff's car.

"She looks and smells terrible," he said after I closed the door. I explained that Trudy had been deathly seasick, and that she had insisted on the cuffs. "Oh good. Then she will really appreciate the orange jumpsuit," he laughed. "I'll let the attorney know to be at the station by eleven. That'll give you a chance to freshen up a bit before we start." I thanked him and hustled back down the ramp to find Cal shutting down and cleaning *Sea Pigeon*.

My offer to help clean the wheelhouse was enthusiastically accepted. We worked together swabbing the interior deck until it shined. I apologized to Cal for Trudy's behavior; he acknowledged that she was indeed quite a pill. "See you at the café?" I asked before we parted ways at the top of the ramp. Cal agreed that he needed coffee and breakfast, but that it would be after a shower and a nap. "Good, I'll see you at ten. We can settle up then, too." Cal commented that this particular ride would be expensive.

I realized I had grown numb with exhaustion when I noticed that I was not sensing the cold as I normally would. I scraped frost from the Duster's windshield and climbed behind the wheel, where I marveled at the amount of fog that formed every time I exhaled. The locals referred to this phenomena as "seeing your breath," which was sort of strange but accurately descriptive. Scientifically, I knew it had more to do with dew point than it did with air temperature. The small, short-lived clouds of vapor that disappear as quickly as they form usually made me shiver. But not this morning. Tired and hungry trumped cold, I thought as I drove home and parked the Duster in its usual spot in the Vickersons' neatly plowed dooryard. I felt as though I was dragging myself up the stairs to my apartment in slow motion. I knew that Henry and Alice could react strongly to being wakened too early, so I was as quiet as I could be. I certainly didn't want or need to bear the brunt of what could be hostility caused by lack of sleep coupled with the fact that I hadn't physically been seen by them since . . . I was so tired, I couldn't think. No note on my door indicated that the landlords were really annoyed with me, I thought. Or, maybe I was being oversensitive and reading too much into it. That has always been my prime symptom of sleep deprivation.

Hot water pounded the back of my neck in the shower. I may have dozed off for a split second and was jarred awake by a bar of soap thumping the bottom of the tub when I dropped it. I didn't even bother picking it up. Right now the only thing I cared about was getting a bit of sleep. I pulled a nightgown over my head and crashed into bed. But sleep came neither quickly nor easily. I was on the verge of cracking a murder case. Lists ran through my head. I fact-checked like some people count sheep. I planned and scheduled in my mind until I was comfortable that I had not missed anything. I had a number of tasks for Deloris to tackle—the most urgent being attempting to recover data from the flash drive I had found. I would meet Cal and get breakfast. I had accumulated a few pieces of evidence that needed to go to the lab—shotgun shells, blood and hair samples from the shooting scene, a sock, and a sock doll. I would meet the sheriff and get Trudy's statement, which would result in yet another trip to Acadia to apprehend Roy Knight as well as others who were involved in Mrs. Kohl's death, plus the shooting of someone yet to be identified, and the arson of the Kohls' home. I was haunted by the fact that I had nearly witnessed a murder, and could have had the shooter red-handed if I had known that I would need backup when I ventured to Acadia. I suspected that the victim of the shotgun blast was someone who had witnessed or possibly participated in the crimes, and needed to be done away with to protect secrets.

Although I hadn't logged much in the way of actual sleep, I woke up refreshed, invigorated, and ready to dive into the beginning of the end of the Kohl case. Before doing so, I would check in with the Vickersons. After all, it was 9:30, and thus

189

late enough to be considered "civil." I threw on clean clothes, grabbed my things, and dashed down the stairs. I banged twice on their door, and barged in. "Well, look what the tide left," remarked Mr. V from his seat at the kitchen table.

"What do you know!" Mrs. V said with a hint of excitement in her voice. I suspected that they both wanted to lecture me about the common courtesy of communicating. But they were both genuinely happy to see me, as I was them. "I would say that you're a sight for sore eyes, but you look dreadful, dear. Where have you been?"

I laughed to think how bad I must look for Mrs. V to mention it. I realized that I had gone to bed with my hair wet from the shower, and hadn't looked in the mirror before leaving my place. "I plan to wear a hat today," I joked as I tried to flatten some of the bumps of hair on the top of my head. "I have been to Acadia Island," I said as I accepted the cup of coffee that Alice offered. I sat at my place and gave my landlords the abbreviated version of my activities since our last visit. True to form, they bombarded me with questions, most of which I either didn't know the answer to or couldn't divulge the information they wanted. My insistence that I couldn't tell them what they wanted to know never stopped them from asking.

"So, what have you two been up to?" I asked to switch their focus from my investigation.

I could tell something was up. The Vickersons shared a look and a grin. "Oh, nothing really," replied Alice. "Nothing as interesting as being shipwrecked with a murderess."

"Not shipwrecked, just delayed by weather. And she is just a suspect at this point."

"Tomato, tomahhhto," quipped Henry. "You'll have her singing like a bird before sunset."

"I hope so," I said as I got up to leave. "If that's the way it goes, I'll see you tonight for dinner!"

"We wish you the best of luck! But we will not be home until late this evening. We have an appointment in Bangor and Henry is going to wine and dine me, aren't you, sweetheart?"

"You bet, darling."

I had never known the Vickersons to go to Bangor unless it was a doctor's appointment. So I assumed that Mrs. V, who proudly suffers from a number of ailments of which I am normally privy to, needed a checkup or was due for a treatment of some kind. "Is everything okay?" I asked as I sat back down.

"Nothing you need to worry about," said Mrs. V quite convincingly. "You have enough on your plate. Now scoot. Go on. Get out of here and grill that girl until she pleads for mercy." I had never known Alice to not want to discuss whatever medical issue she might be experiencing or imagining. Her avoidance of the topic made me nervous. I knew I had to leave to keep my schedule, but was reluctant to do so. The Vickersons were like family to me. They were what I thought normal parents would be like. They offered advice and nurtured. And they even scolded me when I needed it. "Really, you need to go. We can discuss our appointment later."

I thanked them for the coffee, apologized for worrying them, and wished them luck with whatever they were dealing with. I pulled a wool hat on to plaster my renegade hair down, and I left feeling badly. I didn't really care about my appearance. Vanity took a backseat to productivity. I did care about what might be going on with Mrs. V. She had never shooed me off before. In fact, I usually had to tear myself away in mid-conversation. If I thought of the Vickersons as family, why didn't I treat them that way? The fact that my work always came first had been the terminating issue with every relationship I had ever screwed up. Be it boyfriend, gal pal, or fiancé, I had always been accused of "not being there" when needed. I used work as an excuse for emotional avoidance on all levels, and had finally come to realize that I had never had a healthy, balanced relationship of any type. Friendships had come and gone. I did nothing to cultivate nor maintain them. Close friends finally gave up trying when I would not meet them anywhere near halfway in the effort. Everything was on my schedule. I missed weddings, baby showers, birthday parties, and funerals in the name of my career. I had vowed to change that; starting fresh with a move to Maine.

I counted my friends in my head, and came up with two. Cal and Audrey were good friends who expected little from me. Expecting little from me so as not to be disappointed was a strange basis for friendship, I realized, and made me feel even worse. Well, I would be better about relationships after I dealt with this murder case, I thought as I drove to the café. I would have more time to be a friend when the criminals on Acadia Island were taken care of. Justice had to come before relationships.

Cal was in his usual position at the counter. One hand gripped a coffee mug and the other held the newspaper. I was amazed at his appearance—clean-shaven and well-rested. He confessed to having a catnap, and declared that was all he needed to fully recharge his batteries. "That, and caffeine and nicotine," he said, patting the pack of cigarettes in his breast pocket. He quickly produced an invoice for three hundred dollars for his services, hoping that the amount would discourage me from hiring him in the future. I wrote the check and promised to not call on him again unless absolutely necessary. I spoke softly, and explained that I would be heading back out to Acadia after I got Trudy's written confession, and that I would be happy to take the mail boat out of South Haven. As soon as Audrey observed me whispering to Cal, she became very attentive.

"Whispering's lying. Lying's a sin. When you get to heaven, they won't let you in," Audrey recited playfully as she filled our coffee cups. She clearly expected nothing from me, and was not disappointed, which solidified our friendship in my warped definition. "It's also considered rude." Fully admonished, I apologized, and told her that Cal and I were discussing business and didn't want the entire café to know that Cal was on the county's payroll. "The entire café is already aware of seventy-five percent of your recent activities, and the remaining twenty-five percent is being fabricated as we speak," she said nodding to a table where a couple sat with their heads nearly touching each other as they spoke at a decibel level imperceptible to us. They turned their eyes toward us; embarrassed to be caught looking, they jerked their heads away. "Knock, knock, knocking on heaven's doooooor," Audrey punctuated her point with the song. "Everyone in town monitors the VHF," she advised. "They started whispering the second you came through the door. Prior to your entrance, it was like an episode of *People's Court*. They have probably selected the jury already. Of course the other possibility is that they want to inquire about your hairdresser." My right hand flew to my head and pressed down the now matted cow-licks that had grown like horns during my short rest. "Wow. Yeah, that's a lot better," Audrey said, rolling her eyes.

"I need some food," I said, unwilling to acknowledge the fact that I probably looked ridiculous with knots of hair stand-ing up every which way. Each time I patted a spot down, I felt it spring back into the unwanted shape.

"Your private captain has already taken care of that for you. Coming right up!" A shout from the kitchen signaled Audrey to scurry through the swinging doors to grab whatever Cal had thoughtfully ordered in anticipation of my arrival, which he had come to learn was always punctual. Audrey was back before I was done telling Cal how much I appreciated him. "Look at those eggs!" Audrey exclaimed as she placed a plate of fried eggs, bacon, and home-fried potatoes in front of me. "Cooked to per-fection. . . . And Cal is certainly a man who knows how to treat a lady. Judging from the size of that breakfast, I'd say the two of you had quite a night!"

"Don't you dare go there, Aud," I said sternly. The last thing Cal needed was a rumor of monkey business with me, I thought. "It's one thing to tease me about Marilyn and Marlena, but Cal is a married man whose wife doesn't deserve that type of untruth."

"Who was teasing?" And off she went again, making wise-cracks as she cleared plates, took orders, poured coffee, and served meals. I was too embarrassed to look at Cal, so I fiddled with unwrapping my silverware, which was rolled up in a white paper napkin. And Cal was too much of a gentleman to ac-knowledge that he had heard or comprehended what Audrey had implied. I quickly forgot about Audrey's needling and dug into breakfast while Cal flipped to the sports page of the newspaper. Audrey was right about one thing: The eggs were amazing. In fact the entire breakfast, although simple fare, was quite delicious. I vowed to splurge on a full breakfast at least once a week as I dabbed egg yolk with a corner of homemade, buttery, rye toast. I hadn't really developed a taste for home-fried potatoes. Grits are to Florida what fried potatoes are to Maine, I thought as I squeezed ketchup on them. These small chunks of starch, brown and crispy, were part and parcel of every meal served at the café and every eating establishment in the state of Maine from what I could tell. They can't be very healthy, I thought as I speared half a dozen chunks onto my fork. But neither was the bacon that I enjoyed.

I polished off the entire meal in record time. I wiped my mouth with the napkin, balled it up in my fist and tossed it onto my empty plate. I checked my wristwatch and announced that I had to run. I thanked Cal for breakfast to which he replied, "It's the least I could do after last night." Then he winked at me.

Much to my dismay, Audrey heard and witnessed Cal's antics. She doubled over in laughter, which drew the attention of all diners. As I left, Audrey called out, "Wait till Marilyn and Marlena get wind of this! Peyton Place has nothing on us!" I pulled the wool cap over my ears, this time in an attempt to subdue the voices from inside the café rather than the renegade curls on my head. I never imagined that I would be counting the days in anticipation of the end of Clyde Leeman's banishment. As soon as I put the Duster's transmission into drive, I cleared all shenanigans from my mind. It was time for seriousness. Twenty minutes later I was rolling into the Hancock County Sheriff's Department, with fifteen minutes to spare before the eleven a.m. interrogation of Trudy Proctor. Prompt as usual.

I found the sheriff at Deloris's desk in the lobby, fumbling through a file cabinet. "I can't wait for her to get back here," he said of the convalescing secretary/dispatcher. "Her friend Jackie is coming by to grab work for her to do at home. And the phone company has diverted all calls to the station to their home number."

I quickly gathered the items from my bag that needed Deloris's expertise—namely the damaged flash drive—and asked the sheriff to add them to whatever he was sending to her.

"Miss Proctor is in the conference room with her attorney. Let's give them another fifteen minutes, shall we?" I agreed that this was good, and was happy to have time to gather my police-issued tape recorder and a fresh yellow pad. The sheriff reported that Deloris was doing well, and would be returning to the job in a wheelchair in a few days, which reminded me of my quest to get to the bottom of the chemicals from China and whatever drug-related scheme was being woven around and through them. All in good time, I thought. This murder investigation would be a cake walk. I would pass all information and evidence to the DA for a slam dunk.

Islanders might be self-policed, and somewhat lawless, but that meant that they had little to no experience in *my* realm of legal work. They were overconfident, and thus sloppy. Living in their own secluded world, they were not accustomed to being held responsible and accountable for things they might not even perceive as illegal. Islanders had lived for generations without any official police presence. They took care of trouble in their own island way. And islanders had cultivated and maintained a reputation for abusing law officials who dared step foot on their beloved and barbaric haven, resulting in few visits from the law. That is, until I intruded. What a ridiculous situation to subject ex-convicts to, I thought. Islanders were relaxed in their protective bubble within which they did whatever they chose without consequence. I was ready to burst that bubble, exposing many degrees of criminal activity, at the top of which was cold-blooded murder. Justice would prevail. I was certainly getting myself pumped up for Trudy, I thought as I entered the conference room at 11:15.

I was not at all surprised to see that Trudy was represented by a female attorney. I imagined that finding a female attorney in Down East Maine had been an effort. I introduced myself to the young, smart-looking woman, and said good morning to Trudy, who looked overwhelmed and agitated. When I removed my hat and sat down across the table from them, neither woman could look me in the eye as they were both distracted by my hair. It made me a bit self-conscious. The sheriff joined us, sitting at the end of the long table and stating that he was in attendance to act as a witness only, and that this was my show.

I started the tape recorder, stated the date and time, my name and title, and purpose of the conference. I began the conversation by explaining that I had placed Trudy under arrest for her involvement in the murder and botched cover-up of Midge Kohl.

Trudy's attorney responded with, "I understand that my client has been placed under arrest, she is here to cooperate."

I have always understood that cooperation means that alibis have been rehearsed and will be forthcoming. But in this case, I was hoping for real cooperation in the form of a full confession.

"Let's start with what you meant when you stated that things had gotten out of control," I said. "And you also said that you acted alone and that you got caught up in something, which indicates that you may not be the Lone Ranger after all." I waited through a minute of silence before continuing. "Are you protecting someone?" I asked, knowing that this would get a response.

Trudy took a deep breath and looked at her attorney. The woman advised her client to remain calm and tell the truth—the whole story. Her attorney assured Trudy that everything was going to be fine, and that she would be heading home to Acadia this afternoon. I doubted that.

"No, I am not *protecting* anyone!" Trudy sounded indignant. "Quite the opposite."

"Well, the opposite of protecting is endangering or harming," I said. "So, how does that definition fit with your connection to Roy Knight?"

"I just wanted to teach him a lesson. He and Midge Kohl both have blood on their hands. I couldn't stand it any longer. I can't sleep. I am sick to my stomach. I *had* to do *something*. I have spent way too much time *talking* about cruelty and senseless killing for financial gain. Part of being committed to a cause is to do more than pay lip service to it."

Trudy sounded like a campaign slogan, and was no doubt quoting verbiage from whatever cultish faction on whose behalf she had acted. "That's the difference between the truly devout and those who like to wave a flag or hold a banner." She spoke as if she was explaining why she had committed crimes; as if I already knew what had happened, and she was justifying.

"Devout?" I asked. "A lot of blood is shed in the name of any number of gods. But I suspect that your actions were not driven by a religious calling. I need you to walk me through what you have done."

"Well, I can start by telling you what I didn't do," she snapped, sitting bolt upright. Her attorney shot her a look, and she relaxed back into the seat and sighed. "I had nothing to do with the death of Midge Kohl. In fact, I have never been in her house or inside the plant."

"I find it hard to believe that you are totally innocent. I have text messages and email evidence. I have a voodoo doll with a PETA pin stuck through its heart. I have the matching sock from your bedroom. I have your computer, your cell phone, should I continue?"

"And we do not argue that," the attorney interjected. "My client may be guilty of harassment, but you have nothing that connects her to the murder. Look, Trudy needs to get home and organized before heading back to school. What do you need to release her?"

"I need a statement. I need the truth. I want to start with Roy Knight."

The attorney told Trudy that she had nothing to hide, and encouraged her to be honest and thorough in her statement. Trudy launched into a long explanation of her relationship to Roy Knight. It seemed fairly rehearsed, which I expected. She eventually got to the substance of what I was looking for.

"Roy is a vicious killer. Some islanders are afraid of him, so they turn a blind eye. Others are simply desensitized." Finally, the long and agonizing boat ride was going to pay off in spades, I thought. "I wanted to stop him."

"Have you witnessed him killing?" I asked, trying to maintain a flat tone in spite of my mounting excitement.

"Of course. Everyone has. He slaughtered two bucks and a yearling right in our front yard!"

My stomach churned. Deer?

"Roy Knight is a deer hunter?" I asked, putting the pieces of what I had witnessed on Acadia together, and feeling quite deflated. Thank God I hadn't yet sent the blood and hair samples to the lab, I thought. Although I avoided looking at the sheriff, I sensed his presence.

"Oh yeah. Big time. He sneaks the meat ashore and sells it on some black market. He's killed so many beautiful and innocent animals . . . And out of season, too. He is a poacher, but the game wardens will not come to Acadia to bust him." My heart sunk as I tried to figure out how to salvage this interrogation to get some useful information. "I started following him around and blaring an air horn every time he took aim. The next thing I knew, there was a deer head stuck on a post outside my bedroom window. I want him arrested!"

Trudy had just provided Roy Knight with an alibi for the woods shooting that I had hoped to loop into the Kohl case. Trudy had to give me more than this, I thought. Trudy Proctor was guilty of more than scare tactics and sending a few nasty notes, Roy Knight was off the hook for the time being. But she was not. I needed to play hardball. Back to the basics. Criminal Investigation 101.

"Where were you the night of February twelfth?" I asked.

"Oh, let's see." Trudy was back to her cocky, arrogant self. "That was the night they burned old Dixie down, right?" She had misquoted the lyrics, which was annoying in itself. That coupled with her attitude nearly sent me over the edge. I could've roughed her up a bit, if only her attorney was not in attendance. I was so disappointed and agitated by the realization that Roy Knight had not shot a human that I was ashamed of myself.

"'And the people were singing. They went la, la, la, la, la, la, la, la, la, la, lalalalaaaa.'" Her attorney interrupted the song and advised that she answer the question. "As you will see when you hack into my computer, I was in my room the entire day and night of the period in question. Can you say WEBCAM? Yup, I video-record my existence—asleep or awake. Looks like you and your theory are screwed, doesn't it?" She turned to the sheriff, cocked her head to one side, putting on her best coy show, and said, "Lucy's got some 'splainin' to do, doesn't she?" She then put her back to the shell-shocked sheriff and addressed me again. It took all of my restraint to not slap her across the face. "Back to the drawing board, Sherlock."

TEN

I guess Captain Cal was right," Trudy sneered. "The word 'pig' does bring bad luck . . . to you!" Trudy actually gave me the finger; a gesture that I always thought of as the ultimate sign of disrespect. Her attorney appeared to be embarrassed by Trudy's attitude and actions, but remained silent—something I was certain she wished her client would do. From my seat, the view of the entire situation was poor. If she was telling the truth about being on her webcam at all times, Trudy had not only provided a rock-solid alibi for herself, but had also inadvertently gotten Roy Knight off the hook. And now that I knew the story (which included Trudy's admitting to tormenting Roy Knight), I could almost sympathize with the deer poachers.

I scrambled to salvage something from this interrogation that might help me move forward with the Kohl case. Of course I would have Deloris confirm that Trudy had indeed been in her bedroom during the time in question. But that seemed to be a formality at this point. I wished the sheriff had not been here to witness the botched interrogation. He sat quietly while I wondered what he must be thinking. Although I was relieved to learn that I had not witnessed a person getting killed, I now had no suspect in the Kohl murder in spite of the overwhelming suspicion that nearly *everyone* had motive.

"Are you going to arrest Roy Knight?" Trudy asked.

"No," I answered. She sighed audibly in disgust and rolled her eyes. "On what grounds would I arrest him?" I asked. Might as well continue the fishing expedition before the attorney realizes that they are free to leave.

"Oh, let's see . . . Should I make a list for you? Hunting out of season, hunting at night, hunting in posted areas, selling venison illegally. He is a killer who has murdered hundreds of innocent white-tailed deer for profit."

"That's a case for the game wardens," I said. "Not my jurisdiction."

"Oh, right. I forgot that you are some big-shot detective. Wow, you sure are good at your job," she said sarcastically. "Well, Roy Knight will never be arrested. The last time a Marine Patrol boat came to Acadia was in 1997. They came to arrest Sid Watson for hauling other fishermen's traps. The state's forty-six-foot patrol boat disappeared without a trace while the officers walked to Sid's house to find him. Very expensive for the state of Maine to lose a patrol boat. That's just one example of why Islanders are above the law. They are untouchable. And the Hancock County Sheriff's Department is no exception."

"Need I remind you that you are doing nothing to help that situation?" I asked. "You could have provided your alibi before things got this far, and you would never have been brought in for questioning. You have not only cost me time that should have been spent looking for the murderer of Mrs. Kohl, but you have cost the state a pretty penny as well. This could be seen as obstruction of justice," I said.

"Whoa. That's enough, Detective Bunker," the attorney spoke up. "Trudy is here to help. She is cooperating. Do you have any more questions for her? Because if you are done, we will gather her things and leave."

"I think your client has intentionally led me astray. I think she knows something or is protecting someone. She allowed me to haul her off Acadia Island in a storm rather than provide an alibi," I accused. "So let's hear about her relationship to the deceased, shall we?"

"I am not protecting anyone," replied Trudy. "I just don't care to help you. I think whoever killed Midge Kohl deserves thanks, not prosecution." The attorney shuddered. "You know that I was harassing her. You can prosecute me for that. I'm proud of it. She and Roy Knight are both guilty of killing living creatures in the cruelest of ways."

"Other than you, who else do you think wanted Midge Kohl dead?" I asked.

"Everyone at the plant. Every year-round resident, and most summer people. We have been through this before, right?"

"I understand that Mrs. Kohl was not well liked. I get that many people had an axe to grind with her. But that is far from carrying out a murder. Who wanted her dead, and could actually follow through with killing her?"

"No idea."

"You have no idea, or you're unwilling to talk?"

"All of the above."

Trudy was not about to budge. And I was beginning to think that she really knew nothing more than I did. She was sly about indicating that she was keeping some information from me. But I now suspected that she was toying with me for her own entertainment. I needed to put an end to this. I needed to cut Trudy loose and get back to Acadia Island to dig up some new leads. There were certainly plenty of possible suspects to question, according to Trudy. I would start at the plant. After all, that is the scene of the crime, I thought as I listened half-heartedly to the attorney explain to her client that I had no evidence with which to keep her any longer.

Trudy may be correct about Roy Knight never being arrested for his illegal hunting and other activities. But someone would be arrested and convicted for the brutal murder of Midge Kohl. I just didn't know who yet. I would release Trudy so she could catch the late boat back to Acadia, which meant I would avoid sharing the trip tomorrow morning with her. I would regroup, reorganize, get some rest, and make the early boat tomorrow, I thought.

Finally the sheriff chimed in. "Okay, I think we have all we need here from Miss Proctor. If Deputy Bunker is in agreement, you are free to leave." I nodded and sighed in exasperation.

When the women got up to leave, the attorney asked to have the handcuffs removed from Trudy's wrists. "No, you can't wear them back to the island," she advised her client, who seemed reluctant to offer her wrists to me for unleashing. "And the jumpsuit belongs to the state of Maine."

"No souvenirs?" Trudy smirked as I removed the cuffs from her frail wrists. "Can I borrow your phone for a quick selfie before I lose the orange outfit?" she asked her attorney as they left the conference room and headed back to the jail to collect Trudy's clothes.

"Wow," said the sheriff. "She's obnoxious."

"Yes. But unfortunately not guilty of anything substantial enough to keep her here," I answered.

"Do you think she's capable of murder?" he asked.

"I did. But now I don't think so. This was fun and exciting for her. She can go back to school with bragging rights about her fight for the cause. An arrest and handcuffing will set her apart from her bleeding-heart friends."

"What's your next move? And what do you need from me?"

"I'll have Deloris scour the flash drive I recovered from the fire scene at the Kohls' place. And I'll have her go through everything on Trudy Proctor's phone and laptop just in case there's something there." The sheriff walked with me to the lobby as I thought out loud. "I'll go back to Acadia after I get every bit of information that Deloris can dig up. *Someone* killed Midge Kohl in a cold-blooded, brutal way, and I won't rest until justice is served." I realized that I was giving myself a much needed pep talk.

As I opened the main door to leave, I heard a siren. Funny, I thought, I had never noticed sirens or flashing lights in Miami. They were so commonplace that they were just part of the sound-scape of life there. As the sirens got louder in their approach, I guessed I wasn't yet fully acclimated to Maine. I zipped my coat and pulled the hat over my messed-up hair, when an ambulance appeared and pulled up to the entrance of the jail. This would not be remarkable in any way if I had been in Dade County. But here in Ellsworth, Maine, the presence of an ambulance meant something more.

I pumped the Duster's gas pedal to the floor three times, turned the key, and was pleased that the engine cranked right up in spite of the cold. It seemed that my car had adjusted to Maine better and faster than I had, I thought as I pulled the collar of my coat tighter around the small exposed ring of skin around my neck. I turned the defroster on high, and waited for the ice to melt from the inside of the windshield while I climbed out and scraped the frost that had formed on the outside with a red plastic scraper shaped like a lobster claw, which advertised the Lobster Trappe and had been gifted by the Vickersons. They never missed an opportunity to promote their business, even in the winter, when the gift shop's door was locked up tight. For people in their eighties, they were high energy. I climbed back into the car, where I had an open view of the ambulance now parked with lights flashing at the front entrance of the jail. As the ice slowly melted, it obscured my view and made it easy to ponder the status of the Kohl murder investigation.

I wasn't starting from square one. I had made progress in obtaining evidence and eliminating Trudy Proctor as my prime suspect. I was hopeful that Deloris would extract some key information from the damaged flash drive that would put me back on the scent. I was more determined than ever to ensure that justice be served. I was optimistic, and I had grown to understand that this was exactly what I loved about my job. The next clue, the next witness, the next lab report, the next interrogation . . .

As small rivulets ran down the windshield and dripped on the dash, I mindlessly mopped them up with the cuff of my coat's sleeve and thought about how my perceptions of things had changed as I matured. A much younger Jane Bunker would be embarrassed and frustrated with the course of events so far. Jane Bunker of previous decades thrived on the cat-and-mouse aspect of each and every case, and was passionate about the end result, living for the slamming of the cell door. And any obstacle or false lead or misstep was humiliating and degrading. I'd had little or no patience with myself, let alone anyone else. I had been quick to anger. A younger Jane Bunker would have roughed up a brat like Trudy Proctor, and would have accepted punishment and reprimand as part of the deal. Luckily, I had matured into a more patient, rational, and level-headed detective who did not discourage or embarrass easily. Not that it hadn't taken some restraint to keep myself from slapping Trudy's obstinate face. The fact that I *did* exercise restraint was evidence of growth, I thought as I watched the jailhouse door open.

The sheriff appeared and held open the door while an ambulance attendant pulled one end of a stretcher through, quickly followed by the other end of the stretcher pushed by a second attendant. I left the car running and rushed across the parking lot to assist if needed. The stretcher held a zipped body bag. The sheriff motioned for the attendants to put the brakes on as I approached. I asked if I could be of assistance. The sheriff unzipped the top of the bag, and folded back a corner to expose the face of the deceased. I remarked that the lip ring and tattoos were telltale, and I immediately recognized them as belonging to the young guy who had run me off the road and threatened me with a loaded gun in the midst of trying to steal the box of chemicals from police evidence. "And now he has a toe tag to add to his various accessories," the sheriff said as he zipped the bag back up and opened the ambulance door. "Overdose. There will be a full toxicology done."

I was horrified to learn that yet another young person had done themselves in with a needle. And this time while in the custody of Hancock County Jail! Anyone with even the most tenuous tie with reality must understand that shooting up, snorting, or smoking home-brewed concoctions is suicidal, I thought. This was another unnecessary reminder that my main campaign was and should always be against drugs. I needed to solve the Kohl case and get on with the business of stopping, or at least slowing the manufacturing, trafficking, and selling of opiates and other illicit substances that were mowing kids down like a serial killer on steroids. Now I was pissed. So much for maturity, I thought as I silently renewed my vow to continue to wage my personal war on drugs. First things first. I asked the sheriff for directions to Deloris's place, where I planned to hang out and wait for her to scour the flash drive that the sheriff had already had delivered to her for evidence that might lead me to Midge Kohl's killer.

I called Deloris and announced my scheduled arrival five minutes before pulling into her driveway. She was excited to get involved and happy to have "something to do." Prior to the sheriff's explanation about Deloris's education, training, and experience, I had no idea what an asset she could be. I had neither expertise nor patience for sifting through electronic devices on a salvage mission. Her strengths were my weakness. Perfect! The likelihood of finding helpful information or key evidence on the damaged flash drive was high, I thought. I really needed something to propel me back to Acadia. A new lead would be ideal.

A good bang on the front door was followed by a cheerful shout from inside. "Come on in." As I closed the door behind me, I was relieved to find a very comfortable Deloris propped up in a reclining chair with a portable dinner tray that served as a desk. "Oh, thank God you didn't bring pastries. Why is everyone compelled to show up with a bag of Dunkin' Donuts?"

"I guess it's good I was thoughtless," I said with a chuckle. "You look good! How are you feeling?"

"Anxious to get back to work. But I can't put any weight on my right heel for another two weeks. The doc has me on some heavy-duty painkillers. I can see how people get hooked," Deloris said as she pointed to the couch, indicating that I should make myself comfortable. I tossed my coat and hat onto the far end, and sat where I could see whatever Deloris wanted to show me on her laptop, praying that she had found something. "You know, before I fell through the ceiling, I felt like I was going to find something. My gut was telling me that I was on the right track to uncover something. But I don't know what."

"Well, we can revisit the scene together once you're back on your feet," I suggested. "But for now, I really need your help with the Kohl case. Please tell me that you have something."

"Oh, I have lots of somethings." Deloris started tapping the laptop's keyboard, quickly scanning and scrolling. "The flash drive labeled AIPIA is fairly benign," she said. "Acadia Island Property Improvement Association has been actively buying properties and renovating. They have transformed a couple of huge summer estates into boardinghouses that are leased by Acadia Lobster Products, I assume to house their employees," she said as she continued to scroll through the pages on her monitor. "I researched assessed values from tax records and see that Midge Kohl was able to buy three estates for pennies on the dollar—she was a real bottom feeder." I processed this as Deloris made notes on a sheet of paper. She continued. "I found email correspondence on another flash drive that indicates displeasure with Midge Kohl. It appears that she is suspected of bringing in ex-cons knowing that their presence would drive property values down, enabling her to purchase at ridiculously low prices. I also found accounting figures that indicate that ALP will have to close their doors soon—for good."

"Are you editorializing?" I asked, hoping to not sound unappreciative of her hard work. "Is this your gut reaction or is there hard evidence?"

"Nope." Deloris continued to sift through the flash drive, making notes while briefing me. "It's all buried here in fragments of deleted emails, text messages, and photo files. Mrs. Kohl's technical skills were unsophisticated. Her generation mistakenly believes that deleted means gone. Looks like wealthy investors were looking for a onetime tax write-off. This of course is upsetting to the ex-cons who have made new lives for themselves that revolve around gainful employment and comfort in a safety in numbers sort of way."

"Good." I breathed a sigh of relief and was grateful for Deloris's skill and candor. "Because I had heard these theories about land transactions and who was affected. It's nice to have real evidence of what Midge Kohl had been up to." By the time Deloris popped the flash drive from her laptop, I understood that there were indeed many people who had been hurt financially by her scheme, and more would get in line when the plant closed.

"Can you print a list of her contacts, and the files that had been deleted?"

"Done. Some of the more encrypted correspondence was sent through the ALP system. So I think it's from an employee with a work email address: M-R-O-D at A-L-P dot net." Deloris quickly shifted her hands to the keyboard of a second of three laptops she had surrounding her. "I was able to hack into the ALP company directory. The email M-R-O-D belongs to Manuel Rodrigues. And here's his company headshot." Deloris spun the monitor so that I could easily see it.

"Manny. I met him at the plant. He's a supervisor and was less than accommodating," I said. "What did you see that was *encrypted* in his emails?"

"Well, basically he alluded to knowing something that Mrs. Kohl would not want made public. And my opinion is that the emails and texts are so similar in content, that the emailer and texter are one and the same."

"Sure sounds like blackmail. Was he coercing her?" I asked.

"Right. And I took the liberty of checking his rap sheet. Here's the story on Manny," she said as she handed me a sheet of paper that listed Manny's vast and varied criminal history along with jail time served for each offense. I noted that Manny had been very active in scams and blackmail schemes. "And he is on the sex offender list, which is how he qualified for the Acadia Island program. The case file appears to indicate that Manuel is *not* a pedophile. But he was willing to help friends who are. Anything for a buck," Deloris said unemotionally. She continued. "I was able to check the plant's security footage through their network, and interestingly, the cameras are shut off every night after the second shift, and started back up at five o'clock the following morning. Sort of defeats the purpose of having security cameras, doesn't it?" Before I could nod in agreement, she added, "And, the only people who had access to manipulate the security system online were Mrs. Kohl and Manuel Rodrigues."

I took a deep breath, realizing how much information I now had to deal with, and that I needed to rush back to Acadia to follow up on the new leads. My head was spinning with the amount of information Deloris had retrieved in a short time. She is good, I thought. She had already scanned the prints I collected through the FBI's biometrics database. Unfortunately, the prints that were identified belonged to people who had good reason to be in Mrs. Kohl's office. There were a number of prints that the registry didn't identify, which was not alarming or telltale in any way. She had already sent hair samples that I collected from Mrs. Kohl's office to CODIS with a red label, and expected DNA results within twenty-four hours.

Mulling over what Deloris had revealed, I realized that any ALP employee had motive *and* greater access to Mrs. Kohl at the scene of the murder then Trudy had. Who had the most to lose from an ALP closure? And who might possess the physical strength to overcome and subdue a struggling woman? Manny was now in the center of my sights. If I hadn't been so bent on Trudy Proctor, I would have considered him before, I scolded myself.

"But this," Deloris said triumphantly, "is far more damning." She pushed a second flash drive into the side of her computer. "I was able to recover bits and pieces of this photo gallery. Brace yourself." She pivoted the monitor so that I could easily see the screen. I am far from a prude. But I must confess that the first picture surprised me.

"Is that what it looks like?" I asked.

"If it looks like two naked bodies in a compromising position, it is."

Deloris slowly clicked through a series of pictures featuring the same two bodies in a standing missionary position. The pictures had been photo-shopped from the necks up; replacing the couple's heads with those of Lucille Ball and Dezi Arnez.

"*Someone* loves Lucy," I said. "The woman has to be Midge Kohl. Look at the boots—monogrammed MK. The question is, who is Ricky Ricardo?" The quality of the pictures was very grainy. Deloris suggested that they had been taken from a distance with a low-quality camera. The next few pictures showed the same couple in a different position; in this one I could see the woman's wrists, which were bound to stainless-steel posts with yellow poly bag tape—the exact color of what I had removed from the corpse's wrist.

"Although her wrists are bound, the sex appears to be con-

214

sensual. Most rapes are from behind," I noted. "It looks like these photos were taken at ALP. The plant is full of stainless steel." At my request Deloris flipped through the series again, very slowly, while I looked for clues as to who the man was. Deloris's professional opinion was that photographs had been taken, printed out, and scanned into the ALP system. Copies on the scans were then forwarded to every internal company email account—of which there were only five. Five seemed like a small number of email accounts until I rationalized that there would have been no reason for the vast majority of ALP employees to be set up with such accounts. "Do you think a third party was involved?" I asked. "A photographer?"

"No way. Look closer. All of the pictures are from the same angle, like the camera was stationary. The various shots are just cut and pasted with different aspects blown up. Even the most inexpensive cameras are equipped with timers. They could even have been taken with a cell phone," Deloris said. "Do you think Manuel Rodrigues seduced Mrs. Kohl so that he could blackmail her?" Deloris asked. "His rap sheet suggests that no job is beneath him."

"No, that's too easy," I answered.

"And the last photo I have," Deloris announced as she brought up another very grainy and dark picture. "Ta da. What do you make of that?" The picture had clearly been cut and pasted together—again very poor quality, and the work of an amateur. It portrayed the man with the Desi face photoshopped as if he were humping a cardboard box covered in Chinese characters.

"Well, I am sure it has significance. But it only adds to the confusion right now," I confessed. "These chemicals from China

215

keep popping up. They have to be a key to the case. Just need to figure out how."

"Of course I have an opinion! I thought you'd never ask," quipped a very pleased Deloris. I was curious, but not about to beg for an unsolicited theory. I waited, knowing that Deloris would offer without being prodded. "Remember the texts that mentioned shipments? All caps? Shipments must refer to the boxes of chemicals, right?"

"Okay, I'll buy that," I said. "But how do the chemicals fit in with blackmail and murder?"

"Beats me. You're the detective. What do you think the Lucy and Desi thing means?" Deloris asked as she shifted her hands back and forth between three laptops and an iPad while I mulled the possible meaning of the boxes of chemicals in the whole scheme.

"I don't know the significance of Lucy and Desi, if any. But I think it does bring Trudy Proctor back into suspicion. She quoted the famous 'splainin' line to the sheriff during interrogation. Just coincidence? Or is she connected to these photos? Did you uncover any correspondence between Trudy and Manny?" I asked while still puzzling over the chemicals.

"Nothing. But Trudy is clever. Her skill level in electronic evasion is higher than most. She would likely have the ability to hack into the ALP system and send email from any address," Deloris said. "And I think Trudy is too young to be quoting a sixties TV show."

"What if illicit drugs were being smuggled into Maine through the chemical shipments?" I blurted out.

"Yes! And Desi wants a bigger cut of the profits! I'll bet Manny is in charge of receiving, right?"

"That is possible," I said. "But it will be difficult to prove who the man in the pictures is."

Deloris giggled. "Yeah, right. I must watch too much TV. Aren't we supposed to ID the guy by a mole or wart on his private parts?" I ignored this, and continued to scroll through the photos. She continued. "You can't actually see any of his compromising bits, but he is taking the pictures! He knows he's on candid camera."

"For that matter, how do we know the woman is Midge Kohl?" I ran quickly through the photos again, and answered my own question. "Oh yeah. Why would another woman be wearing Mrs. Kohl's boots? Does anyone else have the initials MK?"

This was met with rolling eyes and a shrug. "Well, the woman in the pictures does have quite a distinct shape. And I took a look at Mrs. Kohl's medical records, including her height and weight. I'd say it's her. That is my professional opinion. Besides, the background does suggest this took place at the plant. And I was able to track down height and weight info for all female employees through the Department of Motor Vehicles—nobody over one hundred and forty pounds."

I almost mentioned that most women lie about their weight, but realized that I was getting off track. It's funny, I thought, how I knew right away that this picture was of Midge Kohl. I had never met the woman. All I had seen of her were charred remains. And my perception of her had been way off. I had her pegged as a cold, all-business type, and certainly not one who would consent to having an extramarital relationship in the middle of a seafood processing plant. Just goes to show you how wrong assumptions can be. I wondered how badly Midge Kohl would have wanted to keep this affair from her husband. "Do you have access to the financials? Maybe you can find out if money has been withdrawn that is suspicious or unaccounted for?"

"I do. And at first glance there are no red flags. I ran the company books through a software program that I created specifically for fraud cases. The books are clean. Every penny is traceable and legit." Deloris hit a button and a printer started spitting out paper. She reached over and collected the sheets as they fell, and handed them to me. "Here's the general ledger. Other than payroll and lobster, the other big monthly expense is shipping. No surprise there, right?"

"Right. What else do you have for me?" I asked. Deloris reported that she had taken the liberty of pulling together a list of all of the residents of Acadia Island who were there with the relocation program initiated by Midge Kohl. Apparently there were twenty-six ex-convicts enrolled in the program. All convictions had been of Class A or B felonies, which carry five- to fifteen-year sentences. So, all of Midge Kohl's employees at the plant had done a stint in a federal penitentiary, had all been paroled, and were all now on probation. Two of the women in the program had been schoolteachers who had consensual relationships with students, Deloris noted with a sigh. A couple of men had been caught selling child pornography. For the most part, the crimes had been of the nonviolent type, which didn't help narrow the suspect pool. Another interesting twist that Deloris pointed out was the fact that some percentage of all the employees' wages was being garnished and applied to fines imposed as restitution for whatever offense they had been convicted of. All employees also had monies taken from paychecks for rent, which was paid directly to AIPTA. "Wow, Mrs. Kohl had the whole ball of wax," I remarked. "Anything unusual about pay stub records for Manuel Rodrigues?"

"No. Nothing. He receives a higher hourly rate. But he's a supervisor, right? It appears that the only Internet access available on Acadia is through a large satellite dish owned by none other than Midge Kohl. I have been able to scan email from a number of the ex-cons and have found nothing that raises my eyebrows."

"Isn't that an invasion of privacy? Not that I really care. But if you found something, we couldn't use it in our case." I surprised myself with the use of *we* and *our* as opposed to *I* and *my*.

"Sex offenders give up their rights when they offend. This is Maine. Parolees consent to computer searches and monitoring software." I was certain that Deloris was incorrect about this, but as I wasn't a stickler for things of this nature, I let it slide.

"What about social media?" I asked. Deloris responded that Facebook has a policy that prohibits convicted sex offenders from having a profile. Her opinion, after doing some major snooping, was that the residents of Acadia who were there on the work release program were all playing by the book, and not involved in anything that might cost them the privilege of working and living on the island. Deloris interjected her opinion that she suspected that these convicts would even go so far as self-policing to keep the status quo.

When it seemed that we had exhausted all avenues of interest, Deloris promised to keep digging. She would call immediately with anything new. And she would hound the lab for the DNA forensics report on what they had received in the way of hair and fingernail clippings from Mrs. Kohl's office. "You don't have the equipment to run the hair and nail samples yourself?" I asked teasingly.

"No, but I can hack into the lab's system and get the results quicker than they'll contact us with them," she suggested.

"I'm good with that," I said as I got up and prepared to leave. I now had enough new information to head back to Acadia Island with intentions of getting to know Manny Rodrigues better. Even if I hustled, I could not possibly make the late ferry. And doing so would be pointless, as I would have no place to stay for the night once on Acadia. Something told me that Joan Proctor would not be extending any hospitality—and I really wanted to avoid seeing Trudy Proctor. One positive result of not being able to nail her on charges was the fact that I now didn't need to deal with her. I would strike out early tomorrow morning, I thought as I folded my notes and stuck them in my coat pocket. I thanked Deloris for all of her help, and left feeling exhilarated with the prospect of a new, totally legitimate suspect.

I had spent more time with Deloris than I had anticipated. But the time had been well spent. The more I thought about it, the more convinced I was that Manny was guilty of murder. Now, I needed sleep badly. That and a hot shower. Oh, and food. Food first, I thought as I drove from Ellsworth back down the narrow, twisting, and poorly plowed road to Green Haven. I wondered what Mrs. V had on the menu tonight. Mussels of some sort, I knew. It must be quite a challenge to come up with new recipes. She took pride in serving dishes that had "never been created before." And she was unfazed if the experiment was a total failure. She would simply say, "We won't bother putting this one in the book," and then politely clear the plates and offer nightcaps in lieu of dinner. Remarkably, there had been only one or two nights that my belly was warmed by Scotch rather than food.

The sun had set when I pulled into my parking spot. Light pink clouds hung on the western horizon like a thin layer of cotton candy, and held the only warmth in an otherwise stark scene of snow and ice fading in the shadows of the dimming day. Sunrise would bring glistening and twinkling, I thought. And midday would bring glare. But for now, all was gray, dull, and sleepy. I was surprised and disappointed to see that the Vickersons Cadillac was not in its spot. The car, which was home to all manner of knickknacks that didn't make the varsity squad of the house, stood as living proof that good taste is not universal. Not that I would win any prizes for interior decorating. But everyone in town commented on the V's monthly changing of whatever occupied their dashboard. I had noticed that Alice and Henry made a point of "running errands" around Green Haven on the first of each month to show off their new display. The most recent dashboard scene included a bobble head of David Ortiz, or Big Papi, the home run king of Boston. There wouldn't be a scene change until March 1, I knew. So my landlords must be off on other business, I thought as I hustled to get inside and out of the cold.

I grabbed the note that had been taped to the outside of my door, and set it on the table without reading it while I unbundled. The hot shower felt great. I had never appreciated hot water this much when I lived in Miami. I turned the knob to the scald position and closed my eyes, enjoying the solitude. I breathed in the moist, steamy air and felt all tension melt from my body. Relaxing, really relaxing was not in my repertoire. I would have to work on that, I thought as I wrapped myself in a bath towel and hesitantly opened the bathroom door, allowing the relatively cold air to barge in. I picked up the note from the table and read. Of course it was a reminder from the Vickersons. They liked to communicate in writing. Too old for texting, they said. And my cell phone was unreliable, they complained. I recognized the neat and bold printing on the paper as that of Mr. V; Alice wrote in an elegant cursive. The single page explained that Alice and Henry had gone on a road trip to Boston, and would "bring back a surprise." I laughed at my landlord's choice of words. The promise of a treat upon their return made me feel like a little kid.

I recalled the only other time I had been told something similar, the very first stage of my life that I remembered anything. My mother had jarred me from a sound sleep and placed me in her lap with my brother while someone drove us to a dock where we boarded a boat. The next thing I knew I woke up in our family's mainland car, a station wagon. We were going on a little adventure. My mother promised treats and surprises for well-behaved, non-whining children. And she delivered in the form of penny candy at every gas stop we made from Maine

222

to Miami. As it turned out, the real surprise was that we never went back. I stopped asking after a while.

Now, as I pulled on sweatpants and a wool shirt, I wondered if the Vickersons would bring me a bag of Atomic Fire Balls, Squirrel Nuts, Mary Janes, and Smarties (my mother never allowed bubble gum). More likely, they would bring me some samples of whatever new merchandise they would be selling at the Lobster Trappe when they reopened this season, I thought as I stood staring into the open refrigerator.

The only other time the Vickersons had traveled to Boston, they brought back goodies from an Italian bakery. My mouth watered with the memory of cannoli and bruttiboni. The Italian pastry chefs had nothing on the Spanish, I thought as I hankered for pastelitos from my old neighborhood in Miami. How long had it been since I had been to the grocery store?

Not much for dinner, I thought as I closed the refrigerator door in defeat. Maybe a can of soup? Yup! And scoring a ten in the lazy factor, I popped open the lid and shoved the plastic can into the microwave. Two minutes later, dinner was served. I slurped the soup with a plastic spoon, using a paper towel as a place mat, enabling me to toss the entire place setting, dinnerware, and cooking utensils into the trash. No crackers meant no crumbs to sweep off the table. I yawned and glanced at my wristwatch. I couldn't possibly go to bed at seven p.m., could I? Even in kindergarten, I stayed up to watch reruns of *Perry Mason* and *Ironside,* which may have influenced my career path. Either that or I had a crush on Raymond Burr. I needed to force myself to stay awake until nine, I thought as I put on the teakettle and gathered all of my sheets of notes that I had shoved into various pockets of clothing in the past couple of days.

I always slept best when I tucked in feeling organized for the following day. I would jump on the early boat to Acadia Island with a plan and procedure. And I would not return without making an arrest, I vowed as I sipped mint tea and shuffled through my notes and printed sheets from Deloris, looking for anything I may have missed. At eight I was ready to give in to sleepiness, when headlights lit up my kitchen. Oh, good, I thought. Mr. and Mrs. V were home. Now I could go to bed and not worry about them driving at night. Maybe I should greet them and help with whatever they had to carry from the car. And maybe I would enjoy one small treat before bed, I thought as I threw on my coat and slippers. One cannoli, as long as it didn't contain chocolate, would not keep me awake, I thought. And I would have fresh biscotti for breakfast.

By the time I got down my stairs and through the shop to their front door, they were already inside. I could hear voices from within the house. I knocked and waited. I opened the door a bit and called out. "Hi. Anybody home? I haven't seen the two of you in days!"

Whispered voices and scurrying sounds were followed by "Just a minute, Jane." I waited with the door cocked open and imagined that Alice and Henry were arranging the pastries for the best effect when unveiled. The couple opened the door the rest of the way and greeted me with hugs. "Come in," said Mr. V. "We have missed you!"

"Oh, I know," I replied with a smile. "I have missed both of you, too. I've been working too much. Nothing unusual there,"

I said, knowing that they would reprimand me for not communicating once the warm greeting was over.

"All work and no play . . ." Mrs. V started her usual lecture.

"Makes Jane a dull girl," came a familiar voice from the kitchen.

Before I could ask who was with them, Mr. V swung open the kitchen door with a flourish and said, "Surprise!"

I couldn't believe what I was seeing. My eyes welled up with tears as I embraced my brother Wally.

ELEVEN

Neither Wally nor I was willing to release the hug we shared. How long had it been? Although we had spoken on the phone weekly since my move north, I hadn't seen my baby brother in over eight months. I should have been ashamed of myself for that. But I was so taken with the happy emotions that his presence always brought that I ignored the nagging twinges of guilt. Wally possessed nothing that would chide or castigate. He was one hundred percent pure joy. When I finally held him at arm's length, I felt a renewed sense of hope on all levels. Life is indeed good, I thought.

The scene took on a dreamlike quality as the Vickersons explained how and why they drove to Boston to pick up Wally at South Station. Wally had boarded a Greyhound bus in Miami, and somehow managed a thirty-seven-hour trip with three transfers. He called the adventure "fun." And that is only one small example of how my brother and I differ. I could never endure that, I thought as I noticed how great Wally looked. The

Vickersons had taken him to a barber shop where he and Henry got cleaned up while Alice shopped for pastries. His poker-straight, sandy-colored hair had been styled in a way that complimented his youthful, rosy face. Everyone always mistook Wally for a much younger guy then he was, which usually resulted in his reciting of birth date, place, and certain details of various birthday parties he had been given along the way.

While Wally marveled about seeing snow for the first time, Mr. and Mrs. V elaborated on what I knew of the status of the home where Wally had lived for most of his adult life. Loss of federal funding finally caused them to close their doors—for good. They did what they could to help relocate all of the residents. In Wally's case, as I am the only known next of kin, they notified me (or tried, and got Mrs. V on the phone instead). Mr. and Mrs. V had agreed to pay the bus fare (which they were quick to note I could reimburse them for), and were able to collect Wally on my behalf and deliver him to me (where he could live in their spare bedroom temporarily).

It took a minute for all of this to sink in. Perhaps my head was swimming from lack of sleep. More likely, this unexpected event in combination with my fatigue made this situation more surreal than it really was. So my brother was moving in. No big deal. It felt right. The biggest adjustment would be for Wally. He would have to switch his loyalty to New England sports teams. That might be an issue, I knew. Wally was an avid and enthusiastic follower of professional football. His entire interior décor had consisted of banners, flags, and posters of the Miami Dolphins. Most of his wardrobe was aqua and white. Knowing how the Vickersons felt about the New England Patriots, the

227

Miami swag would have to be retired. And Wally's closet would be filled with shirts bearing the number twelve and the name Brady. I knew that Wally would learn to love the Minutemen, who were the NFL's most interesting mascots, in my opinion. I wondered how long it would take for Wally to ask for a musket and a tri-corner hat.

Henry and Alice invited us to sit down and enjoy some of the baked goods Alice scored from a variety of Italian bakeshops from Boston's North End while the guys "got handsome." Wally was quick to dig in. Within two bites, the front of his black sweater was dusted with fine, powdered sugar and tiny crumbs from the delicate-looking pastry he devoured as he murmured what I grew up knowing as "the yummy tummy hummy." Like a contented cat, Wally purred the monotoned, multisyllabic, little ditty, keeping the beat with each chew. When it looked obvious that Wally would polish off the entire box of goodies, I suggested that Mrs. V put them away until morning. I was surprisingly calm, and not annoyed with the landlords' minding of my business. I might even find it in myself to thank them, I thought as I devoured a light, flaky pastry that melted on my tongue like butter. Alice cleared the table and instructed Wally to say good night as she showed him his room. Wally explained that he was afraid of the dark and asked that the door be left open, to which Alice agreed.

I couldn't help but worry about the immediate future. I knew that I had to work as many hours as possible, and put all personal business aside until there was an arrest made in the Kohl case. Before I could verbalize any of this, Mr. V said, "Don't worry. We have plans with Wally, and are happy to have his company while you fight crime." I breathed a sigh of relief and smiled, knowing that my landlords were genuinely doing this because they wanted to. "Our family just got a little bigger!" I could hear Mrs. V telling Wally that she would leave the bathroom light on for him, and promising pancakes for breakfast. When she returned to the table and joined us, I patted my heart and mouthed a silent thank you. "Yup, we have a schedule to keep. Must be time to hit the hay," said Mr. V as he looked at the lobster clock over the mantel. "I have made appointments for interviews for Wally with a couple of the local shopkeepers," he said. "We will be seeking gainful employment."

"I need to pull my own weight," came the excited voice from the bedroom. We all got a chuckle from this, and it reminded me how much Wally enriched my life. I stood and stretched. I apologized for needing to scoot up to bed, explaining that I would be heading to Acadia Island early in the morning, and with any luck would come back with a cold-blooded killer in my custody.

"Janey gets the bad guys," sounded more like a tired campaign slogan now that Wally's head was on the long-awaited pillow. The Vickersons ached for more information. They begged for a detailed update of what I had been up to, and protested that I needn't go to bed this early. I promised a full report upon my return tomorrow night, bid them good night, and thanked them both for being so good to Wally.

My last thoughts as I drifted off to sleep were of family. Odd, I thought, that complete strangers as of last June would treat me like one of their own while I had yet to meet any actual blood relation while on the Bunkers' home turf. From what I had gathered in my short time in Down East Maine, I must certainly share DNA with many of the people who live on Acadia. And everyone out there would know of my comings and goings. But nobody had surfaced to make my acquaintance. Nobody had invited me in. Nobody had asked Cal or the mail boat captain or mate about me. Nobody had even bothered to peek at me from behind closed curtains as far as I knew. Maybe having true, blood relatives was overrated, I thought as I pulled the blankets under my chin.

A crease of mango-colored light seeped under the drawn shade of my east-facing bedroom window, waking me with a jolt. I must have overslept, I thought as I sprang from my warm nest and into the cold tiled bathroom. I showered in record time, dressed in layers to insulate myself from what I knew would be a brisk day, and scurried out to scrape ice and brush fresh snow from the Duster. I now dared to look at my watch, and realized that I would just make the seven a.m. boat to Acadia if I left immediately. I drove a bit faster than I normally would; scrunching down behind the wheel so that I could see through the small clear spot I had managed to scrape in the driver's-side windshield before taking off. Fortunately, Wally was a member of the same sleep pattern as my landlords. He never got up before nine a.m.

As soon as I get back from Acadia, I thought as I pulled into the mail boat parking area in South Haven, I need to follow up with Marilyn and Marlena. Their place could be ideal for Wally, I thought as I hustled down the ramp and boarded the boat. Year-round rents couldn't be as expensive as Miami, I reasoned as I took a seat in the cabin. I would figure it out. But for now, I needed to put Wally on a back burner. I had left him in good hands.

"Good morning, Miss Bunker," said the mate cheerfully. "Headed out to the island again, I see. Sorry we left you stranded last time. But if there's freezing spray in the forecast, my uncle won't leave the dock. It's a matter of safety."

"No problem," I replied with a smile. "I understand and appreciate that. I had a friend come after me. As it turned out, that was not the wisest decision."

"Yeah, so I heard. Cal is one of the best, though. He's had a lot of water under his keel—passed more sea buoys than most people have telephone poles." That was a familiar line that I hadn't heard in years. The captain climbed aboard, nodded acknowledgment of my presence, and asked his nephew to throw the lines from the dock. It was only 6:50, which surprised me.

"I thought this trip left at seven. Or is my watch slow?" I asked out of curiosity, and was genuinely happy to be leaving a few minutes early. I knew I needed every second available to achieve what I intended to do today.

"Nope, we leave at seven o'clock sharp," answered the captain. "I'm just swinging around to the freight dock to grab a pallet that's bound for Acadia. Freight for the general store and the plant are our bread and butter this time of year. Not many tourists," he commented as he backed the boat under a boom with a hydraulic winch. The mate wrapped a line around a cleat at the stern, and climbed a ladder to operate the winch. Within minutes, two pallets piled high with boxes were lowered into the cockpit and the boom was raised and secured. The mate scampered back aboard, and off we went at seven on the dot. One pallet was clearly marked for the island store with boxes of bread, crates of milk, cases of paper products, and a phenomenal number of thirty-packs of beer. As if reading my mind the captain said, "I'll bet the residents of Acadia consume more beer per capita than anywhere else on the planet."

"You should see the monthly trip we make for returnable bottles and cans!" exclaimed the mate. "The cockpit is rounded right up!"

The remainder of the forty-minute trip was silent except for a bit of chatter on the VHF radio, giving me an opportunity to digest the fact that Wally was now here, and I would need to make arrangements for the best life possible for him. It is widely known that living independently of relatives is most beneficial to Down syndrome adults. One of the downsides of residing in a remote outpost is that you sacrifice convenience and opportunity, I was now fully realizing. Wally was fairly high functioning, and might enjoy the chance to try out his wings, I thought. He would also need a job, and it seemed that Mr. V was taking care of that. I was positive that there were no sheltered workshop type of employment opportunities in Down East Maine. But there was work that Wally could do within the right establishment.

Of course Wally would also need a social life; it was lucky that he'd always made friends easily. It would be great to get Wally involved in some physical activity. I knew this would be the biggest challenge. Wally was not competitive—at all. Special Olympics had not been his thing, I recalled with a silent laugh. He fancied himself more cerebral than physical. Wally had armed himself with a camera rather than a ball of any sort at the only Special Olympics he had attended. And he was extremely proud to show off the newspaper clipping with photo credit given to Walter Bunker. Photography was a great hobby, and one that Wally had enjoyed since his sixteenth birthday when he received a disposable camera, until it came time to have the pictures developed, since that required giving up the camera. Wally now had a great digital camera that fit in his pocket for ease of recording anything that caught his eye.

Then there was the possibility of enrolling him in continuing education. I sighed out loud. Nope, not my brother. The first and only adult education class I enrolled him in was culinary arts for single men. Wally assumed he was there in the role of photo-journalist. He refused to participate in the class. But he did get some phenomenal pictures that were later used in the school's literature. I chuckled out loud now with the realization that Wally would photograph every meal that Mrs. V prepared, and be quite vocal about wanting his "work" used in her cookbook.

I stood and looked over the bow to see that we were now rounding the headland that would give way to Acadia's main harbor. Wally had been a good distraction, I thought. But perhaps I should have been thinking about the case. I stretched and turned toward the stern, bouncing on the balls of my feet to wake myself up and energize my sleepy system. Although the second pallet that sat in the cockpit was wrapped in a tarpaulin, one corner flapped in the breeze, exposing a box with red Chinese characters. I figured that this pallet was going to

ALP, as I now was quite familiar with the markings and contents, and recognized them as chemical additives for product enhancement.

"I'll bet the closing of the plant will have a negative effect on your winter income," I stated in an attempt to make conversation.

"Yes. We cart shipping supplies to Acadia weekly, and transport product back to the mainland nearly every day. The plant is our best year-round customer, by far," answered the captain. "And without any island kids needing us to get them back and forth to high school, we'll probably cut our schedule to once a day, or even just twice a week once the plant closes. The contract for the mail barely pays for the fuel to get back and forth. Even the store's freight bill isn't enough to keep us going on a twice-daily schedule."

"Wow. The killing of Mrs. Kohl seems to have affected everyone," I said, hoping for some inside scoop.

"Yes. She sure had control of most of the wheels that turn on Acadia. There's hopeful talk of Mr. Kohl stepping in and running the plant. But he has never loved the island like Mrs. Kohl did. Her roots are here, not his. And we had heard that Mrs. Kohl was considering closing the plant before she passed," the captain replied. "So keeping it going is probably wishful thinking. She and her husband are also the largest shareholders of the boat company. We work for them. Or him now, I guess." I found it interesting that the captain did not refer to Midge Kohl's death as a murder, but rather seemed to think she had died of natural causes. He needed another nudge, I thought.

"Well, whoever killed her must be public enemy number

one. I hope I figure out who that is before people take the law into their own hands."

"Ha," blurted the captain. "Good luck with that." He did not sound very optimistic that I had any chance of success, I thought as the boat came to a soft landing at the dock. I'd show him, I thought as I buttoned my coat and prepared to disembark. "Three o'clock departure. Don't be late, Deputy Bunker." I assured him that I would see him for the return trip and stepped off the boat and headed up the ramp.

At the top of the dock I was greeted by none other than Manuel Rodrigues. His feet, clad in super-insulated Moon Boots, into which the tops of his pants were tucked, looked extremely out of proportion with his small frame.

"Good morning, Miss Bunker. Or is it Detective Bunker today?" he asked snidely. I was nervous that Manny had been tipped off about my visit that I had intended to be kept quiet. Nobody knew of this trip. Maybe the captain or mate had somehow dropped a dime when I wasn't paying attention.

"I'm impressed. You have Googled me and learned that I was once a detective," I said as I stopped at the top of the ramp, looking Manny square in the eye.

"Oh, it was easy," Manny replied. "I came here from Dade County. All I had to do was make one call. I'm surprised that our paths never crossed in Miami before you got the boot."

"Yeah, me too. Except that I was mostly drug enforcement. Not much to do with kiddy porn. You must know my friends in SVU."

Manny shifted his weight nervously from oversized, puffy boot to oversized, puffy boot. Then said, "Yes, we do have a lot in common, don't we? We left Florida at the same time. But I left on *good* behavior."

"All right, let's cut the crap," I said as I followed Manny to a truck he had apparently backed down on the wharf. "You are here to turn yourself in! That must be because you know from your vast experience on the *wrong* side of the law that cooperation makes things easier for *everyone*."

Manny climbed in behind the wheel of the truck, and before he closed the door, said, "I actually did not know you would be on the boat this morning. I'm here to pick up freight for the plant." With this he slammed the door, and backed under the pallet that was now swinging from the end of the hydraulic winch at the very end of the dock. The mate lowered the pallet into the bed of the truck, secured the winch, and hustled back aboard the waiting boat. Lines were thrown and the boat jogged away, leaving me alone on the icy chute directly in front of a running truck with a not-so-nice guy whom I now suspected of murder at the wheel.

He rolled down his window, stuck his head out, and asked, "Need a lift?" The smugness in his voice and face left me cold. I declined the ride, promising to see him at the plant, knowing that I would be more comfortable using the Kohls' Range Rover rather than accepting help from my prime suspect. "Suit yourself. See you there." And with this, Manny hit the accelerator, spinning his wheels all the way up the sloped drive to the parking lot. It was obvious that Manny hadn't mastered driving in the snow and ice as the truck fishtailed back and forth, nearly out of control before making the corner onto the main road.

I found the Range Rover right where I had left it. I brushed a fresh inch of snow from the windshield and mirrors. I climbed in and realized how cold it was. The seats were actually stiff, and the steering wheel was glazed with a thin coating of frost. I found the key under the mat, stuck it in the ignition and turned it with crossed fingers. The engine started right up and ran smoothly. I sat in the parking lot with the heat and defrost blowing until I sensed the slightest bit of warmth, then started toward the plant, where I planned to spend some time with Manny and searching for the area of the processing line that was set up like the background in the scandalous photos Deloris had since texted to my phone. I tensed up a bit as I passed the Proctors' house. I knew Trudy was back home—probably sound asleep, I thought as I caught a whiff of wood smoke that curled from their chimney. I imagined that her parents would be happy to see her heading back to college. Even mom and dad must find it hard to like that child, I thought.

When I rounded the next corner, I saw that the road had not been plowed beyond the Proctors' driveway. The only tire tracks were what I realized must be the coming and going of Manny in the ALP freight truck. Suddenly, the Range Rover's engine began to cough a bit. I glanced down to see that the fuel gauge was on the big "E." Damn, I thought as the engine chugged roughly.

I drove the now bucking vehicle along to a wide section of the road where I could pull off enough for another vehicle to pass. (That is, if anyone else was out.) The engine hiccuped and died. Oh great. I estimated that I was now halfway between the Proctors' and ALP. There was no way was I going to ask Joan and Clark for help. I pumped the gas pedal a couple of times and prayed for a start. I preferred to not have a door slammed in my face this morning, I thought as I limped the Range Rover into the snowbank on my right before the engine stopped for the final time. I could easily walk to the ALP, and then hitch a ride or confiscate the company truck to transport my suspect back to the boat this afternoon. I was optimistic that he would come along peacefully once he came to realize the jig was up. Deloris had been thorough, and would have mentioned any violence in his criminal record, I thought as I slammed the door and started hiking down the road. The walk would do me good.

Once I got over the fact that I was traveling on foot, I actually enjoyed the brisk walk. The realization that any witness to my poor planning regarding gasoline was unlikely helped me to relax. And the below-zero temperature kept me moving. Snow-filled limbs of spruce trees hung heavily over the road on either side, shielding the ditches from glints of sunshine that danced through the shadows. Animal tracks, of which I know nothing, left three different and distinct patterns. Deer, rabbit, and squirrel? I wondered. The tracks were so precise, I imagined creatures skittering off into the woods just ahead of me. I approached an open field on my left where the tire tracks pulled off the road. Large, human footprints with an aggressive tread pattern surrounded the tire tracks on the off-road side. As there were only two sets of tire tracks—one coming and one going—and the footprints looked like they were made with Moon Boots, I reasoned that Manny must have stopped here on his way to the dock. But why?

I looked around for a telltale yellow spot, but the footprints left the tire tracks and headed into the open field. I decided to follow them, being careful to step into the packed-down tracks left by Manny, which made it easy to travel through the otherwise knee-deep snow. The footprints lead me through a beautiful, high wrought-iron gate that was marked with ornate black iron posts. Either side of the open gate that jutted above the snow looked like an elegant harp. If the iron craftsmanship hadn't been so fancy, I supposed the gate would have looked more like a jail cell door. Once I entered through, I saw that I was in a cemetery. The tops of tombstones poked through the otherwise pristine white blanket like pale gray islands floating in milk. The footprints appeared to have been made by someone being respectful of the dead; circumnavigating the area and not intruding within the realm of actual graves. I stayed in the footprints to the far edge of the cemetery, where they stopped and lingered by what appeared to be very old tombstones that had been brushed clean of snow, enabling me to read names and dates. BUNKER. A chill ran from the base of my neck to my tailbone.

What could Manny have been up to, I wondered? Other than trying to freak me out, I couldn't imagine why he might have stopped here at the Bunker family graveyard. Snow had been cleared from the faces of several stones, allowing me to read names, dates, and connections to one another until I found it. "Jane Bunker. December 16, 1844-April 09, 1935. Daughter of Percy Bunker and Eloise Lord." I have no problem admitting that I was spooked. I took a deep breath with intentions of slowing my heart down. I could feel my own pulse as I looked around nervously and fought the impulse to scream or run. I knew that I had been named for my father's great aunt, but that was the extent and depth of my knowledge of the Bunker family tree. Was someone watching me? If so, I had to control and manage my actions. I never imagined what feelings could be stirred by happening upon my own name on a grave marker. I took a minute to collect myself, then continued to brush snow and read engravings on stones marking my familial legacy, heritage, and even some obituary information. There, I thought, all calmed down. No reason to be frightened. Dead people never harmed anyone; only the living did.

I followed the footprints around the cemetery, weaving in and out of rows of tombstones and back to the road where Manny must have climbed back into the company truck. I tried to make sense of this bizarre side trip, and what reaction it was intended to produce. Manny couldn't have known that I would run out of gas, could he? And he didn't know me well enough to realize that I would most certainly follow his tracks into the Bunker cemetery, did he? Maybe this was a form of fun more than intimidation, I thought. The best explanation I could come up with was that Manny had intended for me to consider seeing my name on a gravestone as an omen of things to come. Well, I thought, I had news for him. Now that I had shaken the shock and disbelief, I realized that finding and exploring the Bunker family plot was something I should have planned to do. Doing so was perhaps the only way I would ever know anything about my roots, I thought. Short of asking questions of old-time residents of Acadia Island, which I would never do, the only way for me to glean insight into where and who I came from was to do research. And a great place to start was in the cemetery that was now behind me.

I would return in better weather, I thought as I quickened my pace. And I would return when doing so was not contingent upon solving a case of brutal murder. Deep within the crevices of my psyche lay an understanding that the notion of returning to Acadia on personal business would be to soothe what had been triggered at the sight of my name on a gravestone.

All thoughts of graves evaporated upon the doorstep of the plant as I let myself in. I knew the way to the processing floor, where I found Manny. He had changed from his Moon Boots to the knee-high rubber boots worn by his fellow ALP employees. He looked up from a clipboard where he appeared to be looking over a checklist and said, "What took you so long?"

"I decided to walk. And I visited the Bunker family grave-yard for fun," I said. Manny raised an eyebrow, but remained silent. "Is there somewhere we can talk?" Manny knew this was coming, yet was reluctant, as I expected he would be. He was annoyed. I was interrupting his workday. I was on to him. He was buying time, I thought, to work through his alibis and explanations. He indicated with a nod in the direction of the offices that I should follow him. I fell in behind him and felt many eyes on my back as we made our way through two busy processing lines manned by what I knew were ex-cons with a tenuous grip on a second chance at life; a second chance that they knew was slipping away. And my presence added grease to the skids.

I was a little surprised at the appearance of Mrs. Kohl's workspace. It had been transformed into Manny's office in the short amount of time since I'd last been here. The speed of the transformation suggested that this had been planned prior to the office being vacated via Mrs. Kohl's death. He even had a desktop nameplate with "Manny Rodrigues" in an elegant font that contradicted its surroundings. I sat, at his request, across the handsome walnut desk while he got comfortable in a cushy office chair that fit nicely with the desk and other new furnishings.

"Wow. It didn't take long for you to move in," I said, hoping to provoke a response.

"You'll be surprised to know that this has been in the works for some time," Manny replied as he pulled off the rubber boots and stepped into dress shoes.

"Do you mean to say that Mrs. Kohl's demise had been planned?" I asked, knowing this would put Manny on the edge of his seat, which it did. He placed his elbows on the desk and leaned into them, getting as close as he could with the large desk between us.

"No, that is not what I mean to say."

"Well, you had better start filling me in. I have evidence linking you to Mrs. Kohl through some nasty email exchanges."

"She was my boss. Why would I be anything but nice to her? I didn't send anything *nasty*."

"Maybe not. But you were at the very least on the receiving end of some photos that appeared to be within your wheelhouse of activity. And now I see how you may have benefited from her death, so there's motive beyond what I already have. Do you have a new title? It sure looks like you have been promoted from foreman."

"Evidence? Like what?" He snarled. I went through the list of what Deloris had been able to dig up from email correspondence. When I explained the threatening emails that he had sent to his boss that looked a lot like blackmail, he laughed. "You see, English is not my first language. Speaking, I am proficient. But in writing, I am really bad. I'm surprised anyone could make sense of my very poor grammar, spelling, and vocabulary. Maybe you translated my words conveniently for your purposes."

"I don't think so. Most people would find a phrase like 'make you sweat' threatening. No language barrier there," I said.

"Sweat? I meant sweet. I always brought her homemade candies. Really, ask anyone."

That was too easy, I thought. There was no way he could explain his way around the photos of someone having sex with Mrs. Kohl, and how clear it was that someone was using them to blackmail her. And that with his record, he was the most obvious guy. Even with two dozen other employees with similar records, Manny was the only one with a company email account, and ample access to the boss. Manny was well versed in denials and alibis, I was sure. I had to remind myself that he knew his way around legalities and technicalities. I should back up and slow things down. There was no sense tipping my hand.

"It was nice of you to visit my family's burial ground this morning. Would you mind telling me why you were there, just minutes before I landed at the dock?" I asked.

Manny didn't squirm. He didn't even hesitate. Any hardened criminal can stay cool under the gun, I knew. "That was sheer coincidence. I have to say, that it was perfect, though. I mean I didn't know you were coming. I didn't know that I was in your family's graveyard until I cleared snow from the first stone and saw the name Bunker. And I surely did not expect that you would track me like a dog on a scent. That all just fell into place." He smiled and sat back in a more relaxed position. I prompted him again to answer my question as to why he had been in the Bunker cemetery. "Oh, that. Well, I am a graver."

"Okay, I'll bite. What's a graver?" I asked, skeptical that he could deliver any real explanation. That was Manny's opening.

"I enjoy visiting cemeteries. It gives me a sense of the past and history of a place. And I record my pastime by doing stone rubbings," he said.

"Rubbings?" I was skeptical, but was buying some time. I couldn't help thinking of the tendency of murderers to revisit their killings by visiting graves. I wondered if spending time in *any* cemetery brought some vicarious thrill to someone who had killed.

"I place butcher paper over a stone and rub it with charcoal to record inscriptions and designs. Your ancestors . . ." I cut him off before he could report anything that might be about *me*. I wondered if rubbings could have some likeness to souvenirs collected by murderers. A seasoned con artist like Manny had to be a quick thinker, I knew. He tried to convince me that he just happened to have a little time on his hands this morning before meeting the boat, and just happened to stumble upon the Bunker plot, and that I just happened to be on the boat. Pretty unlikely, I thought, and told him so.

"You expect me to believe that? Come on, Manny. You'll have to do better than that. I don't believe in that degree of coincidence—and neither will a judge and jury." I did secretly admire his creativity, though. He may be quick to come up with alibis and justifications, but justice would prevail, I thought as I prepared to launch into my next tactic.

Before I could mention the sexy pictures that were found in his and every other ALP email account, there was a knock at the door. A woman in a white ALP jumpsuit stuck her head in and reported a problem on the processing line that needed Manny's attention. "And there was a message on the main machine for Deputy Bunker to call Deloris as soon as possible," she said, and ducked back out, closing the door behind her.

Manny stood to excuse himself, promising to return after he addressed whatever issue had arisen in the plant. He loosened his shoelaces and was back into the rubber boots. Opening a file cabinet, he retrieved a folder fat with pages, handed it to me, and told me to check it out. When he saw me looking at my phone, he insisted that I use his office phone, as there was no cell service on this side of Acadia Island. Whatever Deloris wanted would have to wait until I could use my cell, I thought. I assumed that Deloris would never try to contact me on the ALP line with anything that couldn't wait for fear of jeopardizing my case. So I reasoned that whatever Deloris needed could not be urgent. Maybe I was paranoid, but if I had no privacy at home on the phone, I wouldn't assume to have any here. On the outside chance that Deloris hadn't considered the potential lack of privacy, and had critical information, I vowed to get back to her ASAP. It's not like I could walk to the opposite side of the island to use my cell phone. Too far. Too cold. No, I would stay here and work on Manny until I arrested him, or he cleared himself, whichever came first. And whichever option tipped the scale at the time I needed to leave to catch the three o'clock boat would prompt my decision.

After about forty-five minutes, I got curious and opened the file folder. Much to my surprise and disappointment, it contained all of the evidence to support Manny's claim of being a "graver." It appeared that he had been actively researching and visiting burial sites since his arrival on the island. He had maps, genealogies, island history and lore printed off the Internet, and he had a number of pictures of stone rubbings he had done. Thumbing through the stack, I found a map of the Bunker plot including a copy of a tax map that showed boundaries and markers of the property. On a separate sheet, there was a diagram of the grave placement with initials on each square that I took to stand for the names of whoever was buried within. There was a crude family tree with several blank spaces that I assumed Manny would fill in when he had time to do the research. As hard as it was for me to believe, it appeared that his visit to the Bunker plot was purely coincidental. I took a small degree of comfort and satisfaction in realizing that nobody had tipped Manny off regarding my trip this morning. I placed the folder on top of the desk and waited.

My anxious wait time was split between mental preparation and strategy moving forward with Manny to get some sort of confession or information that would incriminate him, and the wonderment of graving. I thought it peculiar that someone would devote so much time and energy into total strangers. And it was morbid, to say the least. My discomfort in cemeteries outweighed any intrigue. Although I was not a certified and licensed analyst of criminal behavior, I could not deny what I felt was a connection between a murderer and a graveyard. And I kept going back to rubbings as souvenirs or items to be cherished. Maybe rubbings inspired Manny to create more graves. That might be a stretch, I thought as I grew impatient with Manny's absence. It was more likely that Manny simply wanted to spook me or get into my head through my family roots. I felt myself waffling on Manny's guilt.

Just as I decided to go find him, Manny reappeared. He was drying freshly washed hands with a paper towel as he closed the door behind him with an elbow. Once again he exchanged the boots for dress shoes. I imagined the shoes represented what he wanted, and the boots were his ugly reality. I had no time to waste. "Can you explain why the security cameras here at the plant are shut off every night after the second shift?"

"The cameras were used by Mrs. Kohl as surveillance of crew during work hours. There was no need to have footage of an empty plant. She was mostly concerned with production. Everyone here is aware that they are being filmed."

"But isn't there concern about what might be going on after hours?" I asked.

"Like theft? No. After handling product for eight to ten hours, the last thing anyone wants to do is steal frozen lobster tails or lobster mac and cheese. We are honest, hardworking people; not thieves," he said in a huff.

"No, but there are plenty of other sorts of criminals here," I said calmly, enjoying the fact that I was getting under his skin. "You know how this game is played. You are the conduit between the employees and the management. You are my best source, and frankly, my only suspect. Now *you* have some 'splainin' to do," I put on my best Cuban accent. The reference to Desi and Lucy struck a nerve. Manny's face grew red and he drummed his fingertips on the desktop. "I have gotten a glimpse of what happens here after hours, and it's not pretty." I pulled a printed copy of the most damning picture in the bunch from my bag and put it in front of Manny. "Honest and hardworking, indeed." Manny didn't even glance down at the copy. He crossed his arms over his chest; a red flag in body language, indicating that he was closed off and defiant. "This picture was found in Mrs. Kohl's deleted email file. And it originated from your email account," I said, hoping Manny would overcome what was looking like a case of lockjaw. "This looks like pornography."

"I had nothing to do with killing her. And I don't know who did it."

"No, of course you don't. The brain is an amazing thing. High levels of stress and trauma result in repressed memories. Perhaps placing you under arrest will jog your memory." I said.

"Arrest? For what? You have nothing linking me to the murder."

"I have evidence that you were blackmailing Mrs. Kohl. And I have motive. If Mrs. Kohl pulled the plug on ALP, you would lose your job and your residence." My conviction that Manny was the prime suspect in Mrs. Kohl's murder was eroding. He *could* be guilty. But he also might be innocent. Okay, innocent might be inaccurate. But everything that Manny had shared might well result in more than the shadow of doubt needed to convict. I realized that my interest in Manny was evolving from suspect to informant. People who had spent time behind bars were always the most reluctant snitches. Only the threat of returning to prison would loosen lips.

I pulled two more photocopies from my bag and placed them on the desk with the first. "And I do believe that possession and distribution of pornographic material is illegal, and a violation of your parole. And that's certainly enough to not only arrest, but to send you directly to jail without passing go or collecting two hundred dollars."

Manny took a deep breath and exhaled through pursed lips. I fought the urge to start firing questions at him, since he appeared to be on the brink of becoming somewhat pliable. I let my not-so-veiled threat marinate while I picked up and pretended to take interest in the file folder of stone rubbings and graveyard maps.

I slowly flipped through pages of rubbings, feigning interest while silently praying for Manny to start talking. I didn't look up until Manny cleared his throat. Once the clam opened, I was confident there would be full exposure. And there was. "Okay, I admit to putting pressure on my boss to ensure she would do the right thing regarding the plant."

"What is your opinion of the right thing?" I asked, trying to loosen him up with a benign question before hitting hard-core interrogation methods.

"Mrs. Kohl had agreed to allow ALP to be taken over by the employees, rather than shutting down. The negotiations had been completed, and we were days away from executing the Employee Stock Ownership Plan when Mrs. Kohl got cold feet and was reconsidering her decision. I needed her alive, not dead." Manny stopped short.

I needed to keep him going!

"What caused the cold feet?" I asked with genuine interest.

"Acadia's indigenous, year-round population wanted the plant closed and for us ex-cons involved to be relocated—anywhere but on *their* island."

The origin of the incriminating photos, according to Manny, was unknown. He claimed to have found the pictures in his email, and yes, had used them to his advantage in persuading Mrs. Kohl to follow through with the ESOP. "Who do you think sent you the photographs?" I asked.

"I don't know. Maybe a disgruntled employee. Plenty of those here. Or a disenfranchised local—lots of those, too." Manny claimed to have no idea how the surveillance footage had been hacked into and claimed to have been unaware of the after-hours activities of Mrs. Kohl and the mystery lover until the pictures surfaced. "I didn't understand why Mrs. Kohl wanted the security camera off after second shift until I got the pictures in my email."

"Geez, the photos are of such poor quality, the male could be almost *anyone*. Even you."

"Not if she was the last woman on earth."

"I'm not convinced. If not you, then who?" I asked. A long silence indicated that Manny was done talking. I knew instinctively that Manny was not the mystery lover. I believed wholeheartedly that Mrs. Kohl's lover was also her killer. Manny's reluctance to finger the man in the photos reminded me that there was still a killer on the loose.

While most of Manny's alibi seemed quite believable, it wasn't what I had hoped for, I mused, as Manny eventually filled in more details of the employee ownership plan that he and the entire ex-con community wanted and needed so badly. Desperately enough, I wondered, that perhaps someone had lost control and murdered Mrs. Kohl to ensure the plan continued as they'd originally agreed upon. Manny was more comfortable talking about the foiled business plan than he was about the identity of the man in the photos, which I found telling.

"My IT team found evidence that you had forwarded the pictures to Mrs. Kohl along with threatening notes, and that whoever had sent them to you had done so in a way not to be traceable. Do any of your *teammates* possess *special* technical skills?"

Manny claimed to have no knowledge of anyone with such skill, but admitted that he had no way of knowing what level of computer/cyber technology his comrades had. I pulled the final picture from my bag and slapped in on the desk. Although I knew the picture had not been sent to Mrs. Kohl from Manny's email, I hoped it might shed some light.

"What do you make of this?" I asked of the clearly amateur cut and paste job of the mystery lover humping the cardboard box.

"It means nothing to me other than some real sicko is responsible for the pictures," he replied. I didn't believe that the picture had no significance, and found some humor in the slant of his sensitivities. But I also was losing confidence in my theory that he had killed Mrs. Kohl. I now felt some urgency to find some cell reception. Deloris might have information that would clear Manny altogether, I thought. I asked Manny to show me the area of the plant that was shown in the background of the pictures, and assumed that I could excuse myself at lunchtime to call Deloris.

Back into the rubber boots, Manny led me to the scene shown in the photos. "This is the skinning machine," he said, pointing to a large, stainless-steel contraption with a treadmill-style belt protruding from its side. "It is used to remove skin from fish fillets. We have been processing lobster only, so the skinner has been idle." The belt was precisely where the photos had been captured by the security camera, I noted as Manny motioned my attention to the parallel handrails that framed either side of the belt's entrance to the machine itself. "These are for safety—in case someone gets caught on the belt by clothing—when these railings are pushed, the machine shuts down automatically so a hand or arm doesn't get pulled into the blades; saving the person's skin, so to speak."

I found it ironic that sexual activity had taken place on the skinning machine. At closer inspection, I could see traces of the poly bag tape that I recalled finding melted around the wrist of Mrs. Kohl's charred corpse as well as in the photos. The perimeter of the room was fitted with a gravity roller conveyor system, and I imagined this was used to transport heavy cartons of product in and out of the skinning area (and was easily strong enough to support the weight of a large woman). The conveyors went through plastic-covered ports in the walls that were large enough to accommodate a fully-loaded pallet (and of circumference to easily clear a dead body). I reached under my coat and felt the grip of my gun, which gave me some comfort.

"What is on the other side of this wall?" I asked, pointing to where the conveyor traveled through a window.

"Sorting room. Follow me." Manny took me to the sorting room, where the conveyor split into three tracks. "To the fresh line, freezing line, and cooking line," he said, pointing at each track. I asked to see the other end of the cooking line, and he led me to a large, hot, steam-filled room where one conveyor track ended directly over a huge vat of boiling water (huge enough to contain a volume of water more than ample to submerge a human being).

Manny showed me the hydraulic lift above the strainer that lined the vat and how employees could dump boiled product onto either of two "exit belts," that he defined as cooling and value add. Following the wheeled conveyor system around the plant, I learned the relative ease of killing, boiling, and dumping a body into the back of a truck without getting your hands dirty. Even though I knew that this was where the murder had taken place, the guided tour lent visuals that freaked me out. The attempted cover-up was straightforward, I thought. Once in a vehicle, the corpse must have been driven to the Kohl house, where it was dragged inside and torched with the house to make it look like an accidental death. I was confident that I had now pieced together the timeline and methodology of the murder. This did nothing to soothe my nerves brought on by the knowledge that a murderer was on the loose and may strike again to avoid apprehension.

Manny hesitantly agreed to drive me to the other side of Acadia during his lunch break, where I could purchase a few gallons of gas from the general store to put in the Kohl's Range Rover. We left the plant as the employees were streaming into the break room for their thirty-minute lunch. In the company truck, Manny explained that he had exactly thirty minutes, so he was only able to drop me in town, where I would have to figure the rest out myself. This suited me, as I needed some alone time to check in with Deloris. When we passed the place where the Range Rover sat, I asked Manny to check the truck's odometer and measure the distance to the store. When we pulled into the store's parking lot, Manny reported that we were approximately one and a half miles from the Range Rover. As cold as it was, I figured that I could happily speed-walk that distance, carrying two gallons of gasoline in about twenty minutes just to stay warm. I felt uneasy about thanking Manny for the ride, but did, promising that I would see him back at the plant to resume my investigation, which would include questioning some of his fellow employees. Manny was less than enthusiastic with his reply. The truck was moving away from me before I could close the door.

My plans changed when I read the sign on the store's door: "Closed for lunch. Back at 1:30." I cupped my hands around my face and pressed my nose against the glass, peering into the dark, and indeed empty, Island General Store. Seeing no sign of life deflated my fleeting idea that I could've eaten here, too. I walked around the side of the building where the lone gas pump stood. The cardboard sign taped to the face of the meter read "Report gallons, not dollars," indicating that the antiquated pump couldn't keep up with today's fuel prices. I picked up the nozzle and flipped the lever. Bingo. The pump had been left on. I searched the perimeter for a jerry can or container in which I could put gas. I found nothing. I wandered up the road, looking around for anything I could use. Time was running short.

The first house I saw had a plowed driveway and a large barn that *must* certainly have a few empty gas cans, I thought as I approached the front door and knocked. No answer. I knocked again, more vigorously. I tried the knob. It was locked. I trudged through snow to take a look inside through an open spot between heavy drapes drawn across a picture window, and saw that the furniture had been covered with sheets; put to bed for the winter. Exasperated, I hiked through the snow to the barn to try the door. Looking through the window, I saw two vehicles, and realized that my best bet was to commandeer one of them. A padlock and hasp stood between me and transportation. The only decision I had to make was whether to break a window, or kick down the door. I opted for the door, and gave it a swift kick. It gave a bit. I kicked again and again. On the third try, the door frame splintered, allowing me to push my way in.

The inside of the barn smelled musty; a mixture of automotive oil that had been soaked into the dirt floor over the years, and a briny scent coming from dried barnacles that clung to the bottom of an overturned dinghy. The only light was what seeped through two small windows, and was insufficient. I searched for switches, and found a string hanging from the high ceiling. I pulled, and nothing happened. The power had been shut off for the winter, I imagined. My eyes adjusted enough to give me comfort moving around without fear of stepping into or onto anything. I walked slowly to the barn door to open it for more light. Cobwebs tickled my face, and I waved my hands in front of me to clear them away. With a little effort I was able to release a deadbolt and slide open a wide door, allowing sunlight to flood in, making the place a tad less creepy. I opened the door of a pickup truck and slid behind the wheel. The key was in the ignition. I turned it. Complete silence. I did the same, with the same result, at the wheel of the other car. I popped open the hood, and was not surprised to see that the battery had been removed. I slammed the hood closed, turned to close the sliding door, and nearly ran into Clark Proctor.

"You frightened me!" I said as I regained my composure.

"I'll bet. Can I help you? I care-take for this place, and saw the door open."

I was sure that Clark expected some explanation, and I supplied him with the truth. He agreed to take me back to the Range Rover with a can of gas so that I could stay on schedule and get off Acadia on the late boat, which left in just over two hours. I apologized for the damaged door frame. He said that he would fix it before the owners showed up in the spring.

Once seated in his truck, I pulled out my phone hoping for a signal. "Your best bet is at the top of Annis Hill," Clark said as he pulled onto the main road heading in the opposite direction of the Range Rover and the plant. "I'll take you there." We rode in awkward silence for a few miles, when Clark seemed uneasy and started conversation with, "Any new leads? I mean, I imagine that's why you're here, right?"

"Lots of evidence, but no proof. Not yet anyway. I am making progress, though," I answered. "I hope there are no hard feelings about my taking your daughter in for questioning. She left me with no choice."

"No," Clark laughed. "No hard feelings. *That* was an adventure for her. She's been quite sheltered, and with her rebellious streak . . . Well, let's just say she'll be fine. She's back at school now." Clark slowed down and grabbed a lever that looked like a gear shift. "Need four-wheel drive for the hill," he said as he pulled the lever into place. We crept up a steep hill, and pulled into a turn-around. Clark did a three-point turn and placed the truck in park facing the direction from which we had come. "There's Green Haven," he said, pointing at the mainland across the choppy bay. "Seven miles. May as well be seven hundred."

I stepped out of the truck for some privacy and dialed Deloris. The connection was not great. But she knew it was me, and spoke quickly. "It's about time! You need. . . . But Trudy . . . Careful." The tone of her voice relayed urgency, but I only caught fragments.

"Please repeat" was all I asked, hoping for a moment with enough reception to understand what Deloris was trying to convey.

"First time . . . right track . . . she's not at school. She's," Deloris faded out again, leaving me with more questions than answers.

"Try again," I said, hopeful that I would pick up a few more words to make some sense of what she was saying.

This time all I heard was "Watch your back" before I lost her altogether. I stared at my phone, waiting for service. I dialed again. This time Deloris answered with "Trudy . . . percent match with lab report," before the static took over. I wandered around on top of the hill, staring at my phone and hoping to find a spot from which to make a third call. Clark had opened his window, I assumed to listen in on my conversation, which made me nervous. Now, there was a good chance that Trudy was going to be put back under the microscope from what I had heard in the broken connection of my call to Deloris. I walked a bit farther away and hoped to be out of hearing range when and if I was able to place one more call to Deloris for clarification.

I felt true compassion for Clark and Joan Proctor, and assumed that they knew something, and would do anything to protect their daughter. I should have been suspicious of Clark's willingness to help me with a ride, I thought, after putting them through the ordeal and embarrassment of dragging Trudy off-island. He must surely be hoping that I am way off track, I thought. And he would have been correct had Deloris not gotten the partial message across.

As I approached his open window, I saw that he had pulled a shotgun out from behind the seat. "A big snowshoe rabbit just scampered across the road here and behind that stand of trees," he said quietly. "Mind if I jump out and take a look? Joan makes a mean stewed rabbit."

"Go for it," I said as I climbed back into the passenger side. Clark had left the truck running for heat, which felt good on my feet and lower legs. I would be careful about how I asked, but needed to learn where to find Trudy in the event that I had not misunderstood what Deloris was trying to tell me. I needed the cooperation of Joan and Clark more than ever. And I was running out of time to get back in their good graces and get information before I needed to board the boat.

I continued to stare at my phone hoping for a miracle. My battery was nearly drained, which was not surprising as the phone had been searching for service most of the day. I dug around in my bag for my twelve-volt charger and opened the truck's ashtray hoping to find a functional outlet into which to plug it. Every muscle in my body tensed. I felt heat surge from within my chest as my pulse raged with the excitement and fear of what I saw in the bottom of the ashtray. I picked it up to be sure. There was no mistaking it. I held a thick, masculine, gold chain with a pendant forged in a half-heart shape. I turned the piece over and read the inscription. "And back." Mrs. Kohl's mystery lover had been revealed. And if my instincts were right, so had her murderer.

I slipped the necklace into my hip pocket, pulled my gun from its holster and stepped out of the truck. I needed to place Clark under arrest and get him off-island on the boat that would arrive in approximately ninety minutes. Keeping the pickup truck between myself and the trees where Clark had disappeared in pursuit of game, I waited for him to emerge. When he didn't, I decided to be proactive and go in after him. Aware that he might have his gun sighted on me, I moved quickly in the random zigzags that make the kill zone difficult to hit.

I leaped over a snowbank like taking a hurdle, landing on my feet. I picked the biggest tree on the edge of the thickly wooded area, and dove behind it. I pulled the hammer back, cocking my gun, and waited, not daring to poke my head around and risk being shot. Within a minute, I heard the truck door open. I peeked out to see the interior light on in the cab of the truck with the passenger door open. Clark stood leaning into the truck. I knew he had to notice the ashtray being open and the necklace being gone. He stood and slammed the door shut with great force, and shouldered his shotgun, sending me back into full hiding. Footsteps crunched in the frozen snowbank, then stopped. I knew that it was optimal to take Clark alive in order to discover the whole truth and prosecute *all* guilty parties. I wondered if full disclosure and closure were worth risking my own life. A man who could brutally murder a lover was certainly capable of shooting me. And from what I had learned so far about island justice, he could probably make my death look like a hunting accident or even self-defense. The necklace in my pocket was the single key to linking the murder to Clark Proctor. And I knew that I was the only one besides Clark who held that key. If he could do away with me, he would likely be off scot-free.

"You have something that belongs to me, Detective Bunker," he yelled. "Your handgun is no match for this twelve-gauge." I stayed behind the tree and remained silent. "I know what you are thinking. But you are wrong." A long silence, during which I imagined him shouldering the shotgun in my basic direction, waiting for a shot, was followed by, "Jesus Christ! Come out! I won't hurt you." I didn't believe him. I had to follow my gut. To do otherwise, and be wrong, would be fatal.

I sat in the snow with my back pressed against the trunk of a large spruce tree for what seemed like forever. I held my loaded gun in a ready position in case Clark decided to flush me out of hiding. I could hear the truck's engine idle over the stiffening breeze that sounded like a hoarse, raspy whisper. I glanced at my phone to check the time. Nearly an hour had passed when I heard the truck door open and close, indicating that Clark was now within the cab. I knew that I might eventually have to make a break and head deeper into the woods if there was any chance of making it to the dock to catch the last boat off with or without Clark. As I sat and waited, I contemplated my options. I could come out with my hands up and hope that Clark was telling the truth about harming me. Nope. I could come out suddenly with my gun blazing and hope to get the upper hand in a shoot-out. Nope. I would be an easy target. I needed backup, period.

As I looked at my phone and prayed for one more bar of service so that I could place a call for help, I heard a second vehicle approach. As the vehicle crested the hill, the bang of a backfire startled me. Surely that must be Manny in the ALP truck, so prone to backfiring and sputtering, I thought. I heard the crunching of tires and realized that Manny had joined Clark in the pull-off area very close to where I sat. I strained to hear what was said. I could hear the two voices, but could not make out words. When I heard laughter, I figured that Manny was not in on the "hunt," and that Clark would get rid of him as quickly as he could. I assumed that Manny had the decency to be concerned about me as I had not returned to ALP, nor had I collected the Range Rover from the side of the road. Now was my chance, I thought, to make a move. My best-case scenario now was to get off Acadia Island safely, and return with reinforcement to arrest Clark Proctor.

I slithered on my belly through the snow, making my way deeper into the woods where I could stand and not be seen. When I felt that I was safely behind a pile of blown-down trees, I stood cautiously and looked toward the road. Sure enough, Clark was sitting with the shotgun perched on the sill of the open window, and Manny was pulling away. I trudged deeper into the woods, knowing that if Clark wanted to track me through the snow, I would get a clear shot at him. He would realize that and would not leave his truck. This gave me confidence to travel. I walked in the direction that I assumed was parallel to the road, down a steep hill and toward the dock area. There was no way to make the late boat. But if I could get to the dock, I could commandeer a boat to get back to Green Haven with. I recalled that two scallop boats were on moorings when I arrived this morning, and knew that I could sneak aboard one after dark. I just needed to remain in hiding until then.

I was getting really cold, and wished I had the hat and gloves that I had left in Clark's truck. I took off my coat and sweater, wrapped the sweater around my head, and quickly put my coat back on. I had to keep moving to keep from freezing. The sun set, taking with it the bit of warmth it held in mid-winter. Dusk was quickly followed by pitch blackness.

I made my way to the top of a small knoll and pulled my phone out for one last look. Wow! A random spot of cell service made my heart race as I dialed Deloris. My heart sunk as I heard a busy signal. I quickly dialed the only other number I knew by heart: the café. My hands were now shaking from cold. I felt weak. Mild hypothermia, I knew. Headlights came slowly down the hill as I hoped for the phone to ring before I lost the signal. To my amazement, the phone was answered on the second ring. "Hello. Harbor Café. Wally speaking." My brother's voice was clear and cheerful. I wondered if I was delirious.

A searchlight from the open truck window blazed a wide and bright beam very close to my position. "Wally, this is Jane. Is Audrey there?" I couldn't believe I was speaking to my brother.

"Hi Jane. I love my new job!"

"Wally, this is an emergency," I said trying not to panic and frighten my baby brother. "I need to talk with Audrey."

"Audrey had to go. She left me to clean up and she is coming back for the dinner rush."

"Is anyone there?" I asked, desperately hoping that he was not there alone.

"Nobody. I am responsible for holding down the fort. And filling up aaaalllllll of the salt shakers."

Oh no, I thought, as the searchlight glanced by my right side. I ducked down hoping to stay out of sight, and said, "Wally. I need you to get a message to Audrey or any adult. Please, this is very important. I am on Acadia Island and need some help," I said calmly. I knew it was senseless to give Wally any more detail. "Can you do that for me?"

"Of course I can. I'm not a baby. I am in charge while Audrey is gone." He seemed hurt that I would question his ability to relay the message. But I couldn't worry about that now. I had to get moving again before the searchlight found me. I thanked Wally quickly and told him I would see him later.

I hung up and moved as stealthily as I could through the snow, praying that Audrey would return to the café right away, and that Wally would get the message right. I tried Deloris again as I lumbered along. My legs were tired and cold. It was getting difficult to lift my feet, resulting in more of a shuffling than a stepping. The phone refused to connect. I considered trying to send a text message as doing so required little to no reception. Then I realized that the only numbers I knew were landlines. A full moon rose over an outline of jagged treetops, slightly illuminating my surroundings, and me, I realized as I saw the headlights coming back from the opposite direction.

The outline of a sprawling summer residence came into view, and I knew I had to get to it. I must be close to the dock. I hated being so unfamiliar with the lay of the land, and knowing that this was Clark's home turf. He probably knew every nook and cranny of this rock, I thought as I reached the back of a main house. Maybe there would be a quick source of heat, or some food. At the very least, this unoccupied structure would serve as a hiding place until I could make a dash for the dock. The place was dark. I tried every door and window before realizing that it was senseless to go inside. There would be no power and no heat source. And Clark Proctor might be the caretaker, and if so would know the place like the back of his hand. My only chance was making it aboard one of the scallop boats.

I painstakingly made my way through another patch of woods and back out to the main road, where I could see the lights of the dock. I hadn't seen headlights for a while and I was making good time walking. If anyone came along in a vehicle, I decided I'd take cover behind the high banks of snow on the side of the road. Fortunately, I knew that I would hear anything coming long before I saw them or they saw me. I couldn't trust anyone. I wondered if Manny had indeed come looking for me when I didn't return to the plant and the Range Rover hadn't moved. And what was his interest in finding me? Pure concern, or some evil intent? I wondered if he might be a conspirator or accomplice in the Kohl case. At the very least, I had him on criminal threatening, harassment, and trafficking of pornography. I realized that I was a long way from knowing the answers.

I was at the edge of the parking lot above the dock when suddenly the lights lining the dock went black. I ducked between two parked cars to collect my thoughts. The lot was full of vehicles, some piled high with snow and others totally clean. I thought I heard an engine far off in the distance, but couldn't be sure.

I worked my way from vehicle to vehicle, darting quickly. Was I being watched? I tore frozen sleeves from around my hands and grasped my gun again. The grip of my gun had been warmed by being tucked in my belt, and felt good in my frost-bitten fingers. The whine of an engine grew louder. Now I could tell that it was a diesel, and it was just off of Acadia. I listened intently as I prayed for the engine to be that of a boat coming into Acadia rather than going by.

A car's headlights flipped on behind me, illuminating everything around me and casting my shadow long and bold down the narrow road onto the dock. The truck's engine started. I bolted.

With nothing else to hide behind, I had only one direction to go, and that was away from the truck that had started to drive toward me. I sprinted to the dock just as a green light rounded the headland at the outer harbor entrance. I recognized the green light as a running light signifying the port side of a vessel—the boat was indeed heading into the harbor. But the boat was still a long way from the dock, and moving slowly now.

The narrow walk that connected the parking lot to the dock was slick with ice. I slipped wildly as I tried to make the ramp that led to the float. I slid by the open gate and just missed grabbing a railing. The truck was literally on my heels now as

265

I neared the end of the dock. Icy banks on either side forbid me to get out of the way. I had no choice than to go over the end of the dock and into the water—it was either that or get plowed into and pushed overboard. This was suicidal, I knew. But I took my chances rather than being run over by the truck.

I flung myself over and felt like I was in midair forever; floating down slowly to the surface of the black water. I had reacted in self-preservation, and had no plan. I heard the splash before I felt the breathtakingly frigid water. I was done for. I took two breaststrokes before surfacing, still gripping my gun in my right hand, and popped up under the dock.

I climbed onto a beam at the base of a piling to the dock's deck, struggling to get my entire body out of the icy ocean that had the ability to kill me quicker than a bullet. I clung to the beam and tried to gather my thoughts. My only chance of surviving was to get back ashore without being seen. And to do that, I might have to force myself back into the water.

The truck had come to a stop at the end of the dock above my head. Headlights illuminated the harbor. I was now shivering uncontrollably, and trying to remain quiet. I looked at the float where the dinghies where tethered, and wondered if I could make it over and into one of them without being seen. I heard a second vehicle coming and knew it was Manny when I heard the loud bang come from the tailpipe. The ALP truck crept down onto the dock directly behind Clark Proctor's truck. I heard two doors open and close. I watched movement between the planks of the dock above me and listened. I had to do something fast. I was becoming extremely hypothermic, and soon would not be thinking clearly. I had to force myself back into the water and pull myself along the pilings to reach the shore, where I could get out of the water while I still had the strength to move. I shoved my gun into the front of my waistband and took a couple of deep breaths.

As I pulled myself toward shore, I could hear the two voices clearly. The men were nervous. "Did you actually see her go into the water?" Manny asked.

"Yes. I even saw the splash when she hit the surface."

"Well then, where the hell is she? She can't be holding her breath."

"Doesn't matter. She is dead. Do you know how cold this water is? No way anyone could survive it," Clark sounded like he was trying to convince himself of my demise. Well, I had bad news for him.

I felt my feet hit the ground. I stood in chest deep water and waded ashore slowly, being careful not to make a sound. I now held my gun and prayed that it had not been submerged long enough to wick through the bullet's sealed cartridge, rendering the primer useless. The Glock was not my worry. Wet ammo was. State-issued firearms were equipped with marine spring cups designed to fire when wet. But I had seen reports where they had failed. I was counting on not becoming a statistic that required the gun manufacturer to go back to the drawing board.

Clark was armed, jumpy, and ready to pull the trigger. It was clear that the approaching boat was coming into the float. I stood in waist-deep water at the bottom of a ladder that led to the top of the dock behind the men. My skin had gone from stinging cold to burning hot, and it itched like nothing I had ever experienced. I was in extreme pain, but that was better than numb, which I assumed was next. "What the fuck is that boat doing here?" asked Manny.

"Looks like it's coming into the dock. We'll have to tell whoever is aboard that they can't tie up here. I'll send them to the dock in Smiths Cove," Clark said.

"What if they are here looking for Bunker?"

"We'll add to the body count," Clark said with the calm of a cold-blooded killer. Before Manny could respond, the boat was nudging the floats. The men were distracted by lines being tied to cleats, giving me time to climb the ladder undetected and hide behind the ALP truck. Although I couldn't see them, I heard familiar voices. Cal and the sheriff were here! I silently thanked Wally and knew that my life might be spared. But now there were three of us in danger. I couldn't allow the feeling of relief to overwhelm me to the point of relaxing.

The sheriff yelled up the ramp. "Hello. Have you seen Deputy Bunker?"

Manny quickly answered. "I haven't seen her since lunch. I think she left on the mail boat." Now I could see Cal and the sheriff coming up the ramp. At the top of the ramp, they were met with a shotgun in their faces.

Manny tried to talk sense into Clark. "Hey, man. I want no part of this. I agreed to scare her off, not kill anyone!"

"Toss your gun overboard," Clark barked at the sheriff. The sheriff did as he was instructed, slowly pulling his gun out of its holster and dropping it over the railing where it splashed and sank. I slowly crawled out from behind the truck. Manny and Clark had their backs to me, but Cal and the sheriff could see that I was there with my gun aimed at Clark's head. My hands shook uncontrollably as hypothermia had reached a more advanced stage.

The sheriff had his hands up in surrender and started talking.

"You know, Deputy Bunker didn't know it was you. She thought it was all your daughter, then she had it all on Manuel. She didn't know that your daughter is an addict, either."

"Shut up! Trudy is a good girl! And if Midge Kohl hadn't been trafficking chemicals from China, we would never have had them here."

"And that's why you killed Mrs. Kohl? Or was the killing to hide your affair from your wife?"

"It wasn't an affair! I needed something against her. I wanted her to leave the island so we could have it back. She ruined everything. I didn't want to kill her, but she refused to leave." Manny quickly shoved his hands in the air along with the sheriff and Cal. Clark shoved Manny toward the sheriff. All three men stood in surrender to Clark, who was clearly preparing to spray them with his twelve-gauge at close range. All three men could now see that I had my gun aimed at Clark's head.

"You don't want to do this," said the sheriff. "You'll never get away with it. And what about Trudy and Joan? They will have to live with your legacy. Do you want to be known as the cold-blooded killer of four innocent people?"

"No, they won't. I have four rounds. The last one is for myself," he said coolly and pulled the hammer back, cocking the gun to shoot the sheriff. I steadied my hands and squeezed the trigger of my gun, catching Clark in the right shoulder.

The sheriff quickly moved in and wrestled the shotgun from Clark. As Clark spun around to face me, I could see the look of surrender in his eyes. He seemed relieved to have been stopped from killing anyone else. He dropped to his knees and cried out loud. "I just wanted to protect my family. I wanted my island back," he said softly between sobs. "*Our* island," he clarified as he looked me in the eye.

TWELVE

Clark Proctor hadn't slept in weeks, I thought. I watched his head sway from side to side as the *Sea Pigeon* made her way over the southern bay, leaving Acadia Island in her wake. I assumed that I was exhausted, too, but was running on pure adrenaline. After bringing me up to speed on more details that Deloris was able to muster, the sheriff sat on the bench seat with his back against the port bulkhead. He placed himself strategically between our two suspects, I assumed to keep them from communicating. Manny sat staring into nothingness with eyes wide open and cuffed hands resting in his lap. I stood directly in front of the bus heater, rotating a quarter of a turn every few minutes to dry my clothes. I draped a wool blanket Cal had aboard over my shoulders that now ached and burned. The side of my right calf felt hot. I spun another ninety degrees to allow the heater to blow onto both shins; positioning myself to look over the bow and toward dim lights that grew brighter and brighter as I slowly stopped shivering.

Cal was the epitome of quiet confidence as he navigated between and around islands, ledges, and buoys. I assumed that this was a first for my trusted friend: transporting a cold-blooded killer and ex-con who, in light of the screaming accusations we had been witness to in the short time between the dock and the deck of the boat, were guilty of several crimes. The café would be buzzing tomorrow morning, I thought as I realized that this may well be the beginning of a long row of dominos to fall. A killer would soon face justice. Not just any killer. This killer had murdered and assumed that his island shield would protect him from due process, as it had . . . Who knows? If what I had been told by my own mother had been true about Acadia, its residents did whatever to whomever, whenever they pleased, without fear. Islanders were, they thought, beyond the reach of the long arm of the law. Their only legitimate form of justice had been retaliation. And retaliation had a habit of escalating. This time it had grown to a frenzy that had done irreparable damage.

I clenched my jaw tight to gain control of my chattering teeth. My muscles were convulsing in response to the extreme cold. The only part of me that was functioning properly, I thought, was my brain. I would use this time on board to thaw out, and to piece together what I knew and what I had just learned from the sheriff. Midge Kohl had paid with her life for her involvement in spearheading the trafficking of illicit drugs and the chemicals used to manufacture them. She and a handful of wealthy summer folks who invested in ALP had constructed a scam of great proportions. I was confident that her fellow investors were ignorant of the drug running, and were only interested in devaluing island waterfront property, enabling them as a legal entity, Acadia Island Property Improvement Association, to scoop it up for pennies on the dollar. Now that the scheme's mastermind had perished, members of the group would never see return on their investments. The future of ALP was grim, thus the future of the ex-cons who had moved to Acadia for employment was also quite bleak.

Deloris had been correct about the activities at Empire Seafood out on The Peninsula. Empire was one of *many* distribution points of the drugs smuggled in from China mixed among bags of legitimate chemicals used in seafood processing. Deloris and I would follow up on Empire, I vowed. According to Manny, the illicit money resulting from drug sales was the only profit realized by ALP. Clark and Manny both had palms being greased to simply remain silent. But that silence was hard to maintain when Trudy came home from college with an addiction to designer drugs. Backing out of drug smuggling was *never* an option. Many dealers had died trying. And when investors and employees were all counting on continued operation of the plant, a secret lover pulls little weight as the sole dissenting opinion.

Mrs. Kohl was willing to walk away from the plant and all activities, signing everything over to the employees. But when it became obvious that Clark would never leave his wife, or his island, for her, she started wavering on giving up ownership. To do so would have put her right back into her former dull existence with a jet-setter husband who was never home, and paid little attention to his wife when he was. It became clear that Mr. Kohl had funded much of the ALP start-up, giving his wife "something to do."

Manny had broken his probation in so many ways that his fate was sealed. He would return to prison where he would likely remain until he was a very old man, I assumed. Old habits are hard to break. He had gotten a taste of a free life on Acadia. He had a job. He had a home. He had family in his coworkers with whom he shared the label ex-con and shame of owing their *one chance* to investors who could pull the plug on their common existence with the stroke of a pen. The plug had been pulled, and Manny had struggled against the floodwaters circling the drain the only way he knew how.

I knew that a full confession was ready to spill out of a despondent Clark Proctor. I had already pieced together the chain of events, and only needed to hear it from him. Linking Trudy's addiction to his involvement with importing and distributing drugs must have driven Clark insane, I thought. And when he couldn't convince Midge Kohl to cease and desist, he flew into a murderous rage. I would need details from Clark of exactly how Midge Kohl went from consensual sex to the vat of boiling water. A bump on the head, or choke hold? Once submerged and dead, the evidence spoke for itself. Clark had transported his victim to her home, and torched the place to cover up the murder. And if I hadn't been sent to Acadia by Mr. Dubois to document the fire damage for the insurance claim, Mrs. Kohl's death would have been determined to be accidental. Clark Proctor would have gotten away with murder.

Clark's life, as he knew it, was indeed over. Once people realize that they have reached the point of no return, well, they don't return. There was no doubt in my mind that Clark would have killed Cal, the sheriff, Manny, and himself had I not been able to squeeze off that one shot, winging him and allowing the sheriff to pounce. Teamwork, I thought. If Deloris hadn't been so persistent and skilled in technical analysis, if Wally hadn't answered the phone at the café and relayed my message, if Cal and the sheriff hadn't shown up when they did, if I had succumbed to hypothermia, if my Glock hadn't fired after submersion. . . . Well, the gun firing was perhaps luck, which bothered me. I knew that if I depended on luck for my survival, that one day my luck would run out. My life has been a long string of close calls. But this one had been a little too close.

When the *Sea Pigeon* bumped against the dock, Clark wakened from his forty-minute nap. The sheriff escorted Manny and Clark to the waiting State Police car and the two uniformed troopers who would transport them to the county jail where they would be processed and locked up until their trials. Clark would be on suicide watch.

Blue flashing lights ricocheted off snowbanks as the State Police vehicle left the parking area at the dock and wound through Green Haven's narrow Main Street. Although it was only seven thirty, most of the town was black. "Can I give you a ride to the hospital?" the sheriff asked as we waited for Cal to finish putting *Sea Pigeon* to bed.

"No, I'm fine. Thanks, though."

"I think you are better than fine," he said with a smile. And that was the first and only compliment I had received from my boss since I was deputized. "But you should get checked out. We don't need you out sick with pneumonia."

"All I need is a hot shower, a hot meal, and a warm bed. I'll grab a ride with Cal. He has to pass my place on his way home,"

I said, dismissing any concern the sheriff had about my physical condition.

"Suit yourself," he said. He looked as though he was waiting for me to say something. So I did.

"You know, Deloris is amazing. She is not being used to her potential as dispatcher and errand girl."

"She is not getting a gun, period." From that I gathered that the issuance of a firearm to Deloris had been a point of heated discussion in the past. I would let it go, for now. "I'll check in with you tomorrow. Good night." And with that, he climbed into his car and drove off just as Cal opened the passenger side of his truck for me.

Cal and I rode in comfortable silence until he pulled his truck up to the door of the Lobster Trappe. "You guys saved my life tonight," I said as I found the handle and opened the door.

"And you saved ours."

"See you at the café. I'll bring my checkbook," I said. The usual $100 boat fare didn't seem like quite enough after what he'd been through. But I knew Cal wouldn't expect anything more. I slammed the truck door and hustled into the well-lit Lobster Trappe.

Before I made it to the stairs, the door of the main house flew open exposing three very relieved faces. The wonderful aroma of something briny and hot wafted into the cool shop, creating a haze of steam that shrouded my "family" like a heavenly cloud.

"We were scared!" Wally shouted as he approached me with arms open for a hug. "Cold! Yuck!" he yelled after shoving off from a quick embrace. "Did you get the bad guys?"

"*We* got 'em."

"Come in, dear," said Mrs. V as she held the door for Wally and me to enter her kitchen. "You must be hungry."

"We waited dinner for you," said Mr. V. "Mussel stew and yeast rolls. Bet you'd drink a wee dram of Scotch first."

"That sounds great! Thank you! Sorry I worried you, Wally," I said as I took my place at the table.

"Audrey likes my name to be Walter. I am too old for Wally," my baby brother said as he took the seat across from me.

"What? I leave you with Audrey for a day, and she changes your name?" I laughed.

I sipped a small glass of single malt and devoured two hot, buttered rolls and a huge, steaming bowl of mussel stew before the interrogation began. I knew it was coming. All three of my dinner mates stared at me, hovering like vultures hungry for a shred of fresh kill. I was nearly ready to excuse myself and head upstairs for a hot shower when Mr. V broke the silence. "We are extremely proud of Walter," he said, patting Wally on the shoulder.

"Me too. Always."

"Maybe you and the sheriff will make him a deputy?" Mrs. V asked.

"Yes, that is a great idea. I'll check into getting you a real badge," I said to Wally. "You have earned it!" I stood, ready to thank Mrs. V for dinner.

"And a real gun," my brother added.

"Well, let's start with the badge, Wally." I almost laughed thinking of Deloris and her quest for a gun.

"Walter," Wally reminded me.

"Yes, sorry. But now I need a shower and lots of sleep. Thanks for dinner and the drink," I said to my landlords. I pushed my chair into the table and started toward the door. "And I will see you all in the morning."

"I love you, Janey," Wally said.

"I love you, too, Wall . . . Walter."